VOLUME ONE

MARTY QUADE
PRIVATE DETECTIVE

AIRSHIP 27 PRODUCTIONS

Marty Quade Private Detective Volume One
"Publish or Perish" © 2019 Gordon Dymowski
"Dogs of War, Angels of Death" © 2019 Chris Bell
"Over Their Head" © 2019 Gene Moyers
"Dead Man's Hand" © 2019 Michael Black

Published by Airship 27 Productions
www.airship27.com
www.airship27hangar.com

Interior illustrations © 2019 Brian Loner
Cover illustration © 2019 Rob Davis

Editor: Ron Fortier
Associate Editor: Jonathan Sweet
Marketing and Promotions Manager: Michael Vance
Production and design by Rob Davis

ISBN-13: 978-1-946183-55-2
ISBN-10: 1-946183-55-5

Printed in the United States of America

10 9 8 7 6 5 4 3 2 1

MARTY QUADE
PRIVATE DETECTIVE

Volume One

PUBLISH OR PERISH

by
Gordon Dymowski

"**W**hen you said breakfast was on you," Marty Quade took a healthy bite of pancake. "You weren't kidding!"

Placing his fork back on the plate, the well-dressed dark-haired detective looked around the Hotel Baltic dining room. Breakfast was always their busiest hour, as hotel waiters and waitresses eagerly served a variety of hotel guests preparing for a typical day of New York City excitement. Glancing back at the variety of dishes in front of him, Marty's face had the delight of a child of Christmas. Huge plates of food—eggs prepared in a variety of ways, bacon, pancakes, doughnuts, and even ham steaks— were spread out on the table in front of him. Across the table from Quade sat a well-groomed, heavy-set man whose spectacles matched his Brooks Brothers finery.

"Let it never be said that Michael P. Trotter of Trotter Publications did not know how to have a good morning." Leaning his white globe-handled walking stick against the table, Trotter scooped a large amount of scrambled eggs from a platter to plate.

Looking Trotter in the eye, Marty shot a wide grin. "You must *really* need me if you're willing to spring for such a spread!"

After chewing a forkful of eggs, Trotter brushed a few crumbs from his beard. "It's a very delicate matter....I need you to find someone."

"That's what I'm good at," Downing a glass of orange juice like a shot of whiskey, Marty gave a sly wink. "So, is this person costing you?"

"Sadly, yes," Slicing off a large piece of ham steak, Trotter chewed before speaking, pointing his fork at Marty to emphasize each word. "One of my editors—Hugh Cranston—has been stealing money from me and my writers. He's also been stealing....sensitive business documents which I need to find quickly."

"Let me guess," Taking a healthy gulp of black coffee, Marty grabbed a slice of buttered rye toast. "Cranston's flown the coop?"

"Yes, Mr. Quade," Dusting off his beard, Trotter sliced off another piece of ham steak. "Two days ago, Cranston stopped coming into the office altogether. I need you to find him and return any information he has stolen. Otherwise, my publishing business is in danger."

Chomping on his toast, Marty mumbled as he chewed, "And what exactly do you publish—girlie magazines?"

"No, Mr. Quade—I publish fiction for ten year olds," Pausing, Trotter contemplated how Marty's hair remained so neatly parted, and continued, "Pulps, as they're referred to in popular parlance. My publications feature tales of adventure, excitement, and intrigue featuring a variety of colorful characters. Many readers need such high-spirited tales in these troubled times…and we provide escape and comfort for the low cost of one thin dime."

"Please—no bumping gums," Marty took in Trotter's moment of confusion, then took another bite of toast. "Tell me what you want me to do once I find this crumb."

"Bring him back so I can prosecute him!" Grasping the ornate globe-topped white and ivory handle of his walking stick, Trotter slammed it on the ground. "The authorities cannot do anything based on allegation, and I want to be sure Cranston *pays* for his crime!"

Gulping down black coffee, Quade speared a strip of bacon with his fork. "You know it's going to cost you more than a sawbuck, right?"

Raising his hand, Trotter snapped his fingers. "You will be well compensated—in fact, let me provide some background information."

On cue, a bellboy approached carrying a bound folder. As the bellboy placed the parcel by Marty, Trotter reached into his lapel pocket and removed a coin purse. Fishing through the purse, Trotter handed the bellboy a nickel. Seeing the bellboy's look of disgust, Marty reached into his lapel, removed a wallet, and handed the bellboy a five spot.

As the smiling bellboy walked away, Marty opened the folder to see a photo clipped on top of several handwritten and typewritten notes. Filing through the papers, Marty examined the photo: a headshot of a thin, balding older man with a mustache and glasses. Moving the pile of papers to one side, Marty thumbed through a pile of magazines with lurid covers and even more provocative titles. Marty couldn't believe how over the top these titles were—titles like *Grey Seal Detective, Valentine Valley, Tales from Zone 4*, and *Special Operative Cavalier*. Clipped to the cover of the top magazine—*Grey Seal Detective*—was a check made out to Marty for $5,000.

Grabbing a doughnut and biting into it, Trotter spread crumbs throughout his beard as he spoke. "I have provided some internal notes and memos, a down payment….and a few complimentary publications."

Marty stared at Trotter dead-on. "Good. I'm definitely the guy for the job—I didn't earn my reputation for *nothing*. I always come well-armed, well-prepared, and able to get the job done."

"I should hope so," Finishing his doughnut in three bites, Trotter scooped a healthy forkful of scrambled eggs into his mouth. "A job like this should be easy for you to complete quickly. And please—continue to enjoy your breakfast—on me. "

Arching an eyebrow, Marty shot Trotter a lethal glance. "That's all well and good, but before you make tracks—let me get this straight: if this is a setup, you'll regret it. *Nobody* gets the drop on Marty Quade. *Nobody*."

"Be assured, Mr. Quade—it's no set-up," Bracing himself with his walking stick, Trotter lifted his considerable girth from his chair. "I have every confidence you're the man to get the job done."

Turning away from Marty, Trotter made his way through the bristling activity of waiters and diners out of the Hotel Baltic restaurant. Glancing through the window, Marty observed Trotter approaching a luxurious sedan with driver waiting patiently. Glancing at a shabbily-dressed man on the sidewalk, Trotter simply turned and ignored him, rushing quickly into the back seat of the sedan. As the sedan pulled away, the poorly dressed man was soon accompanied by a woman with a dress with multiple patches. Approaching the pair were two small children: a boy wearing tattered clothes, and a girl clutching a dirty rag doll. All four looked on with sullen looks as the sedan pulled away.

Catching the man's attention, Marty waved at the family. As the man pointed his wife towards the window, Marty nodded and encouraged them inside. As they made their way into the restaurant, the family of four approached the table where Marty sat amongst huge platters of food. As a busboy attempted to remove the dishes, Marty slipped him a fiver and told him to bring four place settings for his guests.

As the woman and children sat down, the man offered his hand. "Thank you, Mr…"

"Marty—Marty Quade," The detective beamed his brightest smile as he shook the man's hand. "Ace Detective in New York City, Mr…"

"John Kozak," Surprised that he was called *Mister*, the man eagerly shook Marty's hand and took a seat. "This is my wife Melissa, and our two kids—Bobby and Anne."

Melissa—the woman in the patched dress—politely nodded, her head framed by rather long, black hair. Sitting straight in their seats, both Bobby and Anne smiled as waiters brought them clean dishes and silverware.

"New client bought me breakfast," Marty looked at the family of four. "I don't want it to go to waste. Besides, you look like you're new in town, and I could use some company."

Glancing at a clock on the wall, Marty noticed that it was eight thirty a.m.—his meeting with Trotter took much shorter than usual, and a missing person's case would be relatively easy for Marty. Taking a quick glance in the folder, Quade glanced at one of the typewritten notes clipped to Cranston's picture. Around lunchtime, Cranston often frequented an automat, but had not been there in several days. Noticing Bobby eyeing the thick magazines in the folder, Marty flashed him an enthusiastic smile.

With a noticeable gleam in his eye, Bobby asked, "Working a case?"

"Of course," Marty smiled, and the boy smiled back. "You know about detectives—from these magazines, right?"

"Yeah….you're just like Tommy Radcliffe, PI….or maybe even Matt Cavalier!"

"Who?" Marty realized that the boy was referring to the magazines. "Oh, the guys in these stories—you dig these stories?"

"He and I both," John Kozak scooped a healthy pile of scrambled eggs on his plate. "They kept us going on the train from Pennsylvania. We don't have much—in fact, we're here looking for work—but we have some savings, and we always have a few dimes for good reads."

Rolling her eyes skyward, Melissa addressed her husband with some irritation. "…and it's spending money we don't have. We're already squandering our savings in New York, and with trying to find work plus the troubles overseas…."

As their parents squabbled, Bobby squirmed in his seat and Anne cradled her rag doll more tightly. Hoping to break the tension, Marty handed the magazines to Bobby. "I'm working a case in the pulp racket—can you give me the lowdown?"

Bobby smiled, taking the magazines from Marty, "These are great! They're not as good as, say, Operator 5 or Doc Savage, but they're *really* neat!"

"Tell me about 'em," Marty ignored Melissa's disapproving stares.

Holding up one of the magazines, Bobby showed up a cover featuring a robot blasting away at something off to the side while an attractive woman cowered in a corner. Along the top were emblazoned the words *Tales From Zone 4*, and words in a bottom corner announced that the featured tale was *Riddle of the Reckless Robot* by Tate Channing.

"This is my favorite," Bobby flashed a gap-toothed smile. "It has robots, ray guns, and spaceships! It's *really* cool!"

Ignoring his mother's disdainful looks, Bobby placed the magazine face-down and lifted another one—this one with a cover featuring a cowboy and a woman dressed in ranch clothes. "This one's *Valentine Valley*— it's got cowboys, but they meet girls and kiss and stuff. Kind of icky."

"He's right—about the cowboys and women," John took a quick bite of scrambled eggs, quickly chewing them. "In fact, Anne here *really* enjoys that story."

Clutching her rag doll, Anne shook her head and smiled. Catching a waiter's glance, Marty mouthed the words *Get Marcel—quickly!*

Placing the magazine down, Bobby grabbed his fork and shoveled some bacon into his mouth. After swallowing, he lifted a magazine with a gun-toting man on the cover. "This one's *Grey Seal Detective*….and it features Tommy Radcliffe, Ace Private Eye. Kind of like you, Mr. Quade."

"Thanks," Marty smiled at both John and Bobby as the boy placed the magazine on the table.

An awkward grin spread on John's face as Melissa looked on, "They're actually…not well written. Kid's stuff, but they're worth a read."

"Nothing wrong with that," Marty waved his hands.

"And finally, there's Special Agent Matt Cavalier," Revealing a cover with a lantern-jawed blonde man with a gun, Bobby placed the magazine back on the table and swallowed another forkful of eggs. "He's a special government agent, fighting our country's enemies as they threaten to invade us."

Taking a tone of strong disapproval, Melissa nibbled on some toast, "Those kind of magazines are cheap and tawdry…and good people shouldn't be reading them!"

"But Mommy, you *love Valentine Valley*…." Anne defended as she bit into a slice of ham steak.

Within moments, a tall, thin, impeccably dressed man with a mustache approached Marty's table.

"You wanted to see me, Mr. Quade?"

"Yes," Marty pointed at his breakfast companions. "This is the Kozak family, fresh from Pennsylvania. Everyone, this is Marcel—the Hotel's concierge and all around swell guy. Marcel—John's looking for work…. anything available here at the Baltic?"

Marcel smiled, "We have need of a handyman….and of course, if the wife wishes, we can always use part-time maids."

For the first time since meeting Marty, Melissa Kozak smiled.

"Room and board provided, of course," Marcel smiled at Marty. "Anything else I can do for you?"

"No, but thanks for the help," Marty watched Marcel leave, then addressed the Kozaks. "Marcel's a good egg, and I helped his daughter out of a jam some time ago. Keeps bugging me about returning the favor, so this was his chance to do so."

Rising from his seat, John stuttered, "But ....how can we repay you?"

Leaping from his chair, Marty extended his hand, "Handshake. Today's price for a good deed."

Shaking John's hand, Marty turned to Bobby, "Those magazines are *yours* to keep."

As Bobby smiled, Marty released John Kozak's hand and reached into his lapel. Removing his wallet, Marty quickly withdrew a five spot and handed it to Bobby.

"Your assignment, Junior Detective," Marty grinned as Bobby grabbed the bill from his hand. "Head to the corner newsstand and ask for Joe and his nephew Tommy. Buy more of these kind of magazines—the stuff you and your dad enjoy—and take your family, including Joe and Tommy, to lunch at the ice cream parlor across the street."

As wrinkles creased her forehead, Melissa placed her palms out in a defensive manner, "But Mr. Quade, we can't—"

"Look, I just got a healthy retainer and I have a *healthy* bank account," Marty responded despite his doubts about the retainer. "Times are tough for everyone. I'm more than happy to help."

Marcel approached and waved at the family to follow him. Soon, the Kozak family followed the concierge out of the restaurant towards the hotel lobby. Lifting the folder from the table, Marty thumbed through the pages, finding a half-remembered note.

"Automat via Frank G. 11:30 am Monday—Friday."

Glancing at a clock on the wall, Marty decided on his course of action. Folding some notes in half, he placed them—and the headshot—into the lapel pocket of his jacket. After depositing the rest of the file in his room, he embarked on his work.

After all, every case started *somewhere.....*

●●●

New York in springtime is a wonderful time: temperature is pleasantly warm, so people emerge onto the city's streets with confidence. Porches are rediscovered, the breeze has just the right feel, and pedestrians rediscover one simple truth: New York is a city best enjoyed on *foot*.

As he stepped out of the Wertheimer Bank and Trust, Marty Quade took in a healthy lungful of air, enjoying the fact that *this* was *his* city…. and he loved it.

Leaving the check with the bank—and a note to return later—Marty suspected that this was a setup. Although he enjoyed a hearty breakfast out of it, Marty was always suspicious when he got a lot of information— but little disclosure—in a simple missing person's case. However, Marty Quade was never hired to do only a good job—he was hired to be the *best*. That meant *due diligence*, as his lawyer friend would say, whether making sure a check would clear or heading into an automat in the heart of New York.

Approaching the brown-brick framed glass window of the Automat, Marty observed frantic activity. Approaching the automat, Marty saw two medics moving a gurney, its occupant covered by a sheet from head to toe, into the back of an ambulance. Entering the automatic, Marty saw various automat cubicles—containing sandwiches, slices of pie, and beverages— covered in blood. At various places around the room, medical attendants bandaged and cared for a variety of men.

Turning his head, Marty saw a stocky man dressed in a sharp gray suit, burgundy tie, and fedora. Only the worn brown shoes and badge on the man's lapel revealed that he was a detective. Meeting Marty's gaze, the man shot a look of both disappointment and excitement.

"This is a switch," Arching an eyebrow, the man spoke in a cop's dry tones. "Usually, *I'm* cleaning up after *you*."

Already dressed in his best suit, Marty put both hands in his pockets. "Neswick of Homicide—what brings a flatfoot like you here?"

"Shooting," Removing a notebook from inside his lapel, Neswick opened it and read off notes. "Victim was an editor for a local publisher."

Pulling the photo from his inside jacket pocket, Marty flashed it at Neswick. "Was it this guy, pally?"

Returning his notebook to its pocket, Neswick flashed his regulation sardonic smile, "Yes—Hugh Cranston. Worked at Trotter Publications. What…"

"His employer hired me this morning to find him," Marty returned the photo to his pocket.

"Figures. Here's the low down: half hour ago, a man entered seeking Cranston. According to witnesses, Cranston was enjoying a tuna fish sandwich and coffee with his colleagues, who were eating something called "automat soup." The man pulls out a gun, yells gibberish at Cranston, Cranston refuses, man shoots Cranston in the chest. Several of the guys tried to get the jump on him—two men shot, not fatally, but the guy put up one heck of a fight. He takes a powder, and officers are searching for him on foot. Funny enough, Cranston did mumble something before he croaked…-"

"Who do you think I am—Ellery Queen?" Moving towards Neswick, Marty became more excited. "Philo Vance? The dying clue seems a little *too* convenient…."

Checking his notebook, Neswick rubbed the back of his neck. "What he said was something like *Ron…Ron Davison*. Ring a bell?"

Checking a typewritten sheet titled ROSTER: PAID WRITERS, Marty scanned a variety of names and addresses. Finding the name "Ron Davison," Marty memorized the address, corresponding to a street in Greenwich Village.

"On to something?" Neswick arched an eyebrow as Marty returned the paper to his pocket.

"Yes, but you're not invited to this shindig. You and your boys in blue might turn it into a trip for biscuits."

Sighing, Neswick knew Marty was good for a lead, but had no need for a turf war. "Bring us in if it pans out?"

"Neswick, Neswick," Raising his hands defensively, Marty shot the cop his trademark winner's grin. "You know me—I'll buzz you when I get the word."

Shaking hands, Neswick and Marty gave hearty grins. Both men might not have agreed on everything, but when it came to justice were easy allies.

With a quick grin, Marty arched an eyebrow which threatened to crack his neatly-parted hair. Turning on his feet, Marty strode out of the automat and made his way towards Greenwich Village. With his knowledge of New York's streets, Marty took a circuitous route to evade anyone tailing him.

Ducking into a small diner, Marty enjoyed a quick lunch amidst stares at his neatly-tailored suit. As he finished his lunch, Marty checked the address for Ron Davison. As he left a hefty tip on the counter, he made his way into Greenwich Village.

After entering Greenwich Village, he began making his way towards that specific address. The Village, on first glance, was like any other neighborhood—it wasn't knee-deep in poverty, but the mix of hard-working families, immigrants, and others struggling to survive brought home the effects of the current depression. After a brief walk, Marty found himself facing an innocuous-looking tenement whose façade was worn and washed out by the ravages of time. Finding a button labeled "Davison", Marty pressed it with no response.

Discovering that the door was unlocked, Marty made his way inside and walked up several flights of stairs. Odors from a variety of dishes wafted through the halls suggesting a culinary League of Nations. Marty could identify the scent of several specific dishes—corned beef and cabbage, the spicy blood sausage known as *kishka*—but remained undeterred in his quest to find Davison.

Three floors up, Marty walked down a long hall and headed for the apartment number. Tempted to remove his gun from its holster, Marty stopped as he heard an unusual sound—the musical *clickety-clack* of typewriter keys striking paper. Bracing himself for action, Marty knocked on the door with great authority.

Hearing the typewriter stop, Marty stepped back as he heard footsteps approaching the door. Slicking his hair back, Marty looked down one end of the hall, then the other—if trouble was going to come, he was definitely going to be ready for it.

Trouble came as the door opened, and it was the kind of trouble that Marty Quade loved. She was tall, dark-haired, and her plain blue housedress did a poor job of hiding her buxom figure. As she stared at Marty with hypnotic intensity, Marty noted that her hair was tied in a bun, and the bun served as a convenient place for carrying a pencil. Although seemingly modest, the woman's neckline plunged low enough to border on obscenity.

Flashing a grin, Marty puffed out his chest. "Hello, doll. Name's Marty. Hugh sent me—is Ron around?"

Giving a weary sigh, the woman glared at Marty with eyes that bore the weight of weariness and suspicion. "Nice try, pal. Hugh was at Ron's funeral six months ago. Let's try this again, since you're new at this. Who are you and what are you doing here?"

Reaching into his lapel pocket, Marty removed a sterling silver business card case. He handed the woman one of his cards, and she examined it while he returned the case to his pocket.

"Private investigator, huh?" Placing the card in the waistband of her dress, the woman appeared unimpressed. "What brings a shamus like you to the Village?"

"Hugh Cranston was shot earlier this afternoon. He mentioned Ron Davison's name as he croaked. Came here to get the skinny and find myself bumping gums with a swell looking dame..."

Regaining her defiant stance, the woman countered, "Did Cranston send you, or did Trotter?"

Since his obvious charm wasn't working, Marty chose to be blunt. "Trotter hired me to find Cranston. However, I'm thinking that it's too obvious, especially with Cranston now dead. I know the detective working the case, and we both think Trotter's up to something fishy. Why I'm telling you this is simple: you're pretty and you're probably Ron Davison's old lady. So it's in both our interests that I see this through."

"Even if it's Trotter?"

"*Especially* if it's Trotter."

Waving Marty inside the apartment, the woman appeared shocked—but not surprised—at what she just heard. Moving through the dingy-walled apartment, Marty noticed that it was barely big enough for one person: a small living room with a moth-eaten couch with a cheap coffee table in front of it; a small wooden cabinet with a Philco radio in a far corner; and a door along one wall that suggested a pull-down Murphy bed. Along one side was a small stove and refrigerator, with a sink and mirror in another corner. Only a small table with a typewriter surrounded by piles of paper—accompanied by a small wooden chair—seemed out of place.

Turning towards Marty, the woman extended her hand as an introduction. "My name's Rhonda—Rhonda Davison. Ron was my husband."

"Pleased to meet you, Rhonda," Shaking Rhonda's hand, Marty hoped that he could turn this into more than just a pleasant introduction.

Reaching into the cabinet, Rhonda removed two cups and a can of coffee, and headed for the stove. Placing the cups and can on the stove, Rhonda opened the oven and removed a coffee pot. As Rhonda made coffee, Marty took advantage and checked his surroundings—obviously second hand furniture, but this woman was no Apple Annie. If her old man was paying the bills through pulp writing, chances are the typing he heard might be some kind of secretarial work....

Rising from the couch, Marty strode and looked at the half-completed sheet of paper in the typewriter. On the paper was a typewritten conversation between a person named Steve and another per-

"…Rhonda Davison. Ron was my husband."

son named Veronica. Turning over the neatly stacked pile to the right of the typewriter, Marty saw typed and centered along the top page:

MY RODEO ROMEO
A TALE OF VALENTINE VALLEY
By R. Davison

"See anything you like?"

Returning the papers back on the desk, Marty turned to see Rhonda holding a cup of coffee in each hand. She was standing at the couch, leaning to favor one hip. Her tone of voice made her question much more salacious than was intended.

Taking one of the cups from Rhonda's hand, Marty flashed a cocky grin, "I do now."

Gulping some hot, black coffee, Marty saw Rhonda heading for the couch. As she sat down, Marty approached and sat beside her. "What kind of dame writes a story under her dead husband's name?"

After sipping her coffee, Rhonda placed the cup on the table and addressed Marty. "The kind of dame looking to pay the rent. Have a problem with that?"

"No, I don't," Marty countered. "I like my women to be smart, sassy and a little lippy. But I also think it's a bit fishy to pretend to be your dead husband—at least, on paper."

"That's all right," Rhonda buttoned the top button of her blouse. "See.... Ron lost his job in the crash, and we burned through our savings. He started cranking out these yarns for Trotter as a way to get some scratch. I worked some secretary jobs when I met Ron, and when he learned I could type 80 words a minute..."

"Love at first sight," Feeling even more attracted to Rhonda, Marty did his best to keep focused on the case at hand. "But does Trotter..."

Hanging her head somewhat in shame, Rhonda paused before answering, "He knows all too well."

"But how?"

"See," Rhonda lifted her head and held Marty in her gaze. "Some writers are allowed to write under their own name, but for some mags, they write under house names. "Tate Channing", "Rufus T. Hornblow", that kind of thing. Ron hoped to get back to trading stock at some point, so he wrote under R. Davison. You know, 'that's-another-guy', that kind of thing. When he died in a car crash six months ago, I realized I needed to earn a living again..."

"And so Trotter gave you *Valentine Valley*"

"Actually....Ron was writing for that mag. He loved writing Westerns, but Trotter didn't like publishing them. Ron hated writing romance pulps, but I was able to help him with that."

"Listen, sister, this is a great sob story, but why wouldn't Davison—if he's such a great writer—write for other publishers? Trotter's not the only print jockey in town, you know."

"Trotter wouldn't let him," Brushing a tuft of hair from her eyes, Rhonda spoke with a more forceful voice. "Trotter told his writers that he paid the highest rates—our friends have confirmed that's baloney—and in exchanged, his writers worked exclusively for him."

"So Trotter had them under a kind of contract."

"Worse—Trotter kept tabs on his writers, and knew some of their more interesting habits. Drinking, gambling, that kind of thing—but cross Trotter, and he might leak details that would prevent someone from being published elsewhere."

Grasping her cup of coffee, Rhonda took a quick gulp. As she placed the cup back on the table, Marty noticed that there were no lipstick marks on the white porcelain cup. With a sly grin, Marty concluded that her lips really were that deep red in color.

Hanging her head in shame, Rhonda's voice dropped to a near murmur, "After Ronald's death, Trotter came and offered a deal. Either continue writing *Valentine Valley*—same pen name, same royalty rate, or....well, as Trotter put it, I could sell him my words or my body. I chose the former."

As her words hung in the air, Marty Quade kept silent, anger burning in his chest. It seemed like Trotter *was* playing him for a rube, but Marty wouldn't stand for that. Right now, his focus was on Rhonda.

"I wasn't going to let that fat jerk get fresh with me," As she lifted her head, Rhonda's eyes burned with great confidence. "Want to help me break loose of Trotter?"

Shaking his head, Marty pointed at Rhonda. "Listen, sister, I'm not the kind of gumshoe that's easily swayed by a pretty face and a great set of legs. But this shamus has more horse sense than..."

Realizing what Marty was saying, Rhonda interrupted, "Wait a minute—I'm not asking you to kill Trotter. All I want is your help in finding something that can run him out of business."

"Right now, he's my client," Marty asserted. "In fact, he's a paying client."

And that's up in the air with everything that's happened, Marty thought

to himself. Sure, he could let on about his suspicions about the check....
but if this was a setup on Trotter's part, he couldn't risk admitting it.

Rising and walking towards the typewriter table, Rhonda grabbed a
piece of scratch paper and removed the pencil from the bun in her hair.
Returning to the couch, Rhonda made some hasty scribbles and slid the
pencil back into the bun in her hair.

Taking the sheet from Rhonda, Marty glanced and noticed that an
address in a particularly rough area of the Village had been scribbled.
Shooting a glance at Rhonda, Marty saw no indication of a potential double cross, but he was still going to be careful.

Folding and placing the paper in his pocket, Marty looked at Rhonda
with sheer delight. "Listen, dollface, why don't you and I have a little ring-
a-ding after this is all over?"

Fixing her hair, Rhonda cracked her own sly grin, "Why don't you join
me for a ring-a-ding tonight at 7:00 pm? After all, I just gave you the address..."

Flashing a smile that would make a photographer happy, Marty rose
and shook Rhonda Davison's hand. After a long walk down a hallway, and
three floors towards the ground, Marty made his way out of the tenement.

Today had been quite a day: a new client, healthy breakfast, midday
shootout, and an afternoon encounter with a total, full-on doll.

Little could ruin Marty Quade's day right now...

●●●

"What do you mean, my check's no good?"

Standing in the lobby of Wertheimer Bank & Trust, Marty Quade faced
a large, balding man wearing black, blocky spectacles. Even Marty's well-
tailored, sharp brown suit couldn't compete with the man's formal, almost
butler-like attire complete with large, diamond tie pin. Even within the
gray-and-gold marble interior of the bank, the man—who had identified
himself as the manager—stood out as an example of opulence.

"I'm sorry, Mr. Quade," the man announced in a schoolmaster's voice.
"However, Mr. Trotter was quite specific that this check was no good. In
fact, he sent a messenger to deliver this note personally."

Sighing, Marty suspected that this would happen, but didn't let on and
continued the bluff. "Show it to me. Now."

Looking down his nose at Quade, the well-dressed manager scolded,
"This is a confidential matter, and we do not allow regular customers to
view professional correspondence."

Opening his lapel, Marty showed the bank manager his automatic pistol in its shoulder holster. "I think you'll find that this is an all-access pass. I have a license for the gun, a license to be a private investigator, and enough friends on the force to keep you drowning in parking tickets and littering citations. You do realize who I am?"

"You are Martin Quade, the.....self-styled Ace Detective of New York," the manager's voice dripped with disapproval.

"You are correct," Straightening his posture, Marty raised his voice hoping to have someone overhear. "You are not only interfering with my work, you are also interfering in a criminal investigation."

"Perhaps we should consult our attorneys," As a young secretary approached him, the manager turned and addressed her directly. "Miss Calworth, can you please contact Mr. Howe at Dinkham, Lock, and Howe?"

"Kenneth Howe?" Puffing out his chest, Marty shot the young lady a smile. "Please give Kenny my regards, especially since I haven't seen him after that unfortunate incident with Mr. Capone..."

Raising his eyebrows, the man waved the girl off. "Now, never mind..."

Turning back towards Marty, the bank manager worked hard to avoid appearing embarrassed, "Now, Mr. Quade...I think I can make an exception in this case."

As the manager walked back through the door leading into the bank's offices, Marty glanced around the bank lobby. Two men—standing in separate sections of the bank—caught Marty's attention, since both were trying too hard not to be noticed. One was a dark haired man wearing a beige suit, standing at a counter and acting as if filling out a deposit form. Everything about the dark-haired man screamed *G-Man* to Marty. The other—a blonde, slightly less muscular man with a vague, slightly European look—was standing by the door, trying to be hidden. Even in his dark suit, something about the blonde man seemed out of place.

Marty realized that he was knocking over a hornet's nest. That meant he was doing his job *very* effectively. Striding through the door, the manager quickened his pace as he approached Marty. Removing a folder tucked under his arm, the manager handed it to Marty with great speed.

"Read it quick, Mr. Quade," Glancing around the room, the manager whispered. "I don't want Trotter to know about this."

Opening the folder, Marty withdrew a solitary sheet of thick paper with TROTTER PUBLICATIONS INC embossed across the top. Several small blotches on the paper suggested that the note was written in fountain pen. Despite the scratchy handwriting, Marty made out the message with great ease:

TO WHOM IT MAY CONCERN

PLEASE STOP PAYMENT ON CHECK TO MARTY QUADE.
HIS SERVICES ARE NO LONGER REQUIRED; NOR WILL WE
ENTERTAIN HIS INQUIRIES

MICHAEL P TROTTER

Folding the paper in half, Marty slid the note into the same lapel pocket which held his list from Trotter.

"Sir, you can't—that's bank property!" the manager stammered.

"Well, when your butter-and-egg-man Trotter calls," Marty poked the man's chest with each word. "You can tell him you lost it. Used it to wrap fish, whatever you want. Tell him I was here, and you'll have a world of trouble—got it, pally?"

As the bank manager nodded, Marty walked towards the exit. As he approached the door, the European-looking man turned and walked out. Although the blonde man's build looked meager, it suggested that he might be able to kill a man in broad daylight. Out of the corner of his eye, Marty saw the dark-haired maybe Fed move away from the counter and towards him.

Catching the man's approach, Marty turned and offered his hand. "How do you do? I'm Marty Quade, Ace Detective of New York! No, I'm not related to Jimmy Cagney, thanks for asking—how long have you been tailing me?"

Looking around to catch anyone eavesdropping, the man whispered, "I wasn't following you....but you *are* interfering in a Federal investigation!"

"I didn't know," Whispering in similar tones, Marty confirmed that no one was listening. "This has been an unusual day for me. Went from high-end to no-end client in record time."

"Let me guess—Michael P. Trotter, publisher of action adventure magazines?"

"Dead right—I take it you're a regular Philo Vance in the G-Man set."

Regarding Marty with a contemptuous look in his eye, the dark haired man kept silent.

Hoping to stir a further reaction, Marty needled. "Ok, what's the deal?"

"You tell me,"

"Trotter's involved with something shady—something that involves blackmail, larceny, and the kind of good, old-fashioned criminal motive that made this country great five years ago."

"You have no idea," the dark man offered his hand, and Marty shook it. "Name's Draper—Logan Draper. Federal Bureau of Investigation."

"Oh, it's a *Federal* Bureau now," Releasing his hand, Marty stuck both in his pockets.

"You might want to talk with our police contact. He's been advising us on some aspects of the case. He's a homicide cop—name's Neswick."

"Neswick, Neswick...." Letting his voice drift off, Marty feigned ignorance. "Sounds familiar...."

"You spoke with him this afternoon, Quade—the Cranston shooting at the automat." Draper's body tensed, and his voice took on a tone of urgency. "Don't play me for an idiot."

"I never thought you were, but let me tell you something, pally," Standing toe-to-toe with Draper, Marty sneered. "I was hired—and fired—from a case in the same day. The man's murdered when I find him. I've learned things that are none of your beeswax. Stuff's hanging in the air, and I want answers, even if it means running down you glorified beat cops..."

"Let me suggest," Draper reassured Marty, then reached into his lapel and withdrew a business card. "That you meet me in my office—tomorrow morning, nine a.m., third floor. You, I, and Neswick will discuss the case. I'll fill you in on my end, and you can update me with anything you learn— if you choose. But trust me, once you hear what we're looking into....you'll be more than happy to help us."

As Marty attempted to leave, Draper continued, "You have a reputation, Mr. Quade—a reputation that has made its way outside of New York City. Even on our best days, the Bureau cannot hold a candle to what you've accomplished. Hear me out tomorrow morning, and I assure you, you'll be pleased."

"Thanks," Marty responded. "But if you'll excuse me, I've had a long day, and need to take a nap. Hot date tonight."

With that, Marty turned and walked out of the bank.

As he entered the Hotel Baltic, he noticed Trotter sitting in the lobby. Noting the man's seemingly arrogant attitude, Marty chose to play it subtle.

Striding quickly towards Trotter, Marty extended his hand. "Mr. Trotter, good to see you—unfortunately, I have some bad news for you."

"Let me start with my bad news," Refusing Marty's hand, Trotter peered through his wire-rimmed spectacles. "Unfortunately, Hugh Cranston was murdered a few hours ago."

"One of my homicide pals let me know," Hoping to get a reaction, Marty feigned disappointment. "Normally, I don't refund client fees, but in this case, I suppose you want me to mail back your check."

"If you wouldn't mind..." Raising his eyebrow, Trotter spoke with condescending authority. "So I take it you've spent most of your time....in more worthwhile pursuits?"

Feeling slightly insulted, Marty shot back, "Hey, when you hired me, you gained the right to know how I spend my time. Now, my time is my own, and what I do on *my* time is none of *your* business."

"I suppose....after all, some people are born to lead," With every word, Trotter's voice took on a darker, more sardonic tone. "And others are born to serve, if you catch my meaning..."

"I catch it all right," Flashing a slightly evil grin, Marty fought the temptation to perform a public take-down of Trotter. "And let me just say that working with you hasn't been a little slice of heaven....because it hasn't. You should have told me someone was after Cranston. Now, the police think I'm their finger man. You're no longer my client, and you're as welcome as Jack Benny's violin playing."

"Don't take that tone with me, boy!" Shaking with rage, Trotter lifted the walking stick, grasping the handle at one end and the bottom with another.

"Sword stick, huh?" Marty took a necessary bluff. "You know those things are illegal in New York, right?"

Returning the stick to one hand, Trotter forcefully struck it on the ground with each step as he stormed away.

Making his way to his room, Marty took off his jacket and draped it over a chair. Lying down on the bed, Marty planned his evening: early dinner, then his mystery date with Rhonda.

It's going to be a night to remember, Marty thought in silence.

●●●

As the sky grew darker with impending sunset, Marty Quade strode through streets that had seen better days. Even for Greenwich Village, this was a rough stretch that had been worn down by time. Many buildings, including an old mansion, were boarded up and left to be used by squatters. Sidewalk booths, selling everything from apples to Fuller Brushes, were run by various people hoping to catch the nickel of travelers who made a wrong turn. All too well, it was a reminder that although Prohibition had ended two years ago, things still hadn't returned to normal.

Out of the corner of his eye, Marty glimpsed a very curvy woman wearing a man's coat. Although the coat barely hid her feminine figure, the scarf around her head and the dark glasses obscured her features. Despite the oncoming dusk, she seemed confident as she waited alone for someone.

Must be Rhonda, Marty thought as he bounded his way across the street towards her.

As Marty approached, Rhonda turned and flashed a brief smile. Removing her glasses, Rhonda's eyes beamed with enthusiasm.

"Hello, dollface," Marty sauntered besides Rhonda. "Ready for our date?"

Although annoyed at Marty's pass, Rhonda remained composed and unperturbed. "This isn't a date, Mr. Quade..."

"Please—it's Marty."

"Come with me," Rhonda waved towards Marty and both entered the tenement.

Various sounds—kids playing, people arguing—piped through the narrow hallway as Rhonda and Marty walked towards the building's rear stairwell. After heading up one flight of stairs, Rhonda noted the numbers on the doors, and led Marty towards one particular door. Down at the other end of the hall, a shabby-looking old man glared at Rhonda and Marty as he began using a payphone mounted on the wall. Noting the familiar *clickety-clack* sound of a typewriter from behind the door, Marty went to pound on it when Rhonda stopped him, her own knocks reverberating through the hallway. Both heard the typing stop, and then footsteps approaching the door.

As the door opened, Marty was surprised to see a beautiful woman—presumably Chinese—wearing a red silk Chinese-style dress. Long, sleek black hair flowed over her shoulders, and her brown eyes seemed to sparkle. Why this woman lived on the "wrong side" of the Village, Marty thought, I will never understand.

"Glad to see you-" the woman began, and then turned to Marty. "Who's this guy?"

"Marty Quade," Rhonda introduced. "This is Sandra Wong... I mean, Sandra Primrose. Sandra, this is Marty Quade—the detective."

"Oh, the guy who broke the Carlton case last year...." Smiling all too briefly, Sandra's face returned to its usual taciturn appearance. "So what's the infamous 'Ace Detective' doing here?"

"Hugh...has been shot," Rhonda's voice wavered slightly. "Happened this afternoon. Marty's part of the investigation."

Folding her arms, Sandra let out a huge sigh. "Shot? This afternoon? What…"

"The Automat—some guy came in and shot him, getting away before the cops arrived," Marty interrupted. "I know the lead investigator."

"Trotter pulled a scam on him," Rhonda undid the scarf wrapped around her head.

"He also fired me earlier this afternoon," Marty unbuttoned his jacket. "He got a little too high-and-mighty, and so I dropped him like a bad transmission."

"Oh," Straightening herself, Sandra looked relieved that someone *finally* understood her situation. "Come on in."

As Sandra welcomed the pair inside, Marty and Rhonda entered a studio flat that seemed even smaller than Rhonda's place: only a bed, a small stove, a beaten-up chest of drawers, and typewriter table—complete with cheap Remington—in a far corner. Loose piles of paper surrounded the Remington, armed with only a lone sheet standing mid-paragraph. A man of medium build sat on the bed, grasping a small pile of papers. He was scribbling in an awkward manner with his left hand, as his mangled right hand dangled on the bed. Noticing how the wrinkled white button-down shirt clashed with the man's brown skin, Marty observed that the man and Sandra were comfortable and familiar with each other....

Noticing Marty's keen observation, Rhonda chimed in, "Marty, this is Sandra Wong and her husband, Chester Primrose."

"Good to meet you," Extending his hand to Sandra, Marty had a quick realization. "Don't you work at the…"

"Jade Garden, yes," Sandra shook his hand. "Around the corner from the Ventura Diner on 5th. I'm usually working the night shift."

Hearing footsteps approach, Marty turned to see Chester, now standing, extending his left hand.

"Marty Quade, the detective, right?" As Marty shook his hand and smiled, Chester remarked, "Good to finally meet you—I think I saw you at the Club once."

Thinking for a moment, Marty had a flash of memory. "Cotton Club. Two years ago. You tickled the skins for the house band, right?"

"That's right—used to be a drummer. At least, until the head of the Linfero family thought I was checking out his girl."

"Ah, Rudolfo Linfero," Marty shot a sardonic smile. "He probably sent Marco and Pietro after you. They're better known by their nicknames *Tweedledumb* and *Tweedledumber*."

Hanging his head, Chester sighed. "Unfortunately, his boys were smart enough to know how to break the fingers of my right hand, but too dumb to realize I was left-handed. Either way, my timing was off, and I lost the Club gig…"

"…and it was about the time we got married," Sandra interrupted. "Chester and his band mates often hung out at the Jade Garden after the Club closed."

"Best shrimp fried rice in New York," Chester flashed Sandra a smile, speaking volumes of how they felt about each other.

Shooting a quick glance at Rhonda, Marty turned his attentions back to the pair. "The Jade Garden was a great spot—nice, little out of the way place where a guy could go after hours and simply relax…."

"…and my uncle made sure of that," Sandra asserted. "But tell me, Mr. Quade—did you know Linferno?"

"Too well—he was shaking down a client. He sent his goons in my direction."

"And…?"

"I sent them—and Rudolfo—a one way ticket to the cemetery."

"Oh, that's a *good* line," Rushing to the typewriter, Sandra tapped out a bunch of words in rapid succession.

Looking up, Sandra smiled at Marty, who smiled back. *Not the first time I've seen my words in print,* he thought.

As Sandra retuned, Rhonda placed her hand on Marty's shoulder. "That's why I wanted you to come here—both Sandra and Chester work with me. We—and Ron—met through Trotter."

Chester returned and sat down on the bed "Both Sandra and I needed quick money. So we decided to write for the pulps…"

"Wait a second," Marty shook his head in disbelief. "Trotter allows you to write for him…."

"At a cost," Chester replied. "I like writing science stories—you know, rocket ships, planets, that kind of stuff. Hugh agreed, but you know what Trotter did? He assigned me to a different editor who ordered me to write a story titled *Yellow Peril of the Dragon Lady.*"

As Sandra's face soured in disgust, Chester continued, "No, literally—*that* title. In fact, Trotter openly supported it, saying that after all, a check would help me eat more than rice."

Suppressing his anger, Marty turned towards Sandra who explained, "I'm pretty open to writing anything, but I prefer detective stories—used to the tales beat cops would tell over cashew chicken. I'm proud of my

"...ordered me to write...Yellow Peril of the Dragon Lady."

writing, but Trotter won't let me use my own name. Chester and I—for 'accounting purposes'—have to write under house names."

"House—oh, yeah, Rhonda told me about those." Give Marty a thug with a gun, and Marty could handle himself. This pulp stuff was a whole other kettle of fish.

"Some writers are popular enough to write under their own names," Without the scarf, Rhonda revealed herself to be an extremely intelligent and gorgeous woman. "For the three of us—who aren't 'typical' writers—we have to write under house names."

"It makes people think the same four or five guys are cranking this stuff out," Chester asserted. "Other publishers allow some writers to publish under their own name, but Trotter has practically all of his writers use a house name."

"It's true," Rhonda's eyes betrayed desperation and frustration."My husband fought Trotter tooth-and-nail on this, but only got a generic first initial and last name."

"But how do you get paid if you're writing under a false name?" Marty asked. "I can't cash checks that are made out to Jimmy Cagney, although we do look incredibly alike..."

"That's the point!" Fired by anger, Sandra poked at Marty's lapel for emphasis "Trotter's been cooking the books! Most writers—under their own names—get paid a penny a word..."

Rising from the bed, Chester paced towards the trio. "But our checks couldn't buy a bag of circus peanuts. Hugh did some snooping—Sandra..."

Opening a drawer in the beaten chest, Sandra removed a pile of papers clipped together. Handing them to Marty, Sandra then removed a leather-bound ledger.

Marty looked at the papers: one side contained Chinese style characters, but had a large X across the sheet in red grease pencil.

"Cheap printer gave us misprinted menus," Sandra explained. "They wouldn't refund our money, so Chester and I took the menus and use them for notes."

Turning the sheets around, Marty saw the words TITLE: RIDDLE OF THE RECKLESS ROBOT scrawled in pencil across the top. A variety of scribbled notes covered the page.

"Gave Trotter the story," Chester admitted. "His rate's a penny a word, yet I was paid fifteen bucks for a ten-thousand word story. Old man Trotter even handed me my complimentary copy, with the author 'Tate Channing'."

"Now look at this," Taking the ledger from Sandra, Rhonda handed it to Marty. Thumbing through its pages, Marty saw various notes written in red ink: Z4—RIDDLE OF RECKLESS ROBOT/C. PRIMOSE—$15.00/T. CHANNING—$85.00; VALENTINE VALLEY—COLORADO SUNRISE. R. DAVISON, but the amount of $500 had been crossed off with a new rate of $15.00; and GREY SEAL DETECTIVE—RATCLIFFE AND THE MURDER MASTER with S. WONG—$15.00/C.MORGAN—$85.00.

Slamming the book shut, Marty quipped, "Bad enough Trotter's a cheapskate, but he's stealing from his own company—paying others with money due to his writers!"

"But we don't know why," Looking at Marty with great longing, Rhonda took a deep breath. "Trotter's cheating people who are desperate for *any* kind of income!"

"Yeah, and if Hugh hadn't taken this ledger…," Chester asserted. "We wouldn't have any evidence."

"I know how to read ledgers, and I think it's safe to say" Sandra announced. "Trotter's paying these guys for …something."

"Can we…hire you?" Moving closer, Rhonda's green eyes had a slightly intoxicating effect on Marty. "Help us find out what's going on…"

Glancing at the others in the room, Marty spoke with his usual confidence. "Listen, Trotter tried to play me for a sap. He dangled big money in front of me, but not enough for me to fall for his butter-and-egg-man shtick. Now he's treating good, decent people badly."

"So you'll help us?" Sandra asked. "After all, when Rhonda called us earlier, we thought…"

"Look, I'm the best private investigator in the city," Marty shot his usual cocky smile. "Am I going to let this crumb get away with this? Heck, no. Nobody messes with Marty Quade!"

Just then, two loud voices emerged in a commotion. Both were in foreign languages: one a sing-song variety of symbols, the other longer, deeper strings of guttural utterances.

Cocking her ear, Sandra listened and translated, "I can hear something in Cantonese—please don't hurt me, I don't know who you're talking about…"

Removing his gun from its shoulder holster, Marty turned towards the others in the room as he thumbed off the gun's safety. "Stay here—don't leave for any reason!"

"What do you mean?" Rhonda began.

Marty cut her off as he ran out the door. "Trouble's heading our way!"

Leaving the apartment, Marty turned towards the end of the hall. He watched as a large man wearing a sharp, dark suit held a knife. The man was using the knife to threaten an elderly Chinese woman cowering on the floor. As Marty took aim, he caught the man's boyish face, with blonde hair emerging from the brim of the man's fedora.

Looking the man straight in the eye, Marty realized the man was his tail from the bank. Keeping his aim steady, Marty stood his ground. "Why don't you leave her alone, bunky?"

The dark-suited man spoke with a fragmented accent. "Why don't you stay out of things that don't concern you?"

Keeping an eye on man, Marty mentally ran through the accent: *Vhy dun't you stay ut uf things that dun't cuncern you?*

"You're not from around here, are you, pally?" Stiffening his gun arm, Marty spoke with a slight growl. "Let me make one thing clear: I have perfect aim. I'll drop you where you stand. Now drop the knife and let's talk."

"*Dumkoff!*" Twirling the knife in his hand, the man looked poised to stab Marty. "You are interfering! And now, you will die!"

As the man sprang forward, Marty fired three shots in rapid succession. With each pistol shot, the man's body twitched and convulsed in a spastic dance. As he fell, the man dropped the knife and the elderly Chinese woman scampered back to her apartment. Several apartment dwellers—including Rhonda, Chester and Sandra—emerged to see what had happened.

Holstering his gun, Marty pulled a nickel from his pocket and flipped it towards Rhonda.

"Call the police," Marty barked. "Ask for Neswick of Homicide. Tell him a Marty Quade special's racked up and ready to go."

Catching the nickel, Rhonda bolted towards the phone at the end of the hall. As she plunked the coin into the phone and dialed, Chester and Sandra reassured their neighbors. Within a half an hour, Neswick arrived accompanied by several plainclothes and uniformed cops. Approaching Marty, Neswick waved the detective towards a far, private corner of the hallway.

Lifting the brim of his fedora, Neswick arched his eyebrow. "So what's this all about?"

After Marty disclosed what had happened—how Trotter was cheating four people, including Marty Quade—a uniformed policeman approached the two men.

"Look at what's inside!" the uniformed policeman—too old to be a rookie, too young to be a sergeant—handed a cheap wallet to Neswick.

Opening the wallet, Neswick reviewed its contents: a few dollars, some green stamps, and two pieces of identification. One was a New York Driver's license in the name of Charles Q. Morgan; the other was a red-and-white card in a unique script in the name of Johann Gruber. Both IDs contained a picture of the man Marty had just shot.

Waving the uniformed policeman away, Neswick gave a heavy sigh. "Well, that explains the visitor I had this afternoon...."

"Let me guess—G-Man type named Draper," Even after shooting a man, Marty's voice remained unwavering. "Tall, dark-haired, handsome—the kind of guy who should be working Wall Street..."

"You got it, Quade. He's been telling me some rather tall tales....including you spotting him in a bank."

With a broad, arrogant smile Marty whispered, "If he didn't want to be spotted he shouldn't have tailed me so poorly. I went to investigate Trotter's check, and learned that it had more rubber than a Goodyear tire."

Carrying the ledger in her arm, Rhonda approached both men.

Giving her a casual glance, Neswick looked back at Marty and flashed a sardonic grin. "But I take it the bounced check isn't the only reason you're involved."

"I asked him to help," Rhonda caught Neswick's attention with her sparkling green eyes....and held his gaze with her other attributes. "Trotter's been stealing– have a look at this!"

Opening the ledger, Rhonda indicated the figures that Marty had seen earlier. Examining various pages in the ledger, Neswick muttered, "Hmmm.....Morgan. Same's on the driver's license...."

"It's no coincidence, pal," Marty countered. "Guy's accent was slightly European. You know about the stuff that's happening overseas—you know, the tyrant with the square mustache and the bad haircut?"

"Yeah, but what does that..."

"I don't know," Poking his finger into Neswick's lapel, Marty emphasized every word, "But we need to see Draper—pronto!"

"I'm coming with you!" Rhonda declared. "After all, I have a right to..."

Turning towards her, Marty placed his hands on her shoulders. "Listen, dollface, you've done well, but no thanks."

Insulted, Rhonda slugged Marty with a powerful right hook.

A wide grin spread on Neswick's face as he quipped, "I'm impressed."

"Listen, you" Rhonda pointed her finger in Marty's face. "You came to *me*, remember? Trotter may have played you, but I haven't. I deserve a chance to bring this jerk to justice!"

Rubbing his jaw, Marty regarded Rhonda with a new found respect. "Ok, doll-I mean, Rhonda. You earned it. Where'd you learn to hit like that?"

"Grew up with five brothers," Rhonda answered.

As Marty turned to face Neswick, the Homicide detective held the ledger like a schoolboy. "I have a 10 a.m. meeting. You're both invited. It's at the new Federal building downtown. You'll know it when you see it."

All three turned to see another uniformed policeman waving at them. As Neswick and Marty moved from the corner, they noticed that the commotion had died down, with only Sandra and Chester remaining in the hallway with Rhonda. Various plainclothes and uniformed policemen began making their way towards the main stairs, and Neswick soon followed.

As Marty approached the trio of writers, Sandra extended a shaky hand, "I have to go to work soon, but I wanted to thank you for....well, everything...."

Taking her hand, Marty looked her firmly in the eye. "It's my pleasure. I don't like Trotter playing *any* of us."

Chester placed his good hand on Marty's arm as he released his grip from Sandra's hand. "People like us are desperate and simply trying to get by. Trotter made an offer, but it turned out to be a pig in a poke."

Extending his left hand towards Chester, Marty gave him a bright grin. "I'm glad you waited until Neswick left to say that."

Chester regarded Marty's hand unsure how to proceed. Slowly, Chester shook Marty's hand in a limp manner. A shy smile spread across Chester's face, grateful that Marty not only offered his hand....but willingly shook Chester's unbroken hand.

"You're a good egg," Looking at the trio, Marty felt rather proud. "All of you....and as for you, dollface…"

As Marty turned towards her, Rhonda retorted, "My name is Rhonda."

"Rhonda," Marty met Rhonda's gaze, and looked deeply into her eyes. "I look forward to seeing you in the morning."

With that, Marty Quade made his way out of the tenement. As evening broke on New York, Marty Quade walked back to the Hotel Baltic. He was known for two things: being the best at what he did, and helping others in the process. Today, he did *both* things exceedingly well.

In other words, he was doing his job and doing it *right*.

●●●

"Nice digs," Rhonda remarked to Marty outside a newly-constructed beige-brick building.

"Good to know—you might miss that they're the *Federal* Bureau of Investigation now."

Both stood outside the recently constructed Federal building nestled in the heart of downtown New York. Four stories in height, the building had a large metal crest framed by a series of windows. In the crest was an eagle surrounded by the words FEDERAL BUREAU OF INVESTIGATION.

"One of Roosevelt's pet projects," Marty mumbled as he turned towards Rhonda, failing to be inconspicuous in her conservative gray dress and pearls.

Rhonda returned Marty's glance. "Why don't we make our way in?"

Checking his watch, Marty noted the time—9:45. "Might as well. After all, maybe G-Men have better quality coffee and donuts than beat cops."

Taking her by the arm, Marty escorted Rhonda into the building. After a thorough examination by a security guard, Marty and Rhonda headed for the main elevators.

Stopping by a nearby directory, Marty found the floor where Draper's office was located. Entering the cab of the elevator, Marty quickly pushed the appropriate button and the doors quickly closed.

"Must be one of those new automatic elevators I've been reading about," Rhonda declared with delight.

Arriving on the fourth floor, they asked a petite, brunette secretary sitting in a reception area for directions. After Marty handed the secretary a business card—much to Rhonda's chagrin—the pair made their way through the monotonous white halls of the building. Only the numbering distinguished each door, which shared the same frosted-glass-and-wood construction. As they approached the number of Draper's office, they were both relieved when they heard Neswick's sonorous tones emerging from behind the door.

"Listen, I know Quade can be tough to deal with," Neswick's voice declared. "But you need him—trust me, he's helped the department clean up its close rate."

Bursting through the door, Marty quipped, "That's me—the guy who helps the cops do their job better!"

Standing up behind his desk, Draper was sans jacket, clad in a solid white shirt, dark blue tie, and charcoal gray pants. His black hair was slicked back, revealing a sharply angled face that perpetually cast a downward glance. Even without a jacket, Draper's muscular build suggested power and authority.

"Mr. Quade, Mrs. Davison," Draper's deep voice had a slightly hypnotic quality. "I want to thank both of you for coming....please, sit down."

Pointing towards two empty chairs in front of his desk, Draper encouraged Marty and Rhonda to sit. Standing at Draper's side, Neswick seemed more like the G-Man's sidekick than detective.

Clearing his throat, Draper sat back down. "I want to thank you for your time, and more importantly, for helping your country in a time of great need."

Rolling his eyes slightly, Marty spoke with a slight sneer. "Spare us the Jack Armstrong theatrics, pal. Let me guess—Trotter's working for a nasty guy overseas am I right? The funny accent, the fake identification, the cooked books...."

Arching his eyebrows slightly, Draper regained his composure. "Let me just say this—I am working a special joint assignment for the FBI *and* the War Department. As of this moment, all of you are now working under the auspices of both agencies."

"So, what, does that mean we all get a free decoder ring?" Marty gently mocked.

Ignoring Marty, Draper gestured with his hands as he spoke. "Mr. Quade is correct—Trotter is *actively* assisting efforts in Germany, a country now effectively under a military dictatorship and engaged in a reign of terror throughout Europe."

"We all read the news, "Rhonda clutched her purse. "But what does that have to do..."

Rising from his seat, Draper leaned over his desk and spoke with grave concern. "What you may not know is that three months ago, the Germans announced the formation of their own air force—the German word is *Luftwaffe*. American intelligence efforts have learned that much of the funding has come from American sources, one of them being Trotter Publications."

Shaking his head, Neswick was unconvinced. "That's a bit hard to believe—most people want to stay *out* of Europe right now."

"*Believe* it," Draper shot a corrosive look at Neswick. "During the last war, the Germans had a variety of agents hiding in plain sight. Although we were able to stop them."

"We get the picture, chief," Striding beside Neswick, Marty moderated the conversation. "Some Americans—like some Germans—wear shirts that are a nasty shade of brown."

"Quite," Draper went back to his seat, and Marty rushed back beside Rhonda.

Reaching into a desk drawer, Draped removed the ledger and opened it on the desk. Reaching into his shirt pocket, Draper withdrew the two pieces of identification from last night.

"This man—whom Mr. Quade shot last night and whose identification Lt. Neswick so generously provided—is a known German agent," Draper's voice carried a calm chill. "We believe that Michael P. Trotter has been using his publishing company as a front to help German nationals gain new identities in order to undermine American morale and prevent any efforts to assist our European allies."

"So that explains the dual checks!" Rhonda snapped her fingers. "Trotter's been underpaying one set of writers who can't fight back, and using the balance to support these... these spies!"

Folding his hands on his desk, Draper lectured, "One of Trotter's editors, Hugh Cranston, spotted a variety of discrepancies in paperwork which suggested identities for authors who did not exist. He noted these and approached us a year ago."

Biting her lip, Rhonda strained to keep silent. Noticing this, Marty asked, "Does this have anything to do with Ron Davison's death?"

Looking down, Draper avoided Rhonda's gaze but turned to Marty. "Cranston and Davison both had concerns. According to Cranston, Davison had confronted Trotter that afternoon. By that evening...we have harder evidence for Cranston than we do Davison. I'm....really sorry."

Leaning towards Rhonda, Marty whispered, "Sorry, Rhonda."

"But if it's any consolation, Mrs. Davison," Draper adjusted his tie. "Both your husband and Hugh Cranston have done much bringing this to light. In fact, Cranston gave the ledger a few weeks ago to a....Chester Primrose, I believe....hoping that it would be safe."

Confused by these revelations, Rhonda blurted. "But that makes no sense—why hire a detective to find someone you may have already found?'

"Trotter only knew a few of Cranston's hangouts." Marty explained. "My job would either be to find a new hangout or confirm a current one. If I arrive before Trotter's gunman, I'm a finger man; if after, I'm a witness to a homicide."

"What happens?" Neswick chimed in. "Marty finds Cranston—after being shot, of course—and realizes that Trotter's playing a different kind of game."

Rising from his chair, Marty strode towards the cop. "Neswick, I didn't know you cared—you've never called me Marty before."

"I've never been involved in espionage before."

Seeing the warmth between the two men, Rhonda chimed, "And this is the first time Marty hasn't called me *Dollface*."

Turning towards Draper, Marty's voice took on a brisk speed. "Trotter's replacing one set of thugs with another....only *these* thugs ain't exactly home grown."

Allowing the briefest of smiles to play upon his face, Draper regarded Marty with grim determination. "You are correct—we've suspected Trotter for awhile now. We now have concrete evidence of his financial support of foreign espionage. Although we're technically neutral in European matters."

"He's bringing those matters to *our* shores," Marty Quade's voice grew more determined and confident. "And we're gonna stop him!"

"What do you mean, *we*?" Neswick's voice wavered with slight disbelief. "This is a *federal* matter. My badge isn't worth box tops."

Rising from his seat, Draper gave Neswick a look that would burn through steel. "Everyone's got a part to play in this. In other words, you've all been drafted."

Cocking his head back, Marty reclined in his chair as he shot Neswick a sly grin. "Told you—you shouldn't be so eager to get rid of me."

Rising from his chair, Draper walked towards a far corner of the room and removed his jacket from a coat rack. "To use some of the more colorful language in Trotter's magazines, Uncle Sam is more than happy to 'make scratch' on business obligations, including Mr. Quade, Mrs. Davison, and her colleagues."

Shaking her head in disbelief, Rhonda mumbled, "You mean...."

"Yes," Pulling on his lapels, Draper looked powerful in his gray suit. "... but we'll discuss that later."

Flashing his confidence like a badge, Marty Quade rose and stood besides Draper. "So are we going in all stealth and silence....or are we bringing the fight to him?"

"My partner's working on a judge to get federal papers," Draper allowed himself an all-too-brief grin. "We'll pick them up on the way to his office, and we *will* bring the fight to him."

It was the loveliest sound that Marty Quade ever heard—the sound of justice about to be served.

•••

"What's the meaning of this?" Bolting upwards from his chair, Michael Trotter grasped the head of his walking-stick as his office door flew open.

Boldly striding into Trotter's office, Logan Draper reached into his jacket lapel pocket and removed his leather badge holder. Holding it at arm's length, Draper showed the contents—an FBI badge and identification card—to Trotter and his sole companion, a muscular, dark-haired man with a sour face and an equally sour brown-colored suit. Marty rushed in and backed up Draper, and Rhonda quickly entered, closing the door.

"Logan Draper—FBI," Returning his badge holder to his lapel, Draper then removed a folded bundle of papers. "We have a federal warrant, and we're bringing you in concerning to the death of Hugh Cranston."

Stepping forward, Marty flashed his usual don't-mess-with-me grin, then turned and regarded the sour-faced man.

Cocking his thumb hitchhiker-style at Trotter, Marty turned and addressed the sour-faced man. "You got gypped by this carny hack as well?"

Remaining silent, the sour-faced man showed no response to Marty's comment.

Turning back towards Trotter, Marty cracked, "Don't worry, Trotter, I didn't try to cash your check—in fact, I saw your little love note to the bank manager. *Nobody* plays me for an easy mark."

Leaning into his walking stick for support, Trotter sneered at the trio who had just entered his office, "I don't know what this is about, but you have no right..."

"Actually, these papers give us every right," Draper placed them on Trotter's desk. "You've been under investigation for stealing from your own company."

"More importantly—your writers," Rhonda shot Marty a glance, then looked back at Trotter.

Flustered, Trotter's voice took on an indignant tone. "How dare you? You, who came to me after your husband died, who brought others seeking my help."

"And you gypped them," Stepping forward, Marty pointed a finger in Trotter's face as the sour-faced man looked on. "You cooked the books, Mikey. One set of numbers for the typewriter jockeys paying your bread and butter, the other for you to fund an army of foreign thugs."

"And that makes it a *federal* offense," Throwing the papers on Trotter's desk, Draper continued. "In fact, we've been working with local law enforcement on Cranston's shooting. Anything happens to us..."

"And you'll get a world of hurt," Marty patted the holstered pistol be-

"We have a federal warrant…"

neath his jacket. "But nothing's going to happen, is it, Mikey?"

Emerging from his desk, Trotter paced towards the sour-faced man. Nodding to him, Trotter then approached Marty. Both men locked glances while Draper and Rhonda looked on.

"Do you have a problem with me, Mr. Quade?" Despite a meticulously-tailored suit, Trotter looked rather seedy. "After all, I am only a publisher—my magazines provide entertainment for humble souls trudging their way through these times. There are bigger publishers than I—why aren't you investigating them?"

"Because *you* are the problem," Standing his ground, Marty resisted Trotter's attempts at bullying. "You wear your wealth like a cheap suit. You buy me breakfast and hand me a large check....with no intention of following through on payment. The bank manager showed me your little love note, Trotter. Next time you stab somebody in the back, make sure you don't leave fingerprints on the knife handle."

As the sour-faced man moved forward, Trotter waved him back. The sour-faced man stood still.

"I was almost a near-perfect patsy," staring down Trotter, Marty spoke with great emphasis. "If I found Cranston, you could play me as the finger man; if I came across his corpse, I was a witness. Either way, I could help you cover up the fact that you're stealing from your writers to fund a foreign invasion."

Bursting into laughter, Trotter regained his composure and addressed Draper, "That's absurd—in fact, Mr. Channing—the gentleman standing in the brown suit—is one of our best writers."

"That's a lie," Rhonda asserted. "Hugh showed me the ledger! You have two sets of numbers!"

"I don't suppose that you are aware that Mr. Cranston stole that ledger? That he has something he procured illegally?" Sensing an advantage, Trotter flashed a Cheshire grin." Perhaps you would be a good citizen and tell me the whereabouts of that ledger."

"Oh, don't you know already?" Marty stepped up, faced down Trotter. "Your henchman—Charlie Morgan, or is it Johann—tried to grab it last night. Got a few bullets for his troubles."

"Which you donated, of course?" By the look on his face, Trotter assumed victory.

Marty simply grinned—after all, some crooks didn't deserve a straight answer.

"But the important thing, Trotter," Draper asserted, regaining authority.

"Is that we have evidence that links your company with providing financial and logistical support to foreign nationals."

"What—you mean immigrants?" Trotter's sense of indignation seemed counterfeit with each word. "All I'm trying to do....is....is...."

Sunlight drifted in through dusty, rarely-opened blinds. Regaining his composure, Trotter straightened himself. Grasping the end of his walking stick, Trotter regarded the round, white end with a shiny golden tip—as if ready to use it as a club.

Thinking better, Trotter looked up, a malevolent glee spreading on his face. "Why do I bother? After all, none of you will be leaving this room alive."

As Trotter regarded the three people in the room, Channing—the sour-faced man—approached Trotter's side.

As Draper reached under his lapel, Trotter quickly ordered, "Don't think about it, Mr. Draper –my associate—his old name is unimportant, his new name is Mr. Tate Channing....is quite fast on his feet. He has very rapid reaction time, and I would hate for you to be hurt."

Making a side glance at Marty, Trotter continued, "Congratulations, Mr. Quade—you've seen right through my façade. Yes, I am supporting German nationals in this country—and why not? There's a war brewing overseas—a war between perfection and efficiency on one hand, and waste and impurity on the other. Only a few deserve to thrive in the aftermath, and I intend to be one of them!"

"So you're providing money, identities, even an Air Force," Marty quickly regarded the sour-faced man—seems tough, but no need to spring yet—and continued. "The best fascism that money can buy. Am I close?"

"You are dead on correct, Mr. Quade," After giving Rhonda a slightly salacious glance, Trotter's spoke with smug confidence. "Look at our country—people are begging for work and food, and doing little to better themselves. That fool Roosevelt fosters the weak rather than the strong."

"Just like the paper hanger with the cheesy mustache," Marty sneered, with Draper and Rhonda looking on. "You *do* realize he's an idiot, right?"

"Wrong, Mr. Quade—he is a genius." Sitting back down at his desk, Trotter tapped his walking stick for emphasis. "He knows there are two types of people—the superior race and the mongrel hordes. Those who serve and those who command. People in desperate times lead desperate lives....and I intend to use that to my advantage!"

"Some advantage," Rhonda scolded. "You're exploiting others' hard work for your own ends! Worse, you don't seem to believe what you're saying—you're just parroting another guys' baloney. You're spending time building a foreign army for...."

"Takeover," Rising from his chair, Trotter strode over to Rhonda and spoke like a conspirator. "My foreign allies are building military strength, but it is not enough. Building an army of spies here will allow us to....accelerate the moral decay at this country's heart. Strong men must lead us, and I intend to be one of them!"

Quickly glancing at Channing, Marty saw that the sour-faced man was ready to act. "So you're choosing to play this the hard way, aren't you, Trotter?'

"Actually, I'm making it quite easy," Noticing Draper reach again beneath his lapel, Trotter nodded at Channing. Twitching his shoulder, Channing brought his arm upwards then swung it in a sharp, downward motion. With a sickening *whump*, Draper fell as a throwing knife embedded itself into his shoulder. As Draper fell to the floor, Rhonda knelt beside him while Marty approached Trotter.

"See, Mr. Quade," A cruel grin played on Trotter's lips. "Channing is the vanguard of a new movement—a belief that some people are not worth saving. The superior race must prevail!"

"All I see is a thug who got the drop on a G-Man," Pointing a finger at Channing, Quade snarled at Trotter. "And a wealthy thug unwilling to get his own hands dirty!"

"Come, come, Mr. Quade, watch your manners," As his eyes drooped with disappointment, Trotter's spoke with irreverence. "You're going to be on the losing side—why not simply surrender and accept your powerlessness?"

Turning his head towards Trotter, Marty flashed his inimitable cocky smile. It was always the case with Marty Quade—impossible circumstances, difficult situations, and tough choices. Most men folded, but Marty Quade thrived in these conditions– and that's what made him Ace Detective in New York City.

"Because, Mr. Trotter," Marty arched an eyebrow. "In this case, there's no difference between the organ grinder and his monkey."

Snarling, Trotter merely grunted and pointed at Marty. As Channing leapt at Marty, Marty swung a powerhouse right, catching the sour-faced man in the gut. As Channing crumpled to the ground, Marty turned towards Trotter.

"I am part of a new breed, Mr. Quade," Rising from his chair, Trotter held his walking stick like a sword. "This country will be cleansed of wastrels and vagabonds. The world is moving towards a greater unification of thought, action, and purpose—and I am making sure it happens more quickly. That's why this business is a perfect cover—I sell people stories of hope, stories so entrancing that...."

Hearing a loud metallic click, Marty and Trotter looked to see Rhonda, cradling Draper's body in one arm, and the other hand aiming a revolver at Trotter's forehead. As Channing stood up dazed, Rhonda had a look of grim determination.

"As you sell hope, you distract people from what's going on, right?" Holding her gun arm steady, Rhonda looked down at an unconscious Draper, "That's the problem with guys like you, Trotter—you underestimated your staff. Ron and Hugh knew there was something fishy."

"How dare you?" The umbrage in Trotter's voice was thick and dour. "I helped you and your...associates. Gave them an opportunity."

"And cheated us out of our fair share," Rhonda's eyes took on a malevolent glare. "You used us, you exploited us, and for what? Not even greed— just some dumb ideas about superiority."

Holding his walking stick in both hands, Trotter began pulling at either end. With a single shot, Rhonda knocked the stick out of the fat man's hands. As Trotter collapsed in his chair, Marty looked at a patch of metal exposed by splintered wood.

From behind him, Marty heard Rhonda yell, "Marty—look out!"

With a sudden turn, Marty caught Channing rushing him in a bare-knuckle effort. As Channing swung a wild punch, Marty ducked and avoided being hit. As Channing regained his bearing, Marty delivered a few quick jabs to Channing's face. Stumbling backwards, Channing regained his stance and rushed again towards Marty. Attempting a wild uppercut, Channing again missed, and Marty used Channing's momentum against him. As Channing faced the wall, Marty then grabbed the back of Channing's head and slammed the sour-man's face forward. As Channing's face hit the wall with a thud, Marty stepped backwards and allowed Channing to fall to the floor.

Turning back towards Trotter, Marty saw that Trotter had sat back down. Seeing that Rhonda had him covered with Draper's pistol, Marty turned towards the pair on the floor.

Noting a barely conscious Draper, Marty asked, "Is he...?"

"I'm....ok," Draper mumbled in a hoarse voice. "Need .... Take care of Trotter...."

Sighing in disgust, Trotter peered down the lenses of his spectacles. "I am above your petty laws! You are soldiers on the losing side, and I am a general in a growing empire!"

Swinging on the balls of his feet, Marty regarded Trotter with contempt, "Your prose is a bit purple, pal. You've been reading too many of your own magazines."

"Your colleague is down, Mr. Quade…and even if I am 'taken in', there are others like me. We're part of a movement that will rule one continent at a time. It is our sworn duty to rid ourselves of those who are inferior. Only a true race—a master race—will prevail!"

"Really? You're the master race?" Cocking his head, Marty looked at Trotter. "You might want to consider cutting down on the doughnuts. Sugar's gone to your head."

Although facing down Trotter, Quade kept attentive to the sounds around him. At one end, Rhonda was muttering to Draper, softly moaning in pain. In another corner, he heard Channing getting back on his feet, ready for another round.

"Mr. Quade, You're a man of great intelligence," Rising from his chair, Trotter braced himself and leaned forward on his desk. "Why not join us? After all, we could use a man of your skills."

Leaning back, Marty pondered Trotter's offer for a moment. In a brief glimpse, Rhonda felt shocked—would Marty really consider turning sides? Was he playing Trotter?

Straightening his lapels, Marty approached Trotter, staring him dead-on. Marty's dark, well-parted hair was only slightly tousled due to fighting. His suit remained impeccably tailored.

"Sorry, Trotter, no can do," Marty replied, bringing a sigh of relief to Rhonda. "I already have clients. Plus, I prefer staying on this side of the ocean."

Lowering his glance, Trotter shook his head in shame.

"Marty—look out!" Rhonda called.

Turning on his feet, Marty saw Channing wielding the long, sharp steel blade of Trotter's walking stick. With almost superhuman speed, Marty drew his revolver and fired three shots in rapid succession. As Channing fell to the ground, a large red stain spread over his white shirt.

Rushing towards Marty, Trotter reached out as if to strangle the detective. Turning again, Marty was about to aim when he heard two shots. As Trotter fell to the ground clutching his leg, Marty saw Rhonda holding Draper's smoking revolver. As Trotter moaned in pain, Neswick burst into the room with several uniformed police officers.

Taking in the sights, Neswick shouted, "What's going on here?"

"This man needs medical attention!" Rhonda yelled as a policeman approached her.

As a uniformed policeman knelt and yelled at his colleague, Marty helped Rhonda to her feet.

"How'd you learn to shoot like that?" Marty asked.

"Ron was a pulp writer, you know," Rhonda responded. "He took me to a firing range for our first date."

As both Rhonda and Marty smiled at each other, Neswick approached the pair.

"Sorry about the delay," Neswick turned and waved on a pair of men with a stretcher. "Wanted to make sure we had plenty of backup."

As the three of them moved away from Draper, the two men placed Draper on the stretcher and took him to a waiting ambulance below. As they carried Draper out of the room, another uniformed policeman approached Neswick with a pile of ledgers.

"Found these in a secret compartment in a drawer, sir," the cop handed the books to Neswick. "Thought you might want to check them out."

Waving the cop onwards, Rhonda, Marty and Neswick each took one of the large ledgers. Within moments, a hoarse, ragged voice from the floor gurgled, *"Heil Hitler..."*

As everyone turned, Trotter's body began convulsing and shaking wildly. Grasping at the handle of his walking stick like it was a doorknob, Trotter's eyes rolled upwards as thick, white foam spewed out of his mouth. Within a few moments, a heavy sigh burst through Trotter's body, and he stopped breathing.

Handing their books to Rhonda, Marty and Neswick rushed towards Trotter's newly minted corpse. Removing a handkerchief from his pocket, Neswick unclenched Trotter's fingers while Marty, with his own handkerchief, examined the sword cane.

"Puncture wound in Trotter's palm," Neswick turned towards Marty.

Sniffing the round handle, Marty noticed a needle emerging from the tip, "Smells like almonds—cyanide. Trotter took the easy way out."

"Not so much," Rhonda yelled. "Come here, guys!"

As both men approached Rhonda, she had the books open on a table along a far wall of the room.

Pointing to each one, Rhonda explained, "These are Trotter's records—one of them are a bunch of names in German; another is like the journal Hugh gave me, with numbers; and the final is a list of editors who were…. along for the ride."

Wrapping his arm around Rhonda, Marty shot her a grin, "You did good, Rhonda. At least now, we have some hard evidence—too bad Draper's down for the count."

"I wouldn't be so sure, Marty," Neswick's voice took a sour, pessimistic tone as he thumbed towards the back. "Looks like we've got company."

As all three turned, a tall man with a well-coiffed head of gray hair entered the room. Wearing a black suit and tie, he walked with great swagger, and Marty regarded him with some suspicion.

Reaching into his lapel, the tall thin man removed a badge. "John Sterling, FBI. Draper was my partner. He had filled me in on what happened—are those what I think they are?"

As Sterling nodded towards the book, Marty inserted himself between Sterling and the table. As Neswick moved towards the side, Marty warned, "Listen, Sterling—we've been through quite a bit, and we're not gonna give these up."

"Actually, we are going to give this agent the ledgers." Placing his hand on Marty's shoulder, Neswick looked straight into Marty's eyes, "This is their jurisdiction, pal. They're much better qualified than we are."

"And we're very well-prepared to reimburse you for your efforts," Sterling interrupted. "We're very aware of your reputation in this town, Quade—some of us G-Men have often wondered what it would take to get you into the Bureau."

"Nothing doing," Marty poked at Sterling's lapel. "Although I would be best G-Man you hired, I'm afraid my ticket's the street. I'm not giving up my career as a gumshoe for anything."

"Nor would we want you to," Sterling reached into his pocket, withdrawing an envelope which he handed to Marty. "Although it's not as much as Trotter's rubber check, think of this as our small thank you."

Opening the envelope, Marty removed a check made out to his name. Turning away from the group as policemen entered and left the room, Marty saw that it was for less than Trotter's check….but not by much.

Turning back, Marty returned the check to the envelope and shoved the envelope into his lapel pocket. "This isn't going to bounce, is it?"

Laughing, Sterling turned towards Rhonda, "No, it's not….but I have a proposition—a business proposition—for Mrs. Davison."

Standing with arms akimbo, Rhonda regarded Sterling with great skepticism. "Listen, I don't know who you are, but I'm not going to be a G-Man's secretary."

"That's not what I'm asking," Sterling's face, already a long oval, seemed even more pronounced with sunlight streaming through the blinds. "With Draper incapacitated, cleaning up the aftermath of Trotter's activities is going to keep the Bureau busy. We don't know who in Trotter's staff is trustworthy, but we do know that Hugh Cranston was a good egg….and recommended that you run the company until things get settled…"

"Me—run Trotter Publishing?" Shaking her head, Rhonda barely believed what she heard. "What exactly does that mean?"

"You'll work with our accountants to make sure that writers get their full payment," Sterling explained. "But we also need you to keep things moving. Trotter left no succession plan, and quite honestly, we wouldn't trust it if he did. At the very least, you'll be performing a public service."

"Can I hire new staff?"

"Within reason…" Sterling began, and then corrected himself. "And when I say within reason, I mean you can hire whoever you want. After our investigation, you're on your own. "

Standing there, Marty couldn't believe Rhonda Davison's sudden run of luck. The past two days had been a blur—the kind of blur that Marty Quade enjoyed.

Moving towards the tall, thin G-Man, Neswick patted him on the shoulder. "I think, Agent Sterling that you and I should discuss the case at hand—you know, all that bureaucratic nonsense about jurisdictions?"

Noting how Marty and Rhonda were looking at each other, Sterling agreed, "I think you're right, Lieutenant Neswick….and by the way, I never caught your first name…."

As both men left the room, Neswick tilted the brim of his fedora, "My first name's *Lieutenant*. Mama always wanted a policeman in the family."

As the room emptied, Marty turned and wrapped his arms around Rhonda's neck. "Listen, Rhonda—I was thinking that maybe we could do dinner at the Hotel Baltic….maybe a little dancing. Pretend we're Fred Astaire and Ginger Rogers and celebrate our victory. What do you say, kiddo?"

Contemplating for a moment, Rhonda had a sudden flash of recognition. Backing herself out of Marty's grasp, Rhonda had a look of concern on her face.

"I'm—publisher!" Rhonda spoke both to Marty and to herself. "I'm ….I have to finish my story for *Valentine Valley*! Sandra and Chester—I need to call them and ask if they'll join me as editors!"

Another case solved. Another criminal punished. Another good deed performed. For Marty Quade, it was the happiest of endings.

THE END

Bullets, Bad Guys, & Automat Soup

I have always loved hard-boiled detective fiction. Perhaps growing up an only child made me more likely to appreciate those knights errant that walked these mean streets. Maybe it was watching "Spenser: For Hire," which led to reading the works of Robert B. Parker. (I think *Early Autumn* is one of greatest pieces of literature ever written, and yes, I will fight you on that.). Soon, my daily commute to classes in college (and grad school) included trips to various libraries and thrift stores for the works of Raymond Chandler, Dashiell Hammett, Mickey Spillane, Sara Paretsky..... and so began my love of the detective who was "neither tarnished nor afraid."

Another involves a memory from my high school years, and which may be full of shenanigans. While in high school, one of my mother's coworkers claimed to be married to a relative of Frank Gruber's. When Mom mentioned that Gruber wrote the novel *Twenty and Two* (her first "adult" book), and also *The Pulp Jungle*, well...in all honesty, I didn't care at the time. Later investigation into Frank Gruber opened up my eyes to his writing, and it wasn't until recently I got my hands on a copy of the long out-of-print *Pulp Jungle* through the Chicago Public Library (http://www.chipublib.org). When Ron asked me to pitch for this Marty Quade anthology, I had a moment of inspiration.

What if I wrote a pulp story that took place in the pulp era? What if the tale focused on paladins of the typewriter earning their way while surviving on the unique dish known as "automat soup"? (Automat soup, as described in *The Pulp Jungle*, is a combination of hot water, ketchup, other condiments, salt & pepper, and cheap crackers to taste. Composed mainly of free items at the automat, it allowed pulp writers to spend their money on such frivolities as lodging and typing paper).

Crafting the mystery component is easy—you start at the end, but work backwards. (It's like a Sherlock Holmes deduction—you see the results, and then describe how to get there, then flip it so the process leads to the conclusion.) Crafting a motivation was tough: rather than personal, I opted for a very tricky political situation in mid-1930s influenced by a reading of Lynne Olson's *Those Angry Days*. Between the feel of impending war and the desperation of the Great Depression, you have a pretty good brew for a private eye yarn.

Marty Quade is a great character who encompasses everything great about hardboiled detectives. (I'll argue he's the Platonic ideal of private eyes). Throwing him into the pulp "industry" of the time, as it were, made for some really great storytelling opportunities. (As a proofreader for a variety of publishers—including Airship 27—I received a crash-course in the mechanics of writing pulp literature. And yes, there really *were* Western romance pulps. I didn't make that up, although I sorely wish that I had). Creating a "line" of pulp magazines was a bit challenging, but managed to create three pastiches (one an obvious in-joke) and one based on a now public domain character.

Writing this story was not without difficulty—an initial draft was lost due to a corrupted flash drive. Writing some sequences longhand allowed me to rethink the story, and *Publish or Perish* became much stronger and much tighter. In the midst of rewrites, a slight crisis of confidence had me wondering whether my story was rather implausible. While doing research (and by "doing research" I mean "procrastinating"), I came across Peril Press' *Dead Freight* reissue. The story involves Marty Quade, an Egyptian sarcophagus, and heroin smuggling.

My story didn't seem as outlandish after reading.

But this tale is the kind of hard-driving, smart and sassy detective fiction that I thoroughly love. Now its time for me to celebrate with the ideal dish: a large, healthy bowl of automat soup.

●●●

GORDON DYMOWSKI—spends his day hours freelancing as a marketing consultant for non-profits and small businesses. His writing career began with a short story at eight years old, and has taken him through sojourns as a columnist for the **Loyola Phoenix**; writing for the Prodigy online network; and a short-lived humor column for **The Shrubbery.** When he's not editing for Airship 27, Gordon writes for a variety of outlets about a variety of topics, including

I Hear of Sherlock (http://www.ihearofsherlock.com)

Chicago Now (http://www.chicagonow.com/one-cause-at-a-time) and

Blog *This*, Pal (http://blogthispal.blogspot.com)

Gordon made his publication debut with "Out There In the Night" in **Les Vamps,** and has been published in Pro Se's **Tall Pulp.** For more information, a variety of links, and/or a quick and easy way to reach Gordon, please visit http://www.gordondymowski.com

DOGS OF WAR, ANGELS OF DEATH

by
B. C. Bell

Three A.M., Manhattan.

Other than the engines of the city, the only sound on the street was the click of the corner traffic light changing colors. Detective Sergeant Eldon Sayers stood on the sidewalk under the dark awning of a building's side entrance, checking his watch and inspecting the traffic beneath the arcing green and red flashes. Directly across the street from him, leaning against the side of an upscale hotel, stood his partner, Detective Paul Brice, smoking a cigarette between yawns. Both men stared across the intersection only a moment, then, more intently at a car parked in front of a wrought iron gate across the street, as if waiting for something to happen.

"Stake out, huh." A voice said from behind Sergeant Sayers. The Sergeant jumped and spun around, startled.

"Damnit, Quade! Don't do that. Bad enough I have to put up with your surprises at those four-flushing poker games of yours. Why do you have to follow me to the nice part of town and rub it in?"

Marty pulled a toothpick out of his mouth and waved across the street to Detective Brice. Brice waved back, but finished with a flourished pushing motion of his palm, the internationally understood gesture for "get lost."

"All I said was it looked like you guys were on stakeout." Marty shook the sleeves of his suit as he shrugged at Sayers. "Let me guess. Del Raymond, the horse breeder." It wasn't a question.

"How did you know?" Sayers said over his shoulder facing the row of parked cars.

"I have a client of my own."

"Just one? Let *me* guess. One of the board members of Radio Electronic Design Corporation?"

"You ever heard of the Private Eye-Client privilege to privacy?" Marty eyed the parked car over the detective's shoulder.

"Sure, but I know how much you like money. Those people are loaded with it, and I don't believe in coincidences. The only thing that would bring you out this late, besides taunting me, is that you're working the Foucault missing person's case, too."

"Jeez, Sarge, you ought to be a detective." Quade plied a half smile out of his mouth with the toothpick. "You guys keeping an eye on everybody or just Del Raymond?"

"All of 'em. Two prominent society-types missing in three days. One of 'em turns up dead, the commissioner can't afford to sit on his hands."

"So he stakes out bodyguards for every potential victim?" Marty finished for the detective. "Hardly sounds like the picture of economic footwork and deduction to me, but, then again, you guys get paid by the hour. So I won't say anything if you don't."

"You just did," Sayers said. "And detectives are on salary. If they paid us by the hour, we'd be the one's napping in a touring car."

"So what's Raymond been up to?"

"Why didn't you just ask to begin with?" The Sergeant shook his head.

"Because if I didn't make small talk, I knew you'd give me the bum's rush."

Sergeant Sayers did a double take, his head turning sideways. Quade may have been one of the most annoying Private Investigators he'd ever dealt with, but the man was brutally honest.

"See the Duesenberg parked outside the gate of his townhouse. He came home from the stables instead of the clubs tonight, parked there, and passed out."

"Why don't you roust him for drunk driving?"

"Can't do it legally, if he's already parked. Not unless he pulls out on the street. Besides, the detectives shadowing him said he'd only had a couple at the track."

"Huh." Marty massaged his chin with the palm of his hand. Both men stood staring silently at the luxury sedan across the street for a minute. Marty played with the toothpick in his teeth and stuck his hands in his pockets. Turning, he tossed the toothpick in the gutter and said over his shoulder, "I'll be right back."

Sayers nodded without looking. Quade sauntered down the street, his hands still in his pockets, glancing in the windows of the cars parked up and down the block. When he reached the Detective Sergeant's unmarked police car, he glanced both ways. No one was watching when he opened the door and climbed inside.

Sayers glanced at his watch again, sighed, and leaned against the brick wall behind him. Across the street, Brice lit a cigarette, watched the match burn out in the breeze and tossed it in the gutter. Waiting was the hardest part of the job for a Police Detective. Both men looked at each other, and again at the Duesenberg parked outside the gate by the traffic signal.

What they didn't think about, was Marty.

The light in front of the two policemen turned green. Sayers was considering making his way across the street, peeking in the Duesenberg's window and possibly blowing his cover, while Brice contemplated the stub of his burning cigarette.

An engine revved behind them. Spinning tires squealed.

From both sides of the street, the Manhattan detectives' jaws fell open. Brice's cigarette tumbled from his mouth and into his coat, burning his shirt. Brice didn't even notice.

Because passing between them at an illegal speed was their own police car, with Marty Quade at the wheel. Marty spun around the corner of the intersection on two wheels, tires screeching, almost hitting the curb. Brice leaped toward the car and then back, saving his own life. Sayers cussed at Marty and thanked God there wasn't much traffic this early in the morning.

The unmarked car failed to complete the turn on the intersection, peeled up the curb, and across Del Raymond's driveway. Brakes squealing, the detective's cruiser hit the Duesenberg's rear bumper at a right angle, and remained stopped hard, parked inside the rear wheel well of Raymond's luxury Duesenberg.

"Damnit, Quade!" Detective Sayers ran toward the wreckage, trying to yell and whisper at the same time as if his stakeout hadn't been blown already. Brice pulled his gun out and barreled across the street. The Deusenberg's rear bumper fell off. The trunk popped open. Quade kicked open the police car's door and stepped outside.

"Are you crazy?" Sayers grabbed Quade by the lapels, and pulled an arm back, ready to punch. Marty put one hand on the detective's chest and the other on his fisted forearm, and then gently pushed him away. Sayers ground his teeth and Marty turned his jaw toward him, asking if he really wanted to fight. Sergeant Sayers threw both hands in the air and growled, before planting his feet side by side. Quade held his palms out to pacify the man.

"Sorry about that, boys. Seems I accidentally hit the gas when I meant to hit the brake."

Sayers growled and wound his fist in the air. Marty ducked, and Sayers punched Brice in the nose. Quade danced around the both of them as they yelled at each other, and trotted over to where the two fenders had been smashed. Sayers shoved Brice away with both hands and followed. Brice decided to give his superior ample breathing room and checked the back of the car for the point of their stakeout, Mr. Del Raymond, who was just beginning to stir in the backseat.

"Y'know, Quade," Sayers said, "One of these days you're going to pull one of these smart ass moves and it's going to backfire on you. I just hope I'm there to see it."

"Yeah, and one of these days *you're* going to get smart. Me, I don't work by the hour." Quade handed the Sergeant a business card for an auto body shop on 34th Street. "Tell Wendell I sent you, and he'll have the police car fixed by lunch. No paperwork."

Sergeant Sayers nodded, spit into the grass and smiled to himself as if he were starring in a comedy of errors. Marty kicked the Duesenberg's fender out of his way and gazed into the car's open trunk. There was a corpse where the spare tire should be.

"Dylan Gruber," Marty said, feeling the man's neck for a pulse. "The second board member of R.E.D. to turn up missing."

"Get Raymond out here, Brice!" Sergeant Sayers yelled. "And read him his rights!"

Brice yanked Del Raymond off the seat of the car. Del slid out onto the concrete, his legs bending like taffy. Brice smelled the man's breath, and jerked his own head away. Then grabbed him under the arms and laid him across the hood of the car. Del began to slide off again.

"I thought surveillance said he'd only had a couple of drinks." Brice continued to keep Raymond from sliding off the hood of the car with one hand. "This guy's dead drunk."

"And his hitchhiker's just dead." Marty pulled a blanket out of the trunk and placed it over the corpse's face.

Sergeant Sayers slapped Raymond's face back and forth with his hand, but all the playboy millionaire did was moan. Marty, realizing this was the kind of interview that was going to take all night and several pots of coffee, waved at the detectives and made his way back to the street. He had just enough time to grab a few hours' sleep before calling his client to collect.

Case Closed.

●●●

In the last two weeks, two members of the board of directors of R.E.D., the Radio Electronic Design Company, had disappeared only to be found dead later. The first victim, Mr. Mason Foucault, a world famous architect and designer, made headlines when his body had been found floating beneath one of his own Manhattan bridges. Foucault had a history of dark moods, and the body had been so beaten and bloated on the river, that the coroner's verdict had been suicide although there was no note.

Then, only three days ago, Dylan Gruber, an electrical wizard on R.E.D.'s board of directors, had been reported missing. There had been no witnesses nor clues to his disappearance.

Two days ago, Marty had been hired confidentially by Mrs. Vivian Lennox, wife of millionaire Lester Lennox, the founder of R.E.D. and another one of its board members.

The son of an Army General, Lester Lennox had been a hero during the war, and looked to be on the verge of a promising congressional career. The R.E.D. company mission was to revolutionize the radio industry by improving sound through state of the art engineering and materials. The company had been all set to compete with industry giants like Philco-Ford in the radio market, when they made a discovery. A discovery that involved a different kind of broadcasting...and the United States Department of Defense.

While the project was considered "Top Secret" it was the technology that was waiting to be discovered, not the instrument itself. What that meant was that people all over the world, including enemies of the United States, were racing to invent the same product. The first hand-held two-way radio.

A portable radio that would fit into a backpack and could go anywhere. Such an invention would give an army a decided advantage on the battlefield in an instant. Men would no longer have to lose their lives running telegraph wire, or as runners and couriers, dodging shrapnel and enemy fire simply to get word to the soldiers on the front line. It would save lives.

Mrs. Lennox had been positive that the disappearances were linked to the radio contract. However she had no proof, and her husband Lester, a self-made man, wouldn't approve of a bodyguard. So, Vivian Lennox had given Marty a list of R.E.D.'s board members, and suggested he investigate several of them. The most prominent suspect on the list to Marty had been a Mr. Del Raymond, the man he'd just caught with a body in his trunk, a horse-breeder that had made a fortune off bootlegging during Prohibition.

Marty had smiled. He'd known Del since prohibition days, and catching crooks was more his speed than bodyguard work.

After sneaking away from the scene of Del Raymond's arrest the night before, the ace private eye had gone back to his room at the Hotel Baltic, gotten a few hours' sleep, and then called on Vivian Lennox to collect his check. After a big breakfast, he went back to the Baltic.

"Any messages?" he asked the desk clerk.

The clerk searched the cubbyholes behind him and handed Marty a slip of paper. Beneath Marty's name was a phone number and the message:

Have need of your investigative services.

Del Raymond.

● ● ●

"What do you mean it was a frame-up?" Marty said. "They caught you! Stinking drunk with the corpse in your trunk!"

"Marty, I may have done some dumb stuff in my time, but I've never murdered anybody. Certainly not Foucault or Gruber."

"Dead. Man. In. Trunk," Marty repeated, tapping on the chairs backrest in front of him.

They were sitting across from each other in Raymond's city jail cell. Raymond, on the steel platform they called a bed, and Quade on a chair that might better have been called a stool. Marty had come out of curiosity. It had pulled him here. Why would Raymond want to hire the same detective who had just helped arrest him?

"Because we both know that while you're the biggest jerk in the state, you're also the best damned Private Eye."

Quade's curiosity pulled harder.

"Fact is, I went down to the stables last night to check on one of my horses, and something hit me in back of the head. Next thing I know, I'm being pulled out of my car, called a drunk, and arrested for murder."

"You were drunk."

"No, I wasn't. Here, feel this." Raymond leaned forward, parting his hair with his hands to display the lump there. He flinched when Marty barely brushed it. "That ain't no gin blossom, Quade. Somebody hit me and poured alcohol all over me."

"Did you tell that to the cops?"

"Yeah, we had quite a laugh about it."

"You're crackin' me up, too." Then Marty remembered what Sgt. Sayers had said. The detective who had been tailing Del Raymond all night had only seen the horse breeder have "a couple of drinks." One of Marty's eyebrows lowered toward a lopsided grin. "You know I don't work cheap."

"We're talking the electric chair here, Marty! I'll pay you ten grand if you can find out who the real killer is. We got a deal?"

"Plus a hundred dollars a day, plus expenses." Marty counted on his fingers. "Now, if I were you I'd lawyer up. Better a live broke man, than a rich dead one."

Del Raymond nodded his head and shook Marty's hand as the guard came down the hall to unlock the cell door. The jailhouse door rattled behind Marty as he left. Raymond watched him from behind bars with a lonely look in his eyes.

●●●

Marty debated whether or not to go to the scene of last night's stakeout, or take advantage of the office hours still left in the day. When he had first met with Mrs. Lennox, she had mentioned "contracts" and that always set off alarms. Contracts were tricky things, full of the sort of little details that corporate board members like to fight over. And when big wheels fight over big money, big people get run over.

Mrs. Lennox had given him a list of the board members. Now, Marty pulled it out of his pocket and eyed the dozen names on it. He needed more. He had pumped Detective Sergeant Sayers about the victims the night before, and, having wrecked the Sergeant's car, he knew he'd already worn out his welcome there. So, waving down a cab, he headed for the offices of New York Daily News' morgue, where old articles, photographs, and records were kept on all the newsworthy patrons of the city.

Marty had traded information with more than a few reporters in his life, and Sidney "Mole" Muller had been one of them. Muller was not some great bastion of journalism, but rather a man that had found a way to make what he did pay. He traded information with anybody who had the cash, or more information.

"Y'know, Marty, these rich guys have enough money, they're the only ones that pay us *not* to print anything about 'em," Muller said. "In fact, if it doesn't involve evening dress, charities, or patting themselves on the back they tend to want to stay *out* of the limelight."

"So do cockroaches, only they can't pat themselves on the back." Marty pulled the list of board members out of his pocket and pointed at a name. "What do you know about Mason Foucault?"

"Probably no more than you. World famous civil engineer and designer. Cross any bridge outside of Brooklyn, or hold a phone with a mouthpiece connected to the earpiece, and you're familiar with his work. He was famous for adding that extra something that made his work both functional and formal. A well-known perfectionist. So much so, you add that with the fact that Foucault would disappear for about five days a month, and you begin to believe the rumors that he was manic depressive."

"Moody?"

"But always 'up' in public. Behind the scenes he was the tortured artist type, kind of guy that would rather destroy one of his works than leave it less than perfect."

"What about evidence? Associates? Motive?"

Mole handed Marty the front page published two days after Foucault's disappearance.

The civil engineer's financial and family life seemed to be more than stable. There was no suicide note. Again, no signs of foul play, but the body had dropped three-hundred feet below the bridge and spent a day bouncing off rocks in the river. There had been a blow to the back of Foucault's head, but the body's remains were beyond repair. "It was like operating on a bowl of Jell-O," the Coroner had said, off the record. Still, Foucault's head wound had traces of the same limestone on it that had been below the bridge.

"Sounds like he landed tails up," Marty said.

"From that height, heads is a sucker bet."

"Now," Marty held a twenty dollar bill in the air, and waved it in front of Muller. "What more can you tell me about Dylan Gruber?"

"You don't know?" Mole's mouth hung open. "I thought you'd tell me. You're the one busted his corpse out of a trunk last night."

"I'll tell you what I know, if you tell me what you know." Marty pulled his list off the table along with a loose paperclip. He clipped the twenty to the paper and threw it back on the desk. "But I'd like to work my way down the list."

Mole's stare broke from the doorway. He looked at the list then at

Marty, then back across the room blankly.

"Oh, c'mon!" Quade reached for his gun out of habit. "I oughtta just beat it out of you," the Private Eye mumbled under his breath as his hand abandoned his lapel and began searching his pockets for small bills.

"Hey, can I help it if I got wide gauge paper clips?" Mole said, holding his hands in the air. "They only work if there's a thick enough stack of green between 'em."

Marty pulled out a ten, slapped it on the list, and stared down at the Mole like a predator. Muller shrunk in his seat.

Dylan Gruber had been an electrical genius. The inventor had done pioneering work in Ultra-High Frequency research, and already had patents for broadcasting television. But his latest work, the process of shrinking the vacuum tube or finding a way to bypass it in radio amplifiers, was considered revolutionary.

"I suppose nobody knows how Gruber's new electric amplifier works, except for the people over at Radio Electronics Research and Development." Muller flipped through some loose articles cut from the newspaper and glued into a scrapbook file. "I remember one of the copy editor's boys going over to the library to research this one. There's already a gadget patented called the Transresistance Conductor, but nobody can get the thing to work."

"Gruber might've found some new ingredient."

"New element would be more like it, according to the guys in the science department."

"So the victims were both pioneers in their field. I can't see Del Raymond being dumb enough to start knocking off big shots like that." Marty scratched a note on his list, checked off the victim's name and continued. "What about these two listed together, Horvath and Devries?"

"Exactly what they sound like, lawyers, and the guys that really run the firm. Horvath knows all the contract loopholes and DeVries is some kind of patent attorney. Devries has a younger brother who works with the firm but isn't listed as an associate. He's hired muscle. Considering they call him 'Beanie,' I'm guessing he didn't exactly graduate from law school with honors."

"So I should probably talk with these two to get the 'official story.'"

"That would probably be a start." Muller looked up from the table and started to close the scrapbook.

"And I'll probably have to get the real story from Beanie. Ooh, no you don't!" Marty flipped the big book back open. "We're working all the way down the list, Mole. What's this guy do?"

The Mole sighed and shook his head, but couldn't meet the detective's eyes.

"That's Jacob Shockley, owner of Shockley Mining Corporation and worth a fortune in precious metals…"

•••

An hour later, leaving the newspaper's morgue, Marty realized the one thing he didn't have on his list was Radio Electronic Design's address. The bulldog private eye walked half-a-block to a corner drugstore, swept a finger through the telephone book, and came up with two listings at one address. One for their corporate headquarters and one for the laboratory and factory. Back out on the street, he hailed a cab and gave them the address.

Radio Electronic Design's headquarters sat near the warehouse district, a nondescript four-story brick building with yellow letters on the side spelling, Radio E. D. If Marty hadn't known better, he would've thought it was a commercial appliance dealer with a warehouse in back.

Briskly striding through the entrance door, Marty made his way through the lobby, avoiding the desk clerk as if he'd been there before, and headed straight for the elevator. Scanning the office numbers and names framed by the elevator door at a glance, he stepped inside and told the attendant, "Four."

"Hey, I know you. I saw your picture in the paper," the elevator attendant said. "You're Marty Quade, the detective!" Hitting the switch, he chuckled. "Almost like a copper going to see the brass. Get it? Copper? Brass?"

Marty nodded that he did, exited the elevator, and stepped toward an office at one end of the hall. The letters on the door proclaimed it to be the office of Miklos Horvath and Anthony Devries, R.E.D.'s lawyers. Quade stepped inside and, with the door still swinging behind him, strode firmly across the waiting room ignoring the secretary behind the desk.

"Excuse me?" The young lady said, jumping up from her seat. "You can't go in there without an appointment, sir." Marty was already past her, but she stepped toward the door trying to block him with her arm.

"I've already been appointed." Quade waved her arm out of his face like it was a noxious fume and slung open the office's interior door, effectively blocking the secretary. She was still complaining from behind the door, as Marty stepped into the office and slammed the door closed behind him.

Miklos Horvath and Anthony Devries were lawyers pressed from the same mold, just on a different scale. They looked almost exactly alike, except Devries stood a foot under Horvath's six-foot frame. Their clothes were cut from the same cloth, almost the same pattern. Horvath wore gray, Devries blue. Slick pomaded hair, thin mustaches, and cigars seemed to be the order of the day.

The taller one, Horvath, sat behind a large oak desk glancing up from a sheet of paper in one hand as Devries spun around with his bottom lip sticking out, an outraged look on his face.

"We're in the middle of a meeting, Mister...?" Devries said through his teeth. His manner was much less polite than his words, almost threatening.

Trying to defuse the situation, Horvath spoke in a polite pitch. "Didn't Miss Moore...?"

"She tried to, but don't blame her. I'm Marty Quade, Private Investigator."

"And?" Devries hands formed fists at his side. "You say that as if your name is reason enough to walk right in any time you please."

"I know who he is, Tony. I've seen him in the paper. You have too." Horvath said. "Mr. Quade is quite well known his field."

"And a good guy to talk to before the Feds move in," Marty added. "I've got some questions for you two, and we both know they're going to end with me asking about Radio Electronic Design's financials. Am I going to find anything fishy in there?"

"Fishy?" Devries spat. "What gives you the right to stroll in here off the street, and start questioning us like common criminals? Who hired you?"

"I'd think a lawyer might know something about client-investigator privilege." Marty sat down on the couch by the wall and crossed his legs like he was client. "I don't have to tell you, but I will say, it's somebody connected to your board of directors."

"Del Raymond?" Miklos Horvath said. "I saw in the paper last night where you arrested him. He's been the most unpredictable member of the board for years. Gambling, bootlegging during prohibition, why the man spends every night in a club. I hate to tell you Mr. Quade, but it's highly likely Del Raymond is guilty. The man's not ethically fit."

"Nah, Del didn't hire me. Somebody related to somebody else on the board did."

All movement stopped. Both lawyers looked up at Marty, and the room remained threateningly silent.

Marty didn't bother to mention that technically he'd already solved the case for Mrs. Lennox, his original client. "Del may be crazy, but he's a not a murderer."

"How would you know?" Devries countered, pointing a stubby finger at the private eye.

"Oh, I'm not saying Del couldn't murder anybody. Get him angry and he might beat you to death. But I've known Raymond for years, and we're talking systematic, premeditated murder here." Marty counted off on his fingers as he spoke. "A, he's not that mean. B, he's got more money than he knows what to do with. C, Del couldn't plan an evening, much a less a murder spree. And, D, he's not that stupid. He may be mobbed up, but that's *why* he's not that stupid."

"We'll be glad to give you any information we can, Mr. Quade." Horvath stuffed his cigar in a giant ashtray on the desk.

"But it sure sounds like you're working for Del." Devries shook his head.

"What matters is, I'm on this case now, and I'm staying it out." Quade leaned forward and punched the coffee table with his index finger. "There's no way to get rid of me."

Devries' eyebrows hung low over his forehead in a "V." His hands flexed at his sides. The lawyer was both angry and anxious. Horvath stood up behind his desk.

"Mr. Quade, to be blunt, you may have a problem with our financials. We're currently doing government research with funding coming directly from the Department of Defense. To open those files would be an act of treason, as they are currently Top Secret, including the funding."

"You're talking spy stuff," Marty leaned back in his seat. "And this isn't spy stuff. A spy doesn't start knocking off well-known prominent board members. He doesn't want to be noticed. A spy would wait until your little radio doohickey is designed and just steal it."

Horvath sat back down. Devries took the seat in front of the desk.

"What I can tell you, Mr. Quade, is that we have a lot of money wrapped up in this project. A portable two-way radio could make or break this company. A lot of people's futures, both employees and management, are counting on it. But, in answer to your question, while there is a lot of money riding on it, our accounting for the two-way radio project is under inspection of the Secret Service and the Defense Department."

"What about the members of the board? Any of them having trouble with the bills?"

"Not that we would have any way of knowing." Devries stepped toward the door and opened it, signaling it was time for Marty to leave. "We have no control over our board members outside of the business of R.E.D. They are all invested in the company. Del Raymond is wonderful example of that."

Marty didn't move from his seat. Devries continued to show him the door, his eyes burning a path from the detective to the exit.

"Must hurt the bottom line to lose two of the world's foremost engineers in a week. If I were you guys, I'd be wondering whose next."

Horvath and Devries glanced at each other. That was all Marty needed. They were worried about it, too. Marty didn't have a built in lie detector, but he had questioned enough squealers in his time to know when something was up. And something was up. As tough as they acted, the two lawyers were afraid of something besides him. Something besides another murder.

"So, you're sure there's nothing else you want to tell me?" Marty stood up, straightened his tie.

Devries was still looking up across the room at Horvath. Two large men in suits appeared at the door. Marty had seen Horvath press the signal button under his desk. Security, bodyguards, hired muscle; they were all the same to Marty.

"You're either afraid, or you're covering for somebody." Marty now stood by the door but directly across from Devries. Devries was gritting his teeth as he spoke.

"We thought our problem had been solved, along with the entire case, last night!" Devries waved the door back and forth and motioned for the guards to come in with his jaw. "There's Top Secret research going on in this building. Good day, Mr. Quade."

Marty grinned at the security guards. They looked more like hired muscle than professionals, and that's what he had wanted to know.

He had what he wanted. He had stirred something up.

One of the security guards hands reached under his jacket for a gun. Marty shoved the man's elbow down with one hand, forcing the handgun back into its holster, as he drew his own. The private eye's right hand flashed, the barrel of his automatic pressed between the guard's eyes. The guard went stiff. He closed his eyes then his knees started shaking.

"Slow down there, pal. Nobody gives me the bum's rush."

The other guard stood as Marty stuck his gun back in his shoulder holster. The guard under the gun seemed to deflate and shiver, wavering where he stood as the Private Eye stepped back into the hall. Marty strode briskly toward the elevator as the open-mouthed guard pulled the shaking one down the hall behind him.

"I'm sorry, sir. I have to escort you from the building," the guard in the lead said, almost carrying his partner.

"Thanks." Marty pressed the elevator button. "You guys make me feel really safe."

"Nobody gives me the bum rush."

Marty could feel it, he *had* stirred something up. The two lawyers were afraid of murder and more. What could it be? Or, who could it be? Horvath and Devries were both war heroes, so whatever it was had to be pretty frightening. But he'd found out all he could at R.E.D.'s facilities—for now.

●●●

Leaving R.E.D.'s building, Marty wished he could be a fly on the wall in the lawyers' office. If he knew what Horvath and Devries were talking about at that moment, this case might already be closed. He stopped on the sidewalk a second and straightened his hat. A light appeared in his eye and the detective glanced back at the building with the other eye narrowed, as if he were aiming a gun at it.

Making his way around the block, Marty glanced at his watch, then at a train car that had been converted into a hot dog stand. He hadn't eaten lunch, he hated wasting shoe leather, and the place was still in business which, these days, meant somebody had to be eating there. The sign outside said it was a diner, but stepping inside, it didn't take a detective to figure out it would always be a hot dog stand. Marty sat at one of the four seats by the window, the only ones in the place. He ordered the Hot Dog Special and lingered over the fries, reading a newspaper somebody else had left behind and sipping his coffee. Glancing at his watch again, he got up and left. An hour-and-twenty minutes after getting kicked out of the offices of R.E.D., he was standing in front of the building again.

This time, he pulled his hat down low as he strolled past on the sidewalk and glanced inside the lobby's glass front. The same desk clerk was on duty as had been that morning, but so was the hired muscle. Two guards sat at the table in front of the lobby playing cards. If it had been just the desk clerk who had known his name, Marty could have talked his way in easily, but with the goons watching the kid a hypnotist wouldn't be able to talk his way in.

Marty passed the building by with his hat pulled low. Once he'd escaped possible view from the lobby, he noticed the smokestacks on top of the buildings. There were three of them. Two large, one smaller. The weather was warm, so the plant's heating chimneys wouldn't be operating. The two large ones seemed sizable enough to handle factory production, probably more than a radio manufacturer would ever need. With a staff of about a hundred employees, he thought the smaller smokestack might just be R.E.D.'s employee cafeteria.

Rounding the building, he found the employee entrance, next to a small dirt lot—most likely it would be guarded for a while, too. But a hundred feet away, just below the smallest chimneystack stood an open door. Steam escaped from the backroom as a man in an apron leaned against it, smoking a cigarette and staring at the sky. He hid the cigarette behind his back as Quade approached, like he might be taking a break on the clock. Marty straightened his tie, and tried to look like he was management.

"Coffee break?"

"Uh…yeah, coffee break." The man's eyes skittered from one side of his face to the other as he dropped the cigarette butt on the ground and rubbed it out with his foot. He looked at his wrist even though he didn't have a watch on. "Guess break time's about up." Wresting the hinged doorstop off the ground with his foot, the kitchen employee kicked it into the clamp on the side of the door with his shoe.

Marty pressed his hand against the door, effectively holding the cafeteria cook against it, and holding it open at the same time. He lowered his eyebrows with obvious suspicion.

"You wouldn't be trying to keep me out of the kitchen would you, Cookie?" The only real I.D. Marty had on him was a Photostat of his investigator's license. Staring the man down, Marty flipped his wallet open and closed, so quickly that the food worker never really saw it. "Board of Health, Inspector Quade. You haven't been spicin' up the gravy to hide the spoilt meat, have yah?"

"Mister, I just started working here a couple weeks ago. I don't want no trouble."

If he'd paid closer attention the man in the apron would have noticed, Marty's mouth was beginning to curl up at the edges.

"See for yourself." The kitchen worker stood back, holding the door open himself with one arm and waved Marty in with the other. Marty's face broke out in an evil grin as he stepped past Cookie and into the kitchen.

Cookie made eye contact with a man stirring a gigantic pot with a ladle, then with two other employees in the backroom, before shrugging his shoulders and lumbering over to the man stirring the pot. The other man pulled his ladle out and listened as Cookie whispered in his ear. Two more cooks stood behind them watching curiously, their heads tilted the better to hear the conversation with.

Marty marched through the back of the kitchen before they had a chance to figure out who he was. Making his way toward the dining room, he stopped, pulled a spoon from one of the pans and held it beneath his nose. He slurped some sauce off the top, raised an eyebrow at the crew, and the entire kitchen staff went hectically, and very visibly, back to work. Putting the spoon back in the pan, Marty held up a finger in the universal sign for "one moment, please," and stepped through the swinging door.

The dining room stood in an enclosed area of a hundred feet square, with windows that looked out on one of the building's interior hallways. Marty guessed there were still about twenty employees in khakis and work shirts finishing their lunch. The lady at the cash register stared at him in curiosity for a moment, until a few more employees strayed in, picked up cafeteria trays and began working their way down the serving line.

Crossing the room full of lunch tables, Marty followed a row of brightly-colored art deco chairs and perched himself on one of them in the front corner of the room. The man with the soup ladle watched through the wired window in the kitchen door. The detective pushed his hat down from behind his head and leaned the chair back against the wall as if he were about to take a nap. Marty didn't move until the kitchen crew had finally lost interest a half-hour later. When he raised his head again, nobody was watching him.

A young man in a lab coat wearing an expensive tie wandered in the room. The dapper executive didn't grab a tray and line up like the rest of the employees. Instead, he gradually turned his head, scanning the faces in the room. He was looking for somebody, most likely an employee who had taken too long a lunch hour. Marty took in the suit and shoes beneath the young man's lab coat and came to a happy conclusion. He was middle management.

Exactly the man Marty had been waiting for.

Marty was counting on the effect that he was the only other man in the room wearing business attire. He stood up from his chair with a look of recognition on his face, as if he'd suddenly recognized or had an appointment with the young manager. The would-be executive's head tilted in curiosity as Marty stood at attention, then began to approach him with one hand extended.

"Hi there, you must be Mr...?" the Private Eye said, his hand hanging in the air.

The young man shook Quade's hand out of habit, his head still tilted in confusion, as if he thought he should know this man. "Jimmy Gaines, Sound Department. And you are? I'm sorry. I have a terrible memory for names."

"Quade, Marty Quade. I'm a private investigator hired by one of the board." Marty had known this whole meeting would involve his dancing around the truth, but the fact that Jimmy Gaines hadn't yelled out Marty's name and called security meant that Horvath and Devries hadn't notified the staff about their earlier meeting, and Marty's subsequent ejection from the facility.

So, Marty hadn't been eighty-sixed from the building. The lawyers were trying to keep this case under their hat.

"Can I help you?" Gaines asked.

Marty smiled at the magic words.

"I'm sure by now you know about some of R.E.D.'s higher-ups moving on to that great board room in the sky. And, I'm working for them—but you and I both know, the employees of a company sometimes know more about what's going on than the men in charge. They know things first; they're in the middle of the action."

"If you're looking for me to rat somebody out you've got the wrong guy. And, I'm not the gossipy type."

"I just need an employee's opinion on some questions. What are you? A line manager?"

"I'm a sound technician, but around here that's practically working on the line." Gaines waved a hand for Quade to follow him into the hallway, and then into an empty office down the hall. He closed the door behind him. "You've got ten minutes."

Gaines sat down behind the desk. Marty leaned across it from the chair on the other side.

"Mason Foucault, the depressive civil engineer that jumped off his own bridge, what do you know about his personal life? Did he play well with others?"

"I met him a few times, but Foucault was really in on product design—making it look good, easier to use—while the rest of us were trying to cram all the electronics into whatever crazy shape he wanted. They said he was manic-depressive, or shell-shocked from the war or something, but I never saw him out of order. He was like an artist, a perfectionist, and when he got what he wanted, he wanted more. I don't think he killed himself. The two jobs I worked with on him, he was tough. I mean, he was one hard working soldier."

"Huh." Marty had out his notepad. Gaines hadn't looked at the clock on the wall yet.

"What about Dylan Gruber?"

"Dill? Now you're in my territory. Dill was funny, a great guy to work with, nice family. I still haven't gotten over it. Used to listen to ballgames over at his house on the weekend."

"So, pretty normal guy. You think Del Raymond killed him?"

"God only knows. Sometimes I wonder why they let that guy on the board. I'm sure it's because he served with the rest of them in the war, but I don't know. He could have done it. But every time I've seen Mr. Raymond he's been perfectly happy chasing skirts and leaving early for a party. If he did kill anybody, it had to do with money I bet. His horses can't win all the time."

"Any idea what they may have been working on?" Marty checked himself and sat back in the chair. "Nothing Top Secret, just anything that would affect business."

"It's no secret," Gaines said. "In fact, it's something that's already been patented. It's just nobody seems to be able to find the right materials to make it."

"Make what?"

"I don't really have time to explain, but it would be the equivalent of shrinking a vacuum tube. Electronic devices would run instead through a modified conductor, or a semi-conductor."

"Sounds like a short opera maestro to me, kid. I guess what I need to know is, were they having any problems here at work—Del Raymond included—with so much riding on this conductor thing—"

"Actually, it's a 'transistor,'" the young engineer offered.

"Never mind that." Quade sliced the air with the side of his hand. "What's the biggest thing keeping this conductor-transistor thing from being finished?"

"Materials. With the patent already out there, all we need is the right geologic or chemical mixture to form a conductor. Then the 'transistor' will boost electrical power."

"And Gruber thought he could build this thing? The conductor?"

"Pretty much, but it was a matter of time. Like trying to invent the steam engine without having invented all the parts yet." Randy's eyes went back in his head like a thought had struck him. "Actually, there's a mineral that works, Germanium. It's just so rare we can't find enough of it." He scratched his head. "Funny, though, now that you mention it, I remember some of those guys on the board arguing about it. Some of the big shots seemed to think we should have no problem creating some. As I recall Dill used to send them memos with comments about 'hand wavium' and 'hiring a wizard.'"

"Germanium, huh. You remember who was involved in this little debate?"

"Sure. Most of the old soldiers were there. Foucault and Dill, Del Raymond—with liquor on his breath and a racing form in his pocket as usual—Jake Shockley, Lester Lennox... I think everybody was down in the lab that day, everybody but the lawyers and the General."

"The General? You talking about the General Lennox, Lester Lennox's Dad?"

"Yeah, General Mike Lennox. He comes down and visits his son sometimes. Drops by the lab, tells us to keep working hard. Anyway, that's about all I can remember," he glanced at the clock on the wall and began to slide his chair out from behind the desk. Marty remained seated.

"Did any of the men that night seem especially upset?"

Gaines stopped and thought a second as he approached the door.

"Jacob Shockley threw one of the transistor models across the room in front of all of them. Said the whole project was like searching for the Fountain of Youth. I believe his exact words were, '*a legend based on a patented fraud.*'"

Marty needed to find Shockley.

●●●

Heir to a worldwide Mining Company, Jacob Shockley had just earned his geological engineering degree when The World War began, and he became a pilot. Through his own efforts he had saved hundreds of lives—not just by fighting—but by taking thousands of aerial photographs and mapping out enemy territory for the strategists. After the World War, he'd discovered precious metals, and a fortune in jewels exploring South America.

He was a hard-working man, constantly on the move. He was also a very private one. Every piece of real estate Shockley owned was listed under a company name. Even apartments. Nobody knew where the mining engineer was. Marty didn't like the idea of the shoe leather it would cost him checking out a dozen Manhattan penthouses, and he didn't want to walk in on some dame Shockley might be paying the rent for. So he decided to call in a favor.

Stepping into another drugstore, he closed the phone booth door, pulled out a nickel and dialed the Manhattan Police Department. Detective Sgt. Eldon Sayers wasn't on duty. Marty tried the police detective's home number. Nobody answered. Sighing and shaking his head, Marty dialed the number of his own hotel, the Baltic, where he lived.

"Hey, Studs, this is Quade. Is there a poker game going on in my room?"

"Um…" The desk clerk mumbled. "I'd have to go check."

"Dial my room, you four-flusher. I know they tip you when they sneak up there!"

"One moment please." The desk clerk imitated an operator's nasal tone. Marty could hear him fumbling with the phone connections on the other end.

"If you sent the bellboy up to warn 'em, I'll murder you worse than usual, Studs!" Marty yelled in the mouthpiece.

A good deal of the time when Marty was home, and even when he wasn't, there was a card game running in his hotel room. Which might have been illegal, except that most of the men playing were local detectives and reporters. In Marty's words, "half the people there didn't enforce the law, and the other half weren't going to tell anybody about it." Detectives Sayers, Brice, and a handful of others had a habit of "letting themselves in" to Marty's place and playing poker when the private eye wasn't there. Marty didn't seem to be home enough to mind.

The receiver clicked on the other end of the line, and Marty heard the phone ring twice before somebody picked it up.

"Is Sayers there?" he demanded.

"Yup." It was Sayers's partner, Detective Brice. There was a long silence.

"Brice? Brice, I need to call in a favor with Sayers."

"Call in a favor?" Brice laughed. "You wrecked his car last night!"

"And now you're both playing poker in my apartment! If I hadn't come along you two geniuses would still be on the street corner watching parked cars. I solved your case for you!"

"Yeah, and now you're working for the guy we caught. Is that even ethical?"

"Just give Sayers the phone. Let me talk to him." There was a moment of silence then Marty heard muffled voices in the background, most likely through Brice's hand over the mouthpiece.

"Sayers says he doesn't want to talk to you." There was laughter in the background, the sounds of glasses clinking with ice and liquor. Marty could almost smell the cigar smoke.

"Listen, you bonehead!" Marty's voice was more irritated than usual.

"Okay, okay." Brice sensed his sense of urgency. "What's the rush, beside Marty Quade being on a case, I mean?"

"Life or death, and more money than I could ever win stringing you suckers along playing poker. I need to find out where Jake Shockley, the mining engineer is. Guy owns Shockley Steel. He hasn't quit R.E.D.'s board yet, but he seems to have been persona non-grata for a while."

"Jacob Shockley…Mining Engineer" Brice sounded like he was writing it down. Voices muttered in the background. "Call back in about forty minutes."

Marty picked up a grilled cheese sandwich and coffee at the drug store's snack counter and waited. Then called back in thirty.

Shockley was staying at a private residence in New Jersey that bred dogs to some sort of kennel, a dog ranch, racing dogs most likely. Normally, Marty would have taken the train, but not knowing what to expect, he fished the phone book out of the slot under the phone and found a nearby gas station that would rent him a car. Remembering the night before, he decided he would even pay for insurance this time.

●●●

Jake Shockley *was* a private man. His not-so-lavish estate sat off a farm road in upstate New Jersey, surrounded by the sort of impervious, dark forest that serves only to confirm the legend of the Jersey Devil. By the time Marty had gotten there it was dark. The place sat isolated, down another thin dirt road. A dim light burned in the window of a square brick structure, barely visible but for the fact there was open ground in a place where there shouldn't have been. As if there had been some sort of disaster, demolition, or The Devil himself had razed a section of the forest to the ground, thrown some concrete around and put a chain-link fence around it.

He could hear dogs howling in the giant kennel that sat in back of the property, and the occasional bark in the darkness, but it was hard to make out much more than the series of chain link fenced dog runs that ran from the back of the yard to Shockley's square, white fortress.

The gate, however, stood open.

Driving the Ford V-8 he'd rented that afternoon down two tiny slits in the gravel covered ground, Marty passed through the gate and immediately noticed two old pickup trucks and a Daimler parked at odd angles across the yard. Marty pulled the V-8 toward the front of the house. He'd had the windows open all evening in the summertime heat, and didn't bother to roll them up as he shut the engine off. He was pulling on the handle of the door, about to step out of the car, when he heard a barking sound from across the yard and a growl even closer. Something black moved fast to his right.

Marty slammed the car door and began rolling up the window as a frothing black muzzle, all teeth, with two raging eyes afire behind them, bounced off the glass and howled a barrage of barking assaults at him. Dogs. Dobermans. A pack of them.

It took a second for Marty to compose himself and scout out the situation. The dog that had bounced off the car was on a chain. Two more chained dogs sat in a triangular formation, too far away to be an immediate threat. Another two Dobermans bared their fangs, as they howled from inside two pick-up trucks parked askew, their windows rolled halfway down. Marty doubted they were on chains and wondered how easy it would be for the dogs to squeeze out the windows. Something clicked, and the detective heard an electrical power surge as blinding floodlights washed over the entire property.

Marty held a hand up to shade his eyes. The place was a fortress.

"What do you want?" a voice attached to a loudspeaker echoed over the lot.

Marty scooted across the seat to the other side of the car, where the dogs couldn't reach, and yelled out the window.

"Marty Quade, Detective. I'm trying to find Mr. Jake Shockley."

"Who?" the voice echoed into the night like an owl.

"I'm looking for Jake Shockley," Marty announced through bared teeth.

"What if Mr. Shockley doesn't want to be found?" the voice announced from every direction.

"Well, then, I'd get suspicious. A guy locking himself up out here in the middle of a murder spree? I might have to go to the newspapers and tell them everything I know, then, I don't know. Send out for some hired guns?" Marty wasn't gritting his teeth anymore.

Something clicked on the other end of the amplifier and a voice said, "Step out of the passenger door of the car and walk, slowly, toward the entrance. Do not make eye contact with the dogs."

Marty's eyes had barely adjusted to the sudden bright light, but he could make out the front door of the white brick building. Slowly, the private eye wrenched the door open and stepped on the gravel. Every dog on the lot burst into a howling rage of attack, chains stretched to their limits as the junkyard dogs wailed and spat, while the Doberman's locked in the trucks chewed at the windows and doors of their vehicles like they were tearing at flesh. Slowly, Marty strolled for the only door on this side of the building, his hand on his automatic under his lapel. There was a buzzing sound, and the iron grated door on the side of the house clicked as the lock opened.

Marty didn't wait for anybody to answer and stepped inside. There was a pool table and a bar on the left hand side of the room, a long hallway on the right. He heard something jangle in the hallway. Then something growled. He backed against the wall, ready to draw his automatic as the growl erupted into a feral series of howls, and a gigantic blur of black fur and white teeth charged down the hall directly at him.

"Ham Bone," a voice said in a tone that neither threatened nor ordered the dog.

The beast stopped in its tracks, sat down politely and then, looking longingly at his trainer, whined as if he were disappointed he couldn't have Marty for a snack.

Marty didn't realize he'd been holding his breath until he exhaled a sigh of relief.

"I'd advise you to slowly remove your hand from under your coat, Mr. Quade. Sadie doesn't like guns."

"Tell Sadie, I almost used mine."

"That would have been a very poor decision. Sadie doesn't like guns, but she does like chewing the hands off the men holding them. If, she doesn't go for the jugular."

"Unless you're around to say 'Ham Bone' first, huh?"

"Something like that. Sadie's a prodigy. She can almost read my mind. Speaking of which Mr. Quade, what's on yours? I already told the cops everything I know."

"Maybe they didn't ask the right questions."

Shockley sighed and slid toward the bar with a wandering gait that indicated he'd already been drinking.

"I thought this place was supposed to be a kennel. What's with the attack dogs?"

"It's a sideline. We train them for security companies. Safest place I could think of with all of R.E.D.'s board members getting offed. And, yes, I did tell them they're little 'transresistance' element was a fantasy." From behind the bar Shockley poured three-fingers into a tumbler. "Want one?"

Marty didn't even acknowledge the question and kept asking his own.

"So you don't think the 'transistor' will work?" Marty sat down on a stool across the bar from millionaire mining engineer.

"Just between you and me—I don't want to get caught up in any of this Top Secret patent stuff, it's too complicated. We had the element. There's just not enough of it on earth to ever make it profitable."

"Germanium." Marty nodded.

"You got it, and there's not enough of it. Period. R.E.D.'s going to have to wait until somebody has the ability to manufacture a synthetic transresistance converter. That could take years, has nothing to do with mining rare minerals, and so..." He shot a thumb over his shoulder like a baseball umpire, "...I am outta there. Besides, half those guys were crazy over there anyway. Let me tell you, buddy, I made a lot of great friends during the War, but I've lost a lot of them, too. War changes men, sometimes years after the fighting." His eyes drifted up to the single bulb in the ceiling then down into his drink.

"Which men at R.E.D. changed?"

"Everybody in management and half the people in research and development. Foucault and Gruber were part of the half that weren't nuts, and that's why I'm locked up in here. I may not be on the board anymore, but that doesn't make me any safer. I know too much."

"Too much of what?"

"If I talk, I could end up just as dead." Shockley sat his drink down and cupped his head in his hands on the bar. Then he sighed again, leaned back and smiled with a drunken go-to-hell-world look on his face and almost chuckled. "I thought it would be a good idea doing business with my veteran buddies. I mean, these guys and I won some of the same medals, but I never thought one of them would lie about it." Shockley leaned a bit too far over the bar, almost toppled and grabbed the seat behind him, then looked up at Marty's face. "Look, look, I just don't wanna get inna trouble." He picked up the drink again. Marty pulled it out of his hand and set it on the bar.

Drunk, Shockley wasn't making much sense. He certainly wasn't answering any of Marty's questions—but the private eye realized he was telling him a lot more. Marty decided to wait and listen instead of trying to steer the conversation, and find out where that led. Shockley hit the table with his fist, smiled at Marty and stuck a cigarette in his mouth as he muttered, almost talking to himself.

"Didja ever notice how they got that company set up? Every member of the board serves a particular purpose. Like it was a machine or something." Shockley had to close one eye and aim to make the match meet the end of his cigarette. He inhaled deep and plumes of smoke shot out of his nose. "Every part designed to serve a specific end. And we're all just parts."

"What's wrong with the parts, Jake? How come the machine doesn't work?"

"Lennox. Lennox won't work. He lied to win the Medal of Honor. And

I'm pretty sure one of the lawyers on his squad lied for him, too. I still know a few people in Army Intelligence. His story doesn't check out." He stubbed half his cigarette out in an ashtray on the bar. "Lennox didn't take out no behind-the-lines combat unit. He fell asleep on sentry duty, and when he woke up the four men he got medals for killing had already wiped out half his platoon." Shockley spat and drool fell over his lips. "Shell shocked bastards..." The man was fading fast.

So, Lennox was a fraud. Marty still didn't understand what any of this had to do with R.E.D.'s research. Not knowing what questions to ask, he grabbed the mining engineer by the collar and sat the drink in front of him again, goading him with it. Shockley looked up at Marty like he'd just noticed he was in the room. The edges of his mouth turned up. The silence dragged, Marty had to say something or Shockley might pass out.

"Shell shock? Who's got shell shock?"

"All of 'em," Shockley said. "Lennox, Horvath and Devries. Foucault was shell shocked, but he wasn't nuts. Gruber, too, but not so much that it showed. Everybody in Lennox's unit. Those guys dug foxholes and lived on the line for a year. It's amazing they didn't all snap back then."

"So, they're shell shocked. A lot of guys get busted up in the service and heal up okay."

"Yeah, and a lot of men still think they're in the trenches. Only they've been there a long time now. Completely normal, then—" He snapped the fingers of one hand "—they're angry, and they're not takin' orders anymore." Shockley's eyelids began to droop; his eyes began to drift up behind them.

"There are doctors."

"They're on the payroll. Listen, I need to lay down a little while." Shockley stumbled by a couch on the wall and then fell into it. Sadie, the gigantic Doberman, lay down on the ground beside him.

With one eye on the dog, Marty gently slid toward the door. The dog raised its head, looked him in the eye, then huffing a heavy sigh, lowered her jowls to his forelegs and closed his eyes.

Once in the hallway, Marty skirted by the front door and made his light-footed way down the hall to where Shockley and the attack dog had emerged when they first greeted him. Making his way down the corridor, he passed two bedrooms and a bath before coming to a fireproof metal door. It was Shockley's control room for security, where the mining engineer monitored the property from a periscope that extended from above the almost windowless structure.

"What's wrong with the parts, Jake?"

A metal industrial table, large enough to seat eight people, sat affixed to the floor with a few tools and magazines on it. On the far wall sat a control board, with the eye of the periscope hanging down from the ceiling next to a rolling office chair. In the wall next to the control board was a hatch about four feet square, a doggie doorway covered with chain link fencing. The second Marty spotted the chain link, the attack dog behind it began to bay and howl. The dog leaped, tearing at the chain link like it was fabric. The gate held.

As the dog growled, Marty noted the assorted knife switches that decorated the panel on the wall—several for the floodlights in the yard, even one for infrared night-vision on the periscope—but the two switches that really caught his attention sat up on a shelf jutting from the wall upright at a different angle. The handles of the large knife switches were covered with brightly colored yellow and red tape. The bright yellow handle was switched down, but the red handle was up. Marty remembered the dog runs that ran from the back of the property, and figured the yellow switch must open a door to the doghouse in back of the property. That door led to the dog run, and the dog run ran to the gated hatchway in the wall right next to him. All Shockley had to do was throw the red switch, and the house would be flooded with attack dogs. Marty looked into the eyes and down the throat of the beast in the hatch and eyed the red switch gratefully.

"Shaddup, mutt," Marty said in a conversational tone. He remembered the attack dog, Sadie sleeping with Shockley and hastened his search.

The dog in the hatch growled and stopped barking as Marty rifled through the drawers and files. All he found was a bunch of soil samples and some mining reports. In the lowest desk drawer he found a note detailing Shockley's part in the proceedings at R.E.D., but it wasn't much more than Shockley had already told him. Most likely it was an alibi or Shockley's preparation in case he had to make a statement in court.

Marty put it in his pocket. The cops might be interested. Leaving the Shockley fortress, he eased the door open and stuck his head out first, just to make sure nobody had released the hounds, then closed the door behind him.

•••

The Private Eye spent a good deal of the rest of the morning driving back to Manhattan. By the time he got back to his room, Detective's Sayers,

Brice, and a small crew from the N.Y. Daily News had finished their poker game and were gone. Judging by the condition of the room, the game had broken out in either a party or a wrestling match. Marty ignored the empty bottles and stuffed ashtrays. He didn't bother to clean up—one of the reasons he lived at a hotel was that it came with a maid—but he did decide he better get a few hours rest in.

Sheer exhaustion forced him to sleep for a while, but then he began to toss and turn. Quade had the sort of metabolism that enabled him to stay awake for days and sleep whenever he wanted to, but something kept waking him up. After he'd stared at the inside of his eyelids a while, he realized he wasn't going to fall back asleep. Something Shockley had said kept eating at him. The words kept bouncing around in his head.

"Every member of the board serves a particular purpose."

He wasn't sure what to believe about the accusations Shockley had made, but even though the mining engineer had been drunk when he met him, they didn't seem too outlandish. Sometimes a little liquor can ply the secrets out of a man, and Shockley sounded more disappointed than angry. That said something about his character. He wasn't Marty's suspect.

"Every part designed to serve a specific end."

To a private detective like Marty the word "end" might as well have been "intent." Motive.

"Like it was a machine or something. Every part designed to serve a specific..." motive.

He rolled out of bed, grabbed his coat off the radiator he used for a valet, and pulled his notebook out of one of the pockets. Clearing the table of the previous evening's debris with a swoop of his arm, he opened the notebook, grabbed a fountain pen off the bar and made his way down the list, ruling out Del Raymond, his client—who was obviously an uninterested investor—and starting with the victims.

Mason Foucault, the depressive civil engineer who had been the first victim, had been the designer. His design would affect the size, shape, ease of use, and overall enhancements of R.E.D.'s new product, the "walkie-talkie" thing.

If every man was a part, that was Mason Foucault's. Marty grabbed another piece of paper and frantically scribbled two words. Foucault's name and the word "design."

Dylan Gruber, the electrical wizard and second victim, had been research and development. Without him the product, and thus the project, wouldn't have been possible. He wrote down "Gruber" and "R & D."

Horvath and Devries were lawyers, who were also ex-military. Not only could they deal with patent issues, but with military contracts as well. He wrote the words "legal" and "sales" beside their names.

Shockley, the mining engineer, had been there for materials. Marty wrote it down.

That left Lester Lennox. The man who had organized all of it. The number one investor.

Lester Lennox, fake war hero, shell shocked millionaire, industrialist investor—and potential future congressman.

Putting all the pieces in place. Marty tore through the pages of his notebook, back to front, mentally drawing a character sketch of Lennox.

"Every part designed to serve a specific end." What was Lennox's intent?

To go down in history for the creation of a new form of high tech electronics? Sure. To serve his country? Probably. To make some money along with all of his other rich buddies? Definitely. But, after originating the project, the scientists would use their money to fund further research. Lennox's ends wouldn't be much different from Del Raymond's—but he wasn't having any fun like Del was.

Lennox wanted a product, and just like the rest of the board members, he would use it to build a reputation. But Lennox wasn't just part of the machine. He'd created it. He had a different end.

Why had he wanted to create the "walkie-talkie" to begin with? A millionaire war hero running for office—whose father just happened to be a General. That would give Lester Lennox, and R.E.D, a direct pipeline to the United States Defense Department. R.E.D. would know what they wanted before anybody else; they'd be able to specialize ahead of time. The Generals and Majors would be lined up like customers at a hot dog stand.

Lennox's motive had been the defense industry all along. Nothing illegal about that. He'd make a fortune—until word got out he was a fraud—then the whole plan would fail. Not only wouldn't Lennox get elected, but since R.E.D. had yet to get their new "transistor" to work, a fortune would be lost. The project would be called off before it had a chance to start. And it had already passed the point of no return. People kill people over that kind of stuff.

Marty wrote down "Lennox, motive: cover-up."

But why had Lennox's wife hired him to begin with?

•••

A shower, a shave, and a clean shirt, and Marty was back out on the street. He had statements, but no real evidence. Marty hated wasting time, but he needed to think about the case before interrogating anyone else, so he decided to return to the scene of the crime. Waving down a cab, he headed across town to where Del Raymond had been arrested the night before.

Then, leaning back in his seat, he massaged his chin and thought about Mrs. Lennox's motives. Marty had a built in lie detector that leaned heavily toward skepticism, yet Vivian Lennox had seemed genuinely frightened for her husband's life. Going over the scenario in his head though, he considered the fact that she could have been conning him to make her husband look innocent.

Reaching the scene of Del's arrest, Marty paid the cab and then stationed himself at the same corner where Detective Sayers had been on stakeout two nights before. He then crossed the street and observed the intersection from Detective Brice's view.

Shifting his head back and forth, Quade waited for the walk signal, crossed a third of the street and stood still in the crosswalk, unmoving. After staring at the scene a few seconds, he noticed an oak tree with a small copse of bushes around it that blocked both men's view of Del Raymond's yard the night before. A sportster honked at him as traffic began to move again. Quade hopped back on the sidewalk and crossed in the other direction toward the scene of the crime.

He could still see Del's tire tracks in the gravel. His eyes scanned the ground around him, and then he began to circle the area where the car had been parked. Some marks in the gravel, streaks of scattered pebbles, and dusty concrete were the only sign there had been a scuffle. But stepping on the plush, green lawn, the afternoon light reflected off the grass revealing something else to him.

A trail.

Marty wasn't exactly a tracker, but he could easily make out a few heel prints that had torn up the grass going uphill, heading towards the fence in back of the estate. Whoever's prints they were only showed because the grass had torn and then yellowed in the morning dew. Marty picked up one of the torn leaves and scanned the amber edges, trying to determine how long since someone's feet had last skidded across the ground. While a night had passed, it was possible they could have been made shortly before the time Del had been arrested.

Faint as they were, Marty followed the impressions marked in the grass uphill, toward the fence around the estate's garden. Monkey grass and ivy had been planted to block the view from the street, but in the dirt next to the fence Marty spotted a full-fledged footprint. A small one. Somebody nimble and light, Marty guessed, as he followed the trail away from where Del Raymond had parked his car and toward the next city block. Three solid footprints stepped sideways, as if Marty's prey had been hiding with their back toward the fence. Then eight, maybe nine more steps in the dirt. And the footprints disappeared.

It only took Marty a second to look up, instead of down, and figure out they had skipped and jumped, grabbing a limb that hung over the wrought iron fence. They could have stayed in the tree all night, but more than likely climbed over the fence and inside Del Raymond's estate. What could be safer? Who's going to search inside the estate, when the owner is being arrested on the outside?

Marty was convinced Del had been framed. And whoever had done the dirty work had small feet. Of course, given the crowd these murders dealt with, an assassin might have been hired. But something felt personal about this one.

Crossing the street again, Marty walked a block to a corner phone booth. Inside, he dialed the police department and told Detective Sayers to send one of his crime laboratory people out to make a plaster of Paris mold of whatever footprints were left at the scene, and to dust the fence and the tree branch above it for fingerprints. He was about to call Mr. and Mrs. Lennox on the telephone, but decided against it. If he could confront the two of them face to face at their penthouse apartment at the Huntington-Windsor Hotel, he'd be able to watch their reaction.

Sliding the phone booth door open, Marty stopped. One eyebrow lowered and a half-smile broke into a grin on the same side of his face. He turned around and stepped back inside. Closing the door behind him, he reached into his pocket, sat down on the metal seat in the corner, and surprisingly dialed the Huntington-Windsor Hotel.

Marty Quade knew a lot of people, and a lot of people knew Marty Quade. One of the people he knew was the Hotel Detective at the Huntington-Windsor. T.J. McNabb was an old pro who'd gone from the Vice Squad to peeping in keyholes. The kind of tough guy that preferred a fistfight to any kind of arms, he wasn't exactly fond of Marty—the ace Private Eye had shot two thieves in his hotel one time, and hotel detectives are like that.

Unfortunately, hotel detectives are also given a bonus *not* to know anything about what goes on in the ivory upper-floors of Manhattan's skyscrapers, and on a professional level, those weren't the type of people they were hired to investigate. McNabb might know something, but Marty wanted more than information. When he had shot those two thieves in the hotel three years ago, Marty had also rounded up seventeen-thousand dollars' worth of emeralds and a smuggling ring in the Huntington-Windsor, and McNabb had taken partial credit for it. Marty considered that another favor to call in.

After that call, he shoved another nickel in the slot, and dialed the number he had written down for Jimmy Gaines, the sound technician he'd met at R.E.D.'s employee cafeteria. That little change of expression Marty had had outside the phone booth, had been him remembering his interview with R.E.D.'s attorneys—and his wish that he could have been a fly on the wall after the interrogation. There would be no favors to call in with young Mr. Gaines. This time Marty would have to pay cash.

Stepping back out onto the street, he hailed a cab and headed uptown.

•••

The Huntington-Windsor was considered to be one of the finest luxury hotels in the world. Built at the turn of the century, the original owner had designed the upper floor of the hotel as a luxurious home for himself and his family. Lester Lennox had purchased the luxury penthouse and all the amenities that came with it three years ago.

Marty flipped a dime at the woman behind the newspaper stand, took a paper, and strolled through the lushly decorated Art-Nouveau lobby to the reservation desk. Slapping the paper on the counter, he announced himself to the clerk behind it.

"Reservation for Marty Quade."

"Ah," the clerk held up a finger, and pulled a room key out. "Detective McNabb said you'd be by." He winked at Marty as if they had a secret. Marty grabbed the key out of his hand.

"Where's McNabb?"

"I don't know."

"Get him. I'll be right back."

Marty stepped outside the hotel for a minute and met the sound engineer from R.E.D.'s cafeteria, Jimmy Gaines. The private eye handed the keys off to Gaines, and the sound engineer handed Marty a lunch sack with some small pliers and electrical equipment in it.

When Marty went back in the hotel, McNabb was sitting in a chair in the lobby smoking a cigar. They shook hands. McNabb pretended to catch up like they were old pals, but Marty made him get to the point.

"Without the key, the elevator won't go to the penthouse," McNabb said. "The only other way into the Lennox house is the stairs—and unless you got something solid, I ain't wasting my reputation on some crazy hunch."

"All you got to do is look the other way, Mac. Just like before. If I don't find anything, nobody knows. If I find anything, you'll get credit in the newspapers. Just think about that Christmas bonus."

"And if you get caught, I lose my job."

"I get caught—you just hit yourself over the head with something, and say I knocked you out when I came in." Marty slapped him on the back and smiled. "I'll just say I lost my room key and got confused."

"Oh, you're more than confused, Quade. You're delusional. If you think I'm giving you the key to the penthouse elevator, yours doesn't go all the way to the top floor. And, the stairs have an alarm system."

"Funny thing about alarm systems," Marty reached across the table and began to straighten McNabb's tie, making the hotel dick uncomfortable, "you unplug 'em and they don't work." He patted McNabb on the cheek and made his way for the elevator.

"Basement," he told the elevator operator.

"Basement? That's for employees only."

"Do I look like I want to be here?" Marty's eyes glowed angrily under the shadows of his eyebrows.

The elevator operator pulled the switch down.

After finding the light switch in the basement, it took all of thirty seconds for Marty to find a veritable library of pale gray fuse boxes. The builders had even installed an extra brick wall to hang them on.

"Electricians," he muttered to himself, following the room numbers on the electrical boxes as they climbed to his right. He spotted the Lennox residence's wiring long before he spotted the number. The large sheet metal box that held Lennox's fuses had a smaller, green box with curved corners, on the wall next to it. The wiring leading to the green box still had white pieces of paper still stuck between the yellow fabric wound around it, meaning it hadn't had much time to turn brown. Since the Huntington-Windsor had been built at the turn of the century, and not originally equipped with electricity, Marty had counted on the electrical system being exposed—and the Lennox's alarm system having the newest wiring there.

But the electric pliers Gaines had handed him were too small to wrench the locked box open. It took Marty fifteen minutes to find a screwdriver and a pair of work gloves in a tool kit stashed on the opposite side of the room.

The private eye didn't know a lot about electricity. He knew positive wasn't supposed to touch negative, and he knew if he touched the wrong thing, he'd probably be the one to fry instead of the alarm system.

But what's a gumshoe without insulated crepe soled shoes? The gloves from the toolkit would keep anything from touching his flesh, and what harm could unscrewing a few wires do? After he'd unscrewed the three cables inside the box, he stood back, satisfied, and slammed it closed again. Crossing the basement, he stuffed the big screwdriver in his coat, tossed the gloves back across the room, and then signaled for the elevator. When the doors opened, and the attendant asked which floor, he requested the forty-second—directly beneath the luxury penthouse home of Lester Lennox.

●●●

When the elevator doors closed behind him on the forty-second floor of the Huntington-Windsor, the first thing Marty noticed was the lack of sound. The place was soundproofed and the carpet was an inch-and-a-half thick. In a city whose errant radios, elevated trains, and crowds of millions made it the loudest place on earth, it was like a blast of silence.

Strolling down the hallway, he wandered by room 423, the same suite he had given Jimmy Gaines the key to earlier. There was already a "Do Not Disturb" sign on the door. If he were a sound engineer, Marty would have said all systems were go. At the end of the hall stood the door to the staircase.

Climbing to the next floor, Marty took a hallway that veered off to his right and came to a door marked "Private." It was the entrance to the hallway where the Lennox's lived. Marty smiled; there was a hinged metal handle across the front of the door with the same yellow-wrapped wiring as the box Marty had dismantled downstairs.

Hoping nobody else in the building has the same electrician, Marty stabbed the screwdriver into the latch by the metal handle and wrenched with both hands, mashing the wood and shoving the back plating into the wall. The latch popped free.

He stuffed the screwdriver back in his pocket and waited.

No bells rang. No sirens. No jackbooted guards. Unless it was a silent alarm that ran right to the police station, he'd be okay, for now. Shoving the door open, he was again confronted by even more silence and a thicker carpet. A few brisk strides and he was standing next to the only other door in the hallway. It was antique oak, intricately carved, and had a brass knocker the size of Marty's head in the shape of a horse's harness ring on the front of it.

Marty stopped to think for a minute whether he felt like a horse, a mule, or a horse's ass, and settled on the mule. This was the worst part of even trying.

Marty was not a locksmith or a second-story man. There were only two ways in. One of them was nearly impossible and would have to depend on luck, the other one would require Marty to slide the past the help—a butler, houseboy, or maid, whoever answered the door. He hoped it wasn't one of the Lennoxes, or the hired muscle he had met back at Radio Engineer and Design. Marty had talked his way into trickier situations than this. Of course, most of those he had shot his way out of. If some wrinkly, aged charwoman who'd been with the family for years came to the door with a feather duster in her hand, Marty might just kiss the old broad.

He almost knocked but decided to try the doorknob first. It was open. *"The nearly impossible way, that depended on luck!"* Marty wasn't one to look a gift horse in the mouth. Without a sound, he edged the door open and stood to the side so he wouldn't be seen. It was so quiet he heard the hairs stand up on the back of his neck. Nothing moved. None of the help was around.

Marty slid in the door, pulling it almost closed behind him but leaving it ajar. He strode quickly on the balls of his feet across the entry hall and into the coat closet, leaving it open a crack so he could see what was going on.

Peering into the living room, the first thing he noticed was the lack of furniture.

The room was almost empty, other than a nondescript wooden table with two chairs and a stool beside it. It wasn't just the furniture, either. It was building materials and artifacts. He could see where an entire arch had been removed from one wall. Considering the original Huntington Family house had been shipped over in boxes full of artifacts from Europe, and considering the fact that Marty had read a few articles that had been published about them, it was obvious something wasn't right here.

With only the light from the crack in the closet door to work by, Marty pulled the pair of pliers out of the paper bag Jimmy Gaines had given him, and began to tear up the carpet inside the closet door. It was loud work; the only way to do it was to tear out a large strip all at once. He cleared the corner with one loud tear, hoping the door and the rest of the apartment's soundproofing would protect him from discovery. He waited a few more minutes, then popped a piece of the wooden molding from the closet's wall paneling. Marty could hear something rubbing against flooring below him. He stuck the screwdriver through a hole in floor, and broke the hole open wider, so it could be seen from below. Twenty seconds later, two wires already bared at the ends shoved their way up a foot into the closet. Marty attached a small microphone resembling a telephone's mouthpiece, aimed it into the room, and taped it to the wall in a gap where the wood paneling met the rug. He waited a little longer, just to make sure he hadn't been heard, and took another look around the apartment.

No furniture, no fancy architecture, and no hired help that he could discern. Either that or they'd given the butler the night off—"to do either some demolition or brick laying," he thought. From the looks of this place, the help had been let go a while ago.

Marty had seen this kind of thing with the well-to-do before. They were broke, selling off their assets so nobody would know about it. If he were to ask, they'd just lie and say they were getting the place remodeled, but Marty had seen this scene during the economic Depression too many times before. The rich hanging on to the last vestiges of their reputation, by selling the very things they'd used to build it.

The silence was broken by a howling voice in another room. It was Lester Lennox.

"You what? You called Marty Quade? How were you going to pay him?" Before his wife could answer, Lennox kept raving. "Never mind the money, he'll expose us. People will know we're broke…again."

"But the killing, Lester. We still have time to leave, go back home and start over. You agreed—"

"I'm not going to prison! I didn't kill anybody. I promised I'd sell the company, but now everyone knows! I will not fail!" The last word tore down the hall, a screaming wail. Then the sound of something being knocked over and a choking, almost begging sound.

Marty kicked the closet door open and hurtled down the hallway. He rounded the corner to see Lester Lennox clasping his wife's shoulder with one hand and the back of her hair with the other. Her limp body faced her husband, but her head hung awkwardly in the other direction, her eyes open, her face expressionless. She was already dead. Lennox had broken her neck.

"Expose what?" Marty stepped into the room with his automatic in his hand.

Lennox looked up from his wife at Marty with a blank stare on his face. Beads of sweat ran down his forehead as he looked at Marty. His expression changed a moment, his head turning toward the sides of the room like he was trying to figure out where he was. He glanced down regretfully at his wife's head in his hand and then back up at Marty. Then his eyes shifted again, like an animal trying to evade a trap.

"Put her down," Marty said. "Gently. I've got some questions, but I think I have the gist of it."

That's when something hit Marty in back of the head. The private eye swung around, trying to block another pummeling blow, but it was too late. He twisted, trying to dodge the next. It hit him on back of the head again, and Marty collapsed to the floor without seeing his mysterious assailant.

It took Marty about an hour to come around, gaining just enough consciousness to moan or roll over. Then he felt his head throb. Even with his eyes closed the light hurt. He opened one eye. The outside world swayed. His stomach roiled. He coughed. It turned into a retch, as he felt the bloody lumps on the back of his head. If he hadn't been dodging his assailant as he fell, he might not be alive right now. Moaning, Marty's living corpse forced itself through sheer will to sit up. He took a few breaths and opened his other eye. Two worlds swayed.

Bracing himself with a chair, Marty stood up and, knees shaking, looked at his watch. He started to shake his head then stopped because it hurt too much. He couldn't think. He remembered the last thing he'd said being something about having the gist of this case. He'd been wrong.

Marty had thought Mrs. Lennox hired him to set up Del Raymond as a decoy, to take the heat off the real murderer, her husband. Maybe she had, or maybe she'd believed Lester Lennox was innocent all along. Now she was dead—and Marty Quade should be. So, why was he still alive?

Then it hit him. Jimmy Gaines, the sound technician downstairs.

Marty's whole body jerked erect and he ran for the front door. His gun was in his hand before he had time to wonder if Lennox had taken it. The hall closet was open, and part of the carpet and wiring in the corner of the doorway had been torn up. Lennox and whoever Marty's assailant had been had found the hidden microphone. Marty sprinted out the door for the stairs.

Still lightheaded, he had to stop and grab the handrail on the stairs a moment before propelling himself around the landing and out the door downstairs. The door to room 423 was already open, the handle almost ripped from where it had been kicked in. Automatic in hand, Marty booted the door the rest of the way open with the heel of his shoe, and was in the center of the room while the door was still banging against the wall.

The place was empty. The table sat at an odd angle with a broken lamp lying across it. A chair lay sideways on the floor, and all the doors and cabinets were open. A thin streak of blood splatter stood about four feet from the floor, as if someone had been whipped and then fallen. Glancing toward the coat closet, Marty spotted the wires hanging from the corner of the door. On closer inspection, he could see the wires had not been torn from Gaine's sound equipment like he'd thought, but still had a curl in the exposed wire where it had been wrapped around an electrical contact.

The wires hadn't been torn out. They had been disconnected. Maybe even by Jimmy Gaines.

Quickly holstering his automatic, Marty grabbed the wires taught and began tearing the already loose molding to see where they went. After he'd determined which direction the wires had been headed, he knocked on the paneling by the door several times, listening for a hollow sound or anything that the young sound-man may have slipped into the wall. Feeling around the top interior corner of the closet, he could tell both ends of the wiring were above his head—as if Gaines had run all the wiring into the penthouse above.

Marty cursed at the crazy kid, as he tried to figure out what he had done. Pulling on the cord that turned the closet light on, the bulb didn't go off—but an idea struck Marty. Gaines had been in the room ahead of both Marty and Lennox's crowd. He had stored the record recorder in the crawlspace above the closet.

Marty grabbed a chair from the living room, put it in the closet and climbed on top. He found the loose piece of paneling wedged in the corner. As he pulled it out, the recording equipment almost fell on him. Marty caught the bottom of the recorder, and gently slid the record off the top, placing it on a shelf next to him, and stepping slowly from the chair, the record player balanced in front of him.

He put the record player on the living room table, plugged it in, and placed the grooved side of Gaine's recording up. Marty knew a little about the recording industry, but not how a record recorder worked. So he turned it on, dropped the needle, and made sure he could hear the sound of scratches inherent in recordings, to make sure he wasn't recording over the evidence.

He heard a scratchy sound first, most likely himself setting up the wiring, and then almost instantly, the frightful scream of Lester Lennox followed by Marty's own voice.

"Put her down, gently," and the repeated thud of what had to be the gun on Marty's scalp. There was some muttering about R.E.D.'s "funds and reputation," then one of the voices reassured the shell shocked veteran and head of R.E.D.

"Don't worry, Lester. No one will find out. I know she was trying to get you to quit the company, and start all over, but it's too late for that now."

"Too…late?" Lennox sounded almost like a child, scared and confused.

"If the news hounds ever found out you killed your wife, you'll be the first one they go after screaming bloody murder! You've got no choice." Marty recognized the voice. It was Anthony Devries, R.E.D.'s attorney in charge of sales. The voice grew louder as he left the back room and stepped toward the microphone that had been mounted in the closet.

"But it was an accident." Lennox could barely be heard. "I didn't mean to kill her—and I didn't kill Foucalt or Gruber…"

"Look, I don't know who killed those two, but you're the one that's going to hang for it."

A barely audible sound from Lennox's throat was the only response, a protest in the distant background that quickly faded for lack of meaning.

"Waitaminute!" Devries cursed and wheezed. "We've been bugged…"

A ripping sound tore from the phonograph. Marty was about to shut it off, but when he looked at the disc, he noticed more had been recorded. There were some skittering sounds, two electrical arcs, and then the sound a telephone makes when it connects with the operator. A heavy breath wandered over the microphone, then a familiar voice.

"Marty, it's me, Jimmy Gaines," the recording said. "They're headed up here, and there's no time for me to get out. I *cannot* lose this expensive equipment. Ssshhh, they're coming," he said as if Marty were in the closet with him. "You'll get the idea." There were a few more clunking sounds and then Marty heard somebody kick in the hotel room's front door.

"Grab him!" It was Anthony Devries voice again. The voice began cursing. There was the sound of a tussle. "What's with the wires, Jimmy?"

"I was just working on a jingle for the Ralston Purina Cereal contest." There was a punching sound and a whoosh of air, like the little attorney had punched him in the gut. Then he heard the furniture being thrown around, the lamp being broken.

Marty recognized the voice.

"Where's the recording equipment, Gaines?" Devries demanded.

"No, they don't take recordings," Jimmy said. "They want you to write the jingle out."

Another "thud" and "whoosh" meaning Gaines had been most likely been punched in the stomach again, was followed by a few more "thuds."

"What are you doing?" It was Mario Horvath's voice, the taller half of R.E.D.'s legal team. He sounded like he was offended.

"Damned kid's got wiring all over the place, he could've been recording us." Devries sounded insulted. Then the sound of a few more high frequency thuds. "Search the place…"

"We don't have time for this sort of thing. We have to stick to the plan," Horvath said. "Lester, now please, stand over there." The lawyer ordered the owner of the company around like he was speaking to a child, or a pet.

"Plan? What plan? In case you hadn't noticed, Lennox knocked off his own wife before we even had a chance to. I thought you said those drugs and doctors would keep him under control."

"Don't start with me, Devries. He's fighting against the conditioning, and the drugs are having less and less effect. His required dose has climbed to the point where he's not even functional. This was bound to happen, and if we'd allowed him and his wife to back out of the business, we'd be in even more trouble. Hell, by killing her, he just did your job for you."

"I didn't plan on killing her," Devries spat. "I just didn't think she'd call in a Private Eye. Speaking of which, what do you want to do with Mr. Quade upstairs."

"We don't have time to deal with this," Horvath rattled again. "We'll have to leave him and deal with Gaines when we get to Shockley's place. We can drive back tonight, and be on board for South America by six A.M. Besides, Quade's private, and he's got a big mouth. Nothing the cops would love more than to ignore him. Kill him, and they might start asking questions."

There was a moment of silence on the recording, as if Devries were thinking about it. Quade reasoned Jimmy Gaines had already been knocked out, and imagined a brainwashed Lester Lennox standing by himself in the corner of the room as the two attorneys eyed each other. From the sound of cabinets opening and closing he could tell they were still searching the place.

"We don't have time to…"

"Okay, okay, let's go!"

There were a few more scratches and thumps, before the needle began spinning around the blank label in the center of the record. Marty shut off the record player, and took the disc off. Picking a pillow up off the couch, he yanked the stuffing out, gently slid the phonograph inside the pillow case, and headed down to the lobby of the Huntington-Windsor. Luck was with him. He spotted T. J. McNabb, the house detective, still lurking around the back of the lobby with the bellboys. Marty grabbed the hotel dick by the arm, almost dragging him along as they headed for the revolving exit.

"McNabb, I need you to call the police. Contact Detective Sayers or Brice, nobody else. Give 'em this, and be careful with it." He handed the Hotel Detective the pillow case. "There's a phonograph confession inside. Tell them the killers are going after Jake Shockley, and plan to sail to South America tomorrow. You got that?"

McNabb nodded that he did, and stood there still waiting for more information as Marty spun through the hotel's revolving door. The gas station he'd rented the Ford V-8 from was only a block-and-a-half away. Jogging toward the corner car lot, he approached the gas pumps from behind the station, where he'd parked the vehicle to return it. The key was still in it. There was no time for paperwork. He'd do that when he got back to the city.

If he got back to the city.

Marty didn't know what kind of car Horvath and Devries were driving, but the private eye had taken enough time to listen to both policemen and professional getaway drivers, and knew the Ford V-8 would eat up the road. Marty went fast, but he also had to worry about coming up behind the very men he was chasing. Rather than just flooring the gas pedal, he moved with the traffic, keeping a steady pace while maneuvering between other cars.

The sun was setting behind him by the time the skyscraper scenery had been replaced with waves of starkly dark pines and shadowed scrub that blotted out the landscape upstate. The only sign of life beyond the thick backwoods was the dark shapes of mountains in the background. When he hit New Jersey territory, traffic thinned so that he only had to inspect a few cars in the distance as their lights floated behind the sprinting V-8.

His jaw clenched the entire time; Marty battled the road into Jersey Devil territory. He'd seen no sign of the two lawyers and their victim. His prey may have had a good head start, but Marty began to feel better when he hit the farm roads. He'd been here before, so he didn't have to guess what the hand-scrawled wooden signs said. He knew where he was going.

But that didn't mean he could get there.

With several miles left to go, Marty turned the car from one dirt road to another. A shot rang out—or that's what it sounded like. The steering wheel whipped to the right in Marty's hands. He'd blown a tire.

The speedy little roadster shot gravel through the air as it spun through the dirt, sliding head first directly toward a ditch by the edge of the road. Marty wrenched the wheel in the other direction with white knuckled fists as the car lurched sideways across the road. With one last surge of energy, Marty white knuckled the wheel to the right and the car skidded onto the shoulder. Marty climbed out of the car and into the dusty shadows as the last embers of the afternoon sun burned out behind him.

He still had miles to go, he wasn't even off the farm road yet, and had some trailing to do. Without a flashlight, he had to leave the V-8's headlights on to change the tire, and that made him a target. Moving quickly, Marty pulled the spare off the back of the car and the jack stored beneath it. The road had soft shoulders, but since the gas station had provided the right tools, Marty had the spare on the wheel in just a few minutes. He'd spent the entire time cursing, and in between cursing, thinking about one thing.

They got a good head start.

Marty spotted the light of Shockley's private fortress from half-a-mile away. He shut off the Ford's lights, so he wouldn't be seen in the distance, idled the car half-a-mile, and then parked off-trail hoping the car would blend in with the bushes. Using the dense foliage for cover, he stuck to the edge of the trail so he wouldn't be seen, and was soon peeking at Shockley's hideout from atop one of the hills that sealed the Jersey woods in a world of its own.

The floodlights on Shockley's place were easy to see. It was lit up like a fireworks stand. He could just make out a new car on the lot, the only one parked in a straight line. Skirting the edge of the property, Marty had to wait a minute for his eyes to adjust to the brightness. It was like stepping out of a cave and into a spotlight. As his eyes focused, he realized he didn't hear the attack dogs surrounding Shockley's house, just the low barking echoes from the kennels that stood like shadows in back of the property. Nothing on the lot moved.

Eyes narrowed to slits, Marty skirted around the edge of the open gate and ran onto the lot. Legs churning, he raced for cover and tried to evaluate the scene at the same time. The new car on the lot was a late model Terraplane—another car wheelmen tended to rave about. No wonder they'd made good time. The car was empty. The truck nearest the entrance had been shot full of holes, somebody had cut loose with a machine-gun. Blood draped the windshield of the truck where one of the guard dogs had been. That was the reason the yard remained quiet. Marty could smell the sickly quick stench of death, blood and guts quickly fouled in the summer heat.

The ace detective sprinted so fast, he was diving and rolling beneath the old pick-up even as he took inventory of what he'd seen. Whoever had shown up had shot the dogs and were probably already inside. While other detectives may have waited for the criminals to flee, the better to keep themselves safe while apprehending the criminals, Marty didn't work that way. First, he knew it was highly likely Horvath and Devries might decide to kill their victims in the house. And second, Marty's one true joy in life—his only joy in life—was taking out the bad guys. Especially, if they were a couple of murdering stuffed shirts.

Marty skittered through the yard, gun in hand, rolling from beneath car to car till he was beneath the Terraplane, the car closest to the door. Crawling as far as he could into the single shadow on the block white building, Marty slid around the corner, toward the rear entrance he'd discovered earlier. The building really was a fortress; there were no windows to dodge under. He was hoping the lawyers hadn't had a chance to lock up yet, but he also knew two unlocked doors in two days was asking for too much. And he'd already worn out his luck not getting shot in the yard.

He got half lucky.

A bolted, stylish, heavy screen door was all that blocked his way. The kind of thing that might stop a guard dog, but not a gumshoe. Marty pulled the penknife out of his pocket and began to slash through the stylish screen next to the bolt. A voice peeled around the corner from inside the house.

"See anybody?" It was Horvath.

There was an electronic arc and then feedback "—'s ALL CLEAR!" The P.A. system broadcast off the roof so loudly. Marty flinched, accidentally ducking his hat into the doorway as Horvath came into the back room. Horvath's head pitched toward the door. He had spotted Marty.

As Horvath began to open his mouth, Marty burst through the door. Diving across the room and over the kitchen table, the detective ace tomahawked the tall lawyer between the eyes with his automatic. Horvath moaned a vowel and a consonant like he'd been about to say something, but the blow cut him short. Marty rolled in the air, managed to twist one arm around Horvath, and land beneath him, but the half-screamed warning and the resulting thud on the floor had been too loud. Marty slowly crawled out from beneath the tall lawyer as he waited to see if he'd been heard.

"What's taking so long?" Devries voice eked from the back room of Shockley's fortress then blasted from the P.A. system on the roof a second later. "Hurry up."

With his vision still blurry—this time adjusting from the spotlights outside to the darkness inside—Marty positioned himself with his back to the wall and slid down the hall with his automatic at his side. Peering around the corner, he could see Devries in Shockley's control room. Gaines sat beaten and bloody, tied to a chair with one arm askew as if he'd been thrown there. Shockley had two black eyes and was strapped to a metal work table affixed to the floor. His arms and legs were tied over the edge of the table, strapped to its legs so he looked like a human sacrifice.

Something made a scuffing sound behind Marty. He hoped it was Horvath regaining consciousness, but knew he'd hit the man too hard. Spinning as he leaped across the hall, in that split instant the private eye could just make out the silhouette of a man only a few feet behind him. Marty heard the shot and saw the flash of fire from the man's gun hand. The same instant the bullet tore through his coat, Marty fired three shots directly into the face of the shadow.

He recognized one of R.E.D.'s suited security guards as the body toppled to the floor at his feet.

"Beanie, you—" Devries cut the sentence short as he rounded the corner. Marty remembered Beanie was Devries brother's name.

But as he turned to fire, something hit Marty from behind.

•••

As voices drifted in and out of his head, Marty realized there must have been two security guards. His hand was already under his coat, but they'd taken his gun. With Beanie dead, he was surprised to still be alive. Before he'd even had a chance to play possum, something slapped him across the face once, then twice more.

"Where is it, Quade?" Devries sounded anxious. "Where is it?"

"Wh—where's what?" Marty feigned awakening as if it had just happened. There was a long moment of silence.

Marty slowly opened his eyes. Devries stood before him, slapping a chair leg in his hand like it was a Billy club. Behind the short lawyer,

Horvath stood holding a rag to his head where Marty had pounded him with the automatic. The security guard that had knocked Marty out from behind stood in the periphery, pacing and occasionally reaching under his lapel to make sure his gun was there.

"The journal, you idiot! You know Shockley kept a journal." Devries slapped Marty again.

"Why don't you ask *him*?" Marty waved his jaw at the prostrate form of the unmoving Shockley on the table. Shockley scoffed, almost laughing at Marty's joke. The mining engineer was still conscious. Devries swung the homemade nightstick at Marty's head. At the last moment, Marty stuck his head out, took the blow on his neck and fell to the floor, mumbling. "I don't know 'bout no journal."

Devries rushed at him again, winding up the Billy-club for the next blow.

Still sitting on the floor, Marty raised both feet and kicked the lawyer, hard, in the shins. Devries screamed, clutching his knees as he fell backward. The security guard in the background pulled a .45 Auto out of his coat, but Marty was already moving.

As the gunman's arm turned to aim at him, the ace private eye vaulted over the table where Shockley was tied and into his assailant's range of motion. Marty slapped the .45 away with his left and, stepping forward, came up with a quick right cross to the chin. The gunman's head twisted and he stumbled backwards. Still holding the pistol, he dodged to Marty's left. His arm pivoted, swinging the .45 around for another shot. The ace of Manhattan detectives charged again, closing the distance between them.

Slamming his shoulder into the thug's chest, Marty turned as they collided, and seized the man's gun hand by the wrist with both hands. His feet shifting like a dancer's, the private eye twisted under the man's arm and came up behind him, twisting the man's arm. Marty wedged his assailant's wrist between his shoulder blades. He slung his left arm around his assailant's throat and lifted him up in the air by threatening to break his right arm. The .45 clattered off the floor.

"Move and I'll pull it out of the socket." Marty held the guard like a bulletproof shield in front of him.

Horvath extended his arm like an archer's, a .38 aimed at Marty's head in his grip. Devries hopped to his feet. Wincing, he bowlegged his way around the room to pick up the .45 Auto the guard had dropped. He backed up, finger on the trigger, wiped his brow with his coat sleeve and aimed between Marty's eyes.

Marty stared over a muscle-bound shoulder and down the barrel of two guns. He twisted his hostage's arm a little more, and shoved his way around the table. Devries backed slightly toward Horvath. Marty faced them from the opposite side of the table where Shockley still lay tied, barely conscious.

"Don't shoot," Marty's unarmed captive screamed. Horvath and Devries raised their automatics.

"Just tell me one thing, Devries," Marty said, pushing his shield forward. "Those footprints at Del Raymond's house, they were yours weren't they?"

The two lawyers looked at each other.

"Yeah, they were mine," the little lawyer shrugged his shoulders without lowering his gun. "Funny, how a slipper's footprint looks just like a women's flat, huh, Quade? We got lucky on that one. You thought the Lennox dame was setting you up, when all we were trying to do was cover our bases. We set the frame-up for that night knowing the cops would be on stake out. Didn't even know you were on the case." There was a moment of silence as the two armed men made eye contact and exchanged the slightest hint of a nod. "Speaking of cases, I'm going to have to bury Beanie in one, and I'm not very happy about—"

Marty yanked his captive by the arm and slung him to the right, leaping behind him toward the control panel on the wall. Hot lead ripped into the chest of the security guard as Marty flipped the two brightly colored knife switches jutting from the shelf wall. First the yellow one, then the red one.

The gate in the wall shot open with the metallic sound of a jailhouse door. The gunfire stopped. All eyes and both automatics were on the tunnel gate.

There was only blackness inside.

The sound of muffled howls in the distance reverberated off metal and concrete then eked down the dog run into the control room. The edges of Devries lips curled up. Horvath's extended arm pivoted with his partner's to aim at the private eye. Marty clenched back in the corner, holding the hired goon as high as he could. Hiding beneath the dead man's body, he flipped every other switch on the control board he could reach.

Tense fingers gripped hair triggers. Something in the dog run bumped the wall outside the chute. Sirens erupted, wailing across the property at a deafening volume. Alarm bells rang and sirens screamed, as searchlights cut the darkness outside. Red and white bulbs on the walls of the control room flashed in unison with the noise. Horvath covered his ears with his hands. Devries black, bull's eye transformed to a slit over the sight of his gun. He aimed and fired. Bullets slapped the dead man's chest with a *sputting* sound, and red holes popped in his shirt. Stray shots ricocheted off the control board and two holes popped in the plaster above Marty's head.

Devries ejected the clip from his .45. His black eyes shined. His smile, the bared teeth of a predator as he slammed a fresh clip into his automatic. But aiming again, something moved next to the wall. Something big, and black. Horvath's eye's widened as he glanced to his left. He knew it was already too late.

There are tales about the hell hounds assigned to guard the world of the dead, hunt lost souls, and guard legendary treasures. The stories are as old as mankind, and may have something to do with man's instinctive fear of animals. In the legends, the hounds have black fur, glowing red eyes, and mystical powers. The legend also says that if someone stares into a hellhound's eyes more than once they will die.

Horvath did a double take. A glance into the blackness, then at Marty, and then back, into the gates of Hell. His mouth fell open as a wave of black fur and snarling fangs burst into the room like an all-consuming flame.

Two shots skipped across the concrete flooring. As Devries fired at the first black-furred demon, another one seized him by the wrist. White fangs stabbed into tendons and muscle with the hellish pressure of a bear trap, only to snag, yank, and tear with unrelenting force.

Jake Shockley had trained all his attack dogs to dislike guns.

A surge of furred black backs with hackles razed filled the room. Snapping white teeth snarled beneath burning red eyes. Devries fired two more shots. A dog yelped but the little lawyer was engulfed in the tide. He screamed shrilly and fell beneath the flood. Watching as one Doberman's fangs tore him apart and two others held him down, he finally lay back and looked up into the beast's red eyes, as if suddenly realizing he had been sentenced to the world of the dead by one of its guards.

Horvath dropped his gun as two of the dogs nipped at his hands. He held both awkward arms up, but the hell hounds kept coming. He tried to shush them at first. Then he said no. Then he screamed.

In the midst of the action, and unharmed due to the fact that they had taken his gun away, Marty spotted Jimmy Gaines, the soundman, tied to his chair in the middle of the room while a roving gang of Dobermans began to herd around him.

Marty grabbed the back of the chair the sound engineer had been tied to, and twirled, slinging Jimmy into the hallway. With one cursory glance at the attack canines, he headed back to the center of the room to save Jake Shockley.

The dogs snarled, eyeing their dead prey on the ground. Marty heard them licking their chops. Now they were they were considering him. He may not have had a gun, but he was still a stranger.

Marty jumped up on the table between Shockley's feet. Grabbing him by the collar, Marty slapped him across the face, and held him up by his nose.

"Shockley! If you ever needed to say 'Ham Bone' the time is now!"

The engineer's hand slapped Marty's arm. The private eye let go of his nose, and Shockley gasped for breath.

"I ain't talking, I…" Then his eyes flew wide. He was almost conscious. "What the?"

"'Ham bone', Shockley! You gotta say 'Ham bone!'"

"Uhhhh, Ham bone?"

The dogs stopped like a wonder of physics. A gigantic wave of revolving, chomping fur, angry eyes, and bloody teeth, stopped cold. One of the dogs even whimpered as several others circled their dead prey with wagging tails.

Marty remembered to inhale, and then sighed. Shockley looked up at him through blackened eyes and chuckled. Marty began untying him.

"Ham bone," Shockley said again, and all the dogs sat down and looked at him. He waved a hand and they sat down. The whole room was still.

"Remind me never to pick a fight with you, Shockley."

"Good God, Quade!" The engineer stared at the bodies on the floor, watching the ever-expanding pool of blood puddle on the concrete. "What happened here?"

"I'll tell you, if you'll tell me something."

"Shoot. Anything."

"Lester Lennox, he lost it on the front lines didn't he. That night he 'fell asleep,' he didn't fall asleep at all, did he? He was shell shocked on the front, and the rest of you made him a hero, right? The guy gave everything—and all you guys at R.E.D. decided to give back."

"Yeah, something like that." Shockley gagged, but kept looking at the blood on the floor. "Can we go into another room?"

"No not until you answer some more questions."

Shockley put two fingers to his lips, and whistled like a robin. The attack dogs stood up, looked at the two men, then turned toward the wall and began to gather around the gate. Tails wagging, the pack twirled, as the dogs skittered back through the grate in the wall one at a time.

When the room was empty that left only the ravaged bodies to look at. Shockley shuddered again before he spoke.

"The rest of his squad made him a hero, like it was a big joke. Like they were putting something over on command. Even told those of us who knew he wasn't a hero, that he'd fallen asleep. Mason Foucault, Dylan Gruber and I went along with it. I mean, I was just reconnaissance. What harm could it do, right?"

"What harm did it do?" Marty bent over, fished a pack of cigarettes out of Horvath's shirt, wiped the blood off and offered one to Shockley. The mining engineer pulled a lighter out of his pocket and lit up, inhaling like it was oxygen and exhaling smoke with his words.

"Did no harm at all at first. But Horvath and Devries had been on the battlefield that day, too, and Devries is really the crazy one. A few weeks later he was locked away in a German prison camp. Some of the other guys said the Krauts experimented on his head."

"Probably where he learned those brainwashing techniques. Drugs and hypnotic suggestion aren't exactly common knowledge."

"Evidently, Lennox was fine when his wife, Foucault, Gruber and a few others took care of him. Then those two shysters crawled out of the woodwork and gave Lennox the idea for R.E.D. I don't know how, but they had him convinced, either I was going to find the Germanium, or the tech boys were going to come up with a synthetic version in the next two years. And he actually bought into it. He may have been brainwashed, but he truly believed in it."

"It wasn't all brainwashing," Marty said. "A person won't do anything they wouldn't normally do while hypnotized. I'm willing to bet the story that saved Lennox is the same one that killed him. He actually believed he had fallen asleep on the line and suffered tremendous guilt from it. Horvath and Devries gave him hope of redeeming himself through R.E.D.s invention and a political life. Too bad it was a false hope."

"Lennox was spending all his time with those two shysters by the time I came around, and it was easy for them to talk him into their scheme. The chiselers had him convinced the company was going to have a real transistor, without ever telling him it might take decades."

"Guess what?" Marty smiled and patted Shockley on the back. "The one thing all you Radio Design geniuses forgot to get was a real accountant. All the company's fees were run through the legal department. I'm sure after they go through the files there's going to be some fairly non-existent companies in there. Meanwhile, they were setting everything up for the big kill. To do that, they needed two things. One, the promise of some new invention the war department wanted. And, two, a political power that would give them a direct link to military defense. Problem was people began to notice Lennox was cracking up. So, after the two murders made things too hot, Horvath and Devries had to move up their deadline, and were about to become simple everyday swindlers."

"Thank God you were here, Quade." Shockley looked at the floor and gagged again. Marty helped him off the table and to his feet. Guiding him toward the door, Shockley put a hand on Marty's shoulder. They stopped and glanced back at the carnage in the room, then trudged into the hallway and began untying Jimmy Gaines. It took a couple of slaps, but Gaines moaned. He was alive, and probably okay.

It wasn't until Marty was carrying Jimmy toward the couch in the living room that they spotted Lester Lennox. The large figure was huddled into a ball in the corner of the room, rocking back and forth with his arms clenched around his knees, mumbling to himself in a child's voice.

Marty dropped Jimmy on the couch, then he and Shockley stared at the one-time war hero a minute. Shockley opened his mouth and started to say something. Marty put a hand on the mining engineer's shoulder to stop him.

There were no words.

Lennox never even looked up. For the briefest of moments the only sound in the world was the mumbling of a man who was barely in the room. Then Marty made his way toward the phone, Shockley toward the bar.

"Tell me something, Mr. Private Detective," Shockley said. "That dog run in back of the house runs over a hundred yards to the kennels. With no gun, no idea how many men might be in the house, or even what stake I held in the situation, how did you buy the time for the dogs to get in the room?"

"Easy, I asked a question."

"You asked a question?" Shockley tried to smile and put a bottle on the bar. "Must have been one hell of a question."

"Not really," Marty answered. "I just remembered they were lawyers."

"What does that have to do with buying time?" Shockley poured two tumblers half full of whiskey, as Marty picked up the phone and began dial the police.

Mister, if there's one thing I've learned in my experience as a Private Eye, it's that lawyers like to talk."

The End

The Obnoxious Detective

In a strange way I'm partly responsible—or to blame—for this anthology. Airship 27's Chief Ron Fortier said, "We need another Private Eye." And, I'm the one that suggested a Marty Quade Private Eye. I don't know what made me do this. Now, if we had wanted to just dig up some nameless detective it would have been easy. I had a short list of Private Eyes from Detective Fiction Weekly, and of course the oddball stories from Black Mask and other pulps I've read, but Marty kept popping up.

Anybody who's read the work of Emile Tepperman—Operator #5, The Suicide Squad—knows for a fact that Marty was not his greatest creation, so why did he keep popping up? My theory is that Marty was a character in the right place at the right time.

Magazines like Black Mask and Detective Fiction Weekly focused on the original hardboiled style of the 1920's. Minimalism was in. Plot was more important than character, violence was portrayed as lackluster—an everyday event—and to be honest, these knights in black armor walked streets so mean that hopelessness became a state of grace. Then, Ten Detective Aces came along.

Ten Detective Aces Magazine, a penny a story—and, oh, what stories! While her more literary sisters stuck to simple sentences and the unembellished facts of the case, Ten Detective Aces did the exact opposite. They went for high drama, cheap thrills and sensationalism. For my money, Ten Detective Aces kicked off the era of the masked avenger pulp. And they needed a private-eye. A bigger than life private eye.

I was not a Marty Quade fan until I learned this.

In fact, I was really not a big Marty Quade fan at all. He was too brash. He was a braggart. He was greedy. He was a know-it-all part of the peanut gallery. How could he fit in a room with that ego? By modern standards, he's just obnoxious.

But, reading the stories again, I figured something out. That obnoxiousness is Marty's greatest quality. Because other than bragging to get the case, Marty has never failed to solve one. It's a matter of pride. Marty will do ANYTHING to solve a case. Anything. That's why he's obnoxious.

And of course, I said, "Write an obnoxious detective? Oh, hell yeah!!"

Now things get complicated.

I'd plotted out a vague mystery, made a list of characters and their jobs, and I had the perfect opening. Since Marty doesn't have an office, Marty was going to meet his client at the diner. I'd written out a nice little intro where Marty meets Mrs. Vivian Lennox as a client, and she asks him to solve the murders of two men at a radio design company. I thought it was great little scene, and then something weird happened. I got a chance to read Gordon Dymkowski's Marty Quade story for the same volume you're holding in your hand. And, Gordon had stolen my opening act!

Short of cursing Gordon needlessly for hours (It was ten minutes tops, Gordon), sending threatening letters, or taking the time to go hire somebody to beat him up, it was obvious to me I needed a different beginning. So how was I going to start this fantastic, investigative, high drama? What was I going to do?

This being a pulp, I would have to kill the dame walking in with legs-up-to-there scene and move right to the action—without killing the mystery. No problem, I decided, Marty will make his own action. Marty will wreck a Police car to solve a case, and the body in the trunk will open the story.

Now comes the hard part. The story was moving fast, and a true flashback would have brought it to a deadly boring halt. I had to go back and review a few facts for the reader without my original intro, and yet I still had to keep the story moving forward.

What's simpler than 3-2-1? Three days ago, one man was murdered. Two days ago, another one was missing. One day ago, Marty was hired. He finds the second man murdered, and it looks like the case is closed—or is it? Remember, this was originally going to be one of the surprises in the middle of my story, and I was opening the story with it. So much for surprises, huh? But in the end I decided to sacrifice my darling for a better, faster story. *Farewell, ruthless little plot point, ya done me well.* Or at least I hope you did. I had been perceptive enough to give all my characters names that might resemble their occupation in some shape or sound, and hoped the reader wouldn't have any problems keeping them apart if I gave them the occasional reminder. I can only hope it worked.

I'd like to say, the plot involving the transistor came about because I knew the original design had been patented decades ahead of time, but that's not the case. It's more like I had simply been going for something in the radio industry, since that was the cutting edge of the electronics back then, and the transistor seemed like a logical step. Only later did I discover the truth about Germanium and the eventual silicone that made sand a profitable part of the electronic world.

Now, as far as process; I have two for writing a pulp mystery. The first, is that it's no mystery. It's threat up-front, and sometimes you can sacrifice a character at the end just to make it look like one. The danger in this, of course, is that if you make it too big a "reveal," a good part of the audience will think, "Oh, that? Yeah, I didn't know I was reading one of those kinds of mysteries, I thought this was a "thriller." Or even worse, "Who cares?"

But this wasn't one of those kind of mysteries, so I went to my second rule. Now, everybody knows, if you want to write a real mystery, the writer needs to know "whodunit" from the beginning. But over the years, I've found sometimes that makes things a bit too predictable. Leave a red-herring hanging out of the closet the wrong way, and your reader will know it from the very beginning, too. So, unless you're going to go outside the bounds of reality and Agatha Christie, as a friend used to say, "Whatchoo gonna do?"

What I did, was write the beginning of my story just as if the original villain in my outline—who just happened to have Lex Luthor's initials—Lester Lennox had done it. But I left myself a few options open. I hope sending Marty to the lawyers first didn't immediately tip the reader off, but I was also hoping they had been around the block enough to recognize the old Private Eye ploy of "stirring things up." Meanwhile, while I was writing it, I had no idea R.E.D.'s lawyers had done it.

Also, I couldn't send Marty back to the scene immediately, because that was going to be my next big "reveal." So, how would Marty get reliable information about Radio Electronic Design? From the inside. How? Duh, the employee cafeteria.

After writing the line about Marty wishing he could be a fly on the wall, and making the character of Jimmy Gaines a sound engineer, I had a plot angle for my big finish. Jimmy would record his own kidnapping. But as yet Lester Lennox was still too obviously whodunit. So, I decided to take him out mentally. Make him almost a zombie, and put off letting the reader know that, until after we had met Shockley.

I don't know where the idea for the attack dogs came in, but I know it wasn't until I was creating Shockley's fortress in my head. As a musician, I'd once played a gig at a biker bar that raised attack dogs. I remember parking the car and making sure every dog was chained up, but it was still scary as Hell. Once that memory hit the page, I knew my mystery ending would be a whole lot grislier than some detective in a room saying, "I suppose you're wondering why I've gathered you all here today," and unmasking the villain. And I liked it that way.

Thinking back, I don't remember narrowing it down to two or three suspects until I wrote the line at the scene of the crime about "tiny footprints," and at that very moment deciding the killer was going to be either Mrs. Vivian Lennox or the tiny lawyer. In the end, the tiny lawyer became a much larger menace, and, being a complete bastard even pulled his tall partner down with him.

All in all, writing is a crazy mixed up process. I know people that won't put down a word until they have every letter of a story written in their head. I know others that fly strictly by the seat of their pants, and some that have just an ending or a beginning. I plot my stories ahead of time, to save time, but characters take over sometimes, one thing you write reminds you of another, and other times characters and history itself won't cooperate. As hard as I try, I don't think I've ever written a story the same way twice, but I'm hoping this one felt like a nice little hardboiled 30s pulp that didn't stop moving and had a satisfying ending.

Or to say it in the same fashion Marty would:

"Crazy and mixed up? You're just the guy to do it, kid."

•••

B.C. BELL - is the author and creator of the series TALES OF THE BAGMAN, the story of a 1930s Chicago racketeer turned Robin Hood. Volume three, THE BUTCHER BACK O' THE YARDS is next. Bell has written over a dozen pulp hero adventures, ranging from THE AVENGER to SECRET AGENT X. His book BIPOLAR EXPRESS, the story of a madman trapped in a post-apocalyptic Chicago, made the Horror Writer's Association reading list for 2012. Bell lives in Chicago and is currently working on a novel-length Weird Tale.

OVER THEIR HEAD

by
Gene Moyers

"That'll be three eggs over easy, hash browns, bacon, ham, and toast; three slices. Uh, any pancakes Mr. Quade?"

"No thanks, Jimmy. I'm not that hungry this morning."

"Very well, sir." The waiter smiled at the heavy set man and the grey eyed man smiled back. He bowed slightly and left for the kitchen. Marty Quade took a quick sip of his orange juice and poured himself a fresh cup of coffee from the pot on the table and went back to poring over the morning paper. As usual the news was all bad.

The big headline was that another midtown bank had been robbed. A bank guard had been killed and the masked gunmen had gotten away with over twenty thousand dollars. Marty whistled silently to himself at this. The article reported that authorities thought that the robbery was the work of the same gang that had committed a series of high profile and deadly robberies all over the city in the last three weeks. Estimates of their total take were now well over two hundred thousand dollars. The article concluded with the announcement that the insurance companies involved were offering a reward of ten percent of recovered money for information resulting in the return of the stolen funds and prosecution of the men involved.

Now this was something that got Marty's attention. Rewards, especially large ones, were just the kind of thing he was interested in. His bank account was flush at the moment but it was never too early to start thinking about where his next paycheck was coming from. He sipped his coffee thoughtfully.

His thoughts were interrupted by his breakfast arriving. Once plates were scattered across his table he dug in with relish. He helped himself to healthy portions of the delicious smelling dishes and enjoyed his breakfast wondering what the day would bring. As he ate he thought about the bank robberies, wondering if it would be worth his time attempting to track down these unknown hoods. It wouldn't be easy, but Marty was the best there was and New York was his city. He had been working here for a long time and knew where a lot of the bodies were buried. He also knew every lowlife and stoolie this side of the Hudson; somebody must know who these mugs were. Maybe it was time to start spreading some dough around.

Marty was spreading jam on his last piece of toast when he noticed Jimmy talking to a woman at the entrance to the dining room. The waiter gestured in Marty's direction. The woman nodded and waited while Jimmy made his way through the late breakfasters to Marty's table, "Excuse me Mr. Quade but there is a lady here who wishes to speak to you." Marty swallowed his last bite of toast, glanced at the woman across the room and shrugged mentally, "Sure Jimmy. Send her over." He slipped the waiter a dollar who nodded and moved away.

Jimmy spoke briefly with the woman and pointed the way. Marty took a sip of coffee and thought ruefully to himself that in the movies the women walking into detective's offices were always tall, rich, good looking blondes. What did Marty get? A middle aged, mousey looking dame who would have been average looking if not for the haunted look on her face and the dried tears on her cheeks.

As she reached his table Marty stood up and offered his hand. At 5 foot 10 inches and 190 lbs. Marty was not a small man. With his broad shoulders, brown hair and gray eyes he had a confident presence that radiated around him. The woman didn't seem to notice as she took his hand. She wasn't really seeing anything. Obviously in great distress, she shook his hand tentatively and asked in a hesitant voice, "Are you Marty Quade, the detective?"

Marty smiled and announced, "That's me Marty Quade, and if you're looking for a detective you've come to the right place." He continued, "And you are?"

"My name is Cynthia Richards, and I need your help."

Marty gestured to a chair and sat down himself, "Would you like some coffee?" The woman shook her head. Marty sipped his own coffee and said, "What can I do for you?"

"It's my husband…" she trailed off as her face crumpled, into tears. "He's dead," she sobbed into her hands. Realizing this was serious Marty waited without saying anything until the widow Richards got control of herself. Then he asked, "How did your husband die Mrs. Richards?"

She wiped her nose with a handkerchief and sniffed, "He was killed. Shot. I've just come from the police." Marty was poised to ask another question when she blurted out, "They think he's one of these masked robbers." She pointed toward the newspaper, "They said he was shot by his partners." She wiped her eyes. Nonplussed, Marty thought this one over. The paper had said nothing of the death of one of the robbers. "When was your husband killed? And why do the police think he was involved in these robberies?"

She peered at him through swollen eyes and whispered, "He died sometime early this morning. He was found outside of a hospital in Brooklyn. The police claim they found money in his pockets." She sniffed and wiped her nose. Marty's mind raced, "What time was this?"

"I'm not sure. They came to get me early this morning."

"What was your husband's name Mrs. Richards? And what did he do for a living?"

"His name was Sam, and he's been out of work since the factory closed."

Marty nodded, "How long has that been?"

"Over two months. Our savings are almost gone." She wiped her face with her handkerchief and added, "The police think that's why he got involved with these gangsters. But I know that's not true. Sam has never broken the law before."

Marty said nothing. He knew too well what a man might do if he was out of work and desperate. He spoke carefully, "Mrs. Richards, this is a job for the police. I'm not sure that I…"

"No Mr. Quade! The police have already convicted my Sam. Only you can prove he didn't do these terrible things." Marty knew that this poor woman had no money to pay his usually hefty fee and he didn't really want to get involved. Still, he didn't like disappointing people and… there was that reward, "You said something about money."

"I'll find the money to pay you somehow, Mr. Quade. I don't know how or when but…"

"No, I didn't mean that. You said something about the police finding money on your husband didn't you?"

"Uh, yes. They found some big bills in his pockets. I don't know where they came from but they weren't his."

"When was the last time you saw him Mrs. Richards?"

"Yesterday morning. He and his friend Rich Everly were going out to look for work like they did every day."

Marty pulled a notebook from his pocket and wrote down two names, "Where does this Rich Everly live?" Mrs. Richards gave him both her address and the address of Everly, and looked up hopefully, "Then you'll help me Mr. Quade?"

Marty smiled, "I'll ask around a little. If there's anything to be found, I'll find it."

"Oh thank you Mr. Quade. I'll find the money to pay you somehow."

Marty stood up and waved his hand, "Don't worry about that now, Mrs. Richards. We'll talk about it later. I'll call you when I know more." He signaled for Jimmy to put breakfast on his bill and walked the troubled woman out of the dining room. He saw her safely across the lobby of the *Hotel Baltic* and onto the street. He then headed for the elevators. In his room he slipped a leather holster under his left arm, checked his automatic and tucked it into the holster. Throwing on his overcoat Marty took the elevator back down and exited the hotel onto a busy New York street.

It was a beautiful day and Marty decided to walk for a while. He loved the city this time of year. It was a cool October day with a crystal blue sky overhead and a light breeze. The rains and winds had washed away the stench that built up throughout the summer and the city smelled clean and fresh. He knew that winter was just around the corner. But the wind and snows were still a few weeks away. It was a good day to be alive. Spring in the Big Apple wasn't bad either, especially after a long cold winter but Marty liked fall the best. He whistled as he descended a subway entrance to catch a train downtown.

Twenty minutes later he entered the 12th precinct lobby and asked for Sgt. Donovan. Donovan was a long time detective and old friend of Marty's who had been working the 12th for several years now. The uniformed desk sergeant knew Marty by sight. He smiled and made a call back to the detective squad room. Soon a stocky, square jawed red head appeared. The Irishman smiled when he saw Marty and extended his hand, "Marty it's good to see you. What brings you out this early in the day?"

Marty shook his hand and smiled cagily, "I heard that you guys caught up with the gang who have been running wild through the city's banks. Thought I'd see if you arrested anybody I know."

Donovan looked surprised for a moment, "Well, yeah I heard they picked up a body at one of the hospitals late last night. I don't know any details though. That was out in Brooklyn."

Marty nodded, "Could you ask around. It's kind of important."

The detective looked sharply at Marty, "How come you're so interested?" Suddenly a thought came to him, "You're not sniffing around because of the reward are you?"

Marty shrugged non-committedly, "Actually I'm asking around for a friend. I need to know what you boys have on the stiff."

Donovan shook his head and looked at Marty knowingly, "Riiiight… come on back while I make a call." Marty followed the cop down the hall and into the squad room. He took a seat next to Donovan's desk while the detective dialed a number. Marty looked around nodding to a couple of passing detectives while he half listened to Donovan argue into the phone. Finally the Irish detective hung the earpiece back on his candlestick phone and scanned his scribbled notes, "Well, it seems the stiff that was dumped at the hospital was named Samuel Richards, resident of Brooklyn. He's unemployed with a wife and two kids. No record, he's totally clean. He was carried up to the door of the hospital by another man about two this morning. Nothing but a vague description of him though." He looked curiously at Marty, "Does that tell you anything?"

Marty lit up a cigarette and asked, "This guy Richards doesn't sound like the stick up man type. What connects him to these robberies?"

Donovan consulted his notes again, "You mean something other than the two forty five slugs in his chest and stomach? It's probably the money they found stuffed in his pockets; several big bills that have definitely been identified as coming from a couple of the bank jobs." Marty was thoughtful as Donovan continued, "The local boys think he and his partners had a falling out over the loot and they decided to get rid of him."

"Have they talked to anyone who knows him?"

"Yeah, I guess they've spoken to his wife and a few friends. It seems he's been out of work for a while and they think he was getting desperate. One of his out of work buddies is also missing. They think he's probably in on it too."

Marty stubbed out his cigarette in an ashtray and stood up, "Thanks Don, I appreciate you asking around for me."

Sgt. Donovan leaned back in his chair and looked questioningly at Marty, "You don't seem too surprised or… convinced. What do you know?"

Marty smiled and shrugged, "What was the name of that friend?"

Donovan consulted his notes again, "Everly, Rich Everly, also from Brooklyn."

Mary turned to go but stopped and looked back, "If these mugs decided to shoot it out over the money, why would they haul their wounded pal down to the hospital instead of dumping the body in an alley somewhere?" Donovan opened his mouth to reply but couldn't think of anything to say. He closed his mouth and looked sharply at New York's Ace detective. Marty gave him a casual wave on his way out, "Be seeing you Don, and thanks again." He left, the detective frowning after him.

Marty was thoughtful on his way back to the *Hotel Baltic*. Once there he got his car and headed for Brooklyn. His first stop was at the Everly's address. It turned out to be a modest four story brown stone. He checked the mail boxes for an apartment number and knocked at the third floor door. It was opened by a middle aged woman who seemed uncomfortably familiar. The hair and dress were different but she had the same swollen eyes, and tear stained cheeks. This woman could have been a sister to Mrs. Richards. Marty smiled and spoke, "Mrs. Everly? My name is Quade. Could I speak to you for a few moments?"

The woman wiped her eyes with a handkerchief and sniffed, "Who are you?"

"I'm a private detective. Mrs. Richards gave me your address. She's asked me to look into her husband's death." Mrs. Everly looked startled then stepped aside and invited Marty into the modestly furnished apartment. Inside she pointed to sofa and Marty sat holding his hat in his hand. She took a seat also and said, "If Gladys Richards thinks you're okay. That's good enough for me. What do you want to know?"

Marty recounted his conversations with Mrs. Richards and parts of his conversation with Donovan. He then said, "The police seem to think that your husband was involved in these robberies along with Sam Richards. They also seem to think that your husband may be the man who shot Richards." At this the woman burst into tears again. Marty had seen dames cry before but he was still a little uncomfortable as this woman held her head in her hands. Finally she got herself under control and Marty said softly, "That's what the police think Mrs. Everly. I don't necessarily believe it. I need you to help me find out what really happened.

She sniffed and nodded, "I know my Richie couldn't have shot Sam. They were best friends for years. They worked at the shoe factory together. I don't know why the police think they did these horrible robberies. Neither of 'em know anything about guns much less own a gun."

Marty nodded, "When did you see your husband last?"

"Yesterday morning. Sam came by and they went off together to look for work, just like they did almost every morning."

This point interested Marty, "So your husband hadn't done anything unusual lately? Or gone anywhere different?"

She shook her head, "Not that I know of."

"And he hadn't been acting strange? Perhaps nervous or worried?"

"Well, he has been worried about money. He's been out of work so long. It was hard on both Sam and Richie. Not being able to provide for your family is hard on a man's pride. Can you understand that Mr. Quade?"

Marty nodded. He could, he knew very well how many men defined themselves by their jobs. Men out of work could easily become depressed and even desperate. He continued, "So your husband had been depressed?"

"Well yes... but he seemed happier the last few days. When I asked him why, he said they had a line on a job that might pay off." She hesitated for a moment before she added guiltily, "I was glad. We're already behind on the rent. We need something... anything." She stifled another sob in her handkerchief.

Marty didn't want to pester this woman but he needed more. He pulled out a notebook and pen, "Can you tell me any places he liked to go, restaurants, neighborhood bars, anyplace he might have friends that I could talk to?"

Mrs. Everly nodded and quickly reeled off a half dozen names and locations that Marty quickly scribbled down. He put away his notebook and stood up. As she saw him to the door she spoke once more, "I don't know what you're charging Gladys Richards but I can pay too. I don't know when I can get you some money but I promise..." Marty raised his hand and smiled thinly at the worn out woman, "We'll cross that bridge when we come to it. Right now I'm just trying to find out what happened." She nodded sadly. Marty grimaced inside as he added, "I'll let you know if I find out anything about your husband."

He put on his hat and walked toward the stairs. She called out to him one last time, "Find him, please!"

On the way down the stairs Marty shook his head. Times were tough and he met many hardened people who didn't hesitate to take what they wanted or needed. There were also ordinary people caught up in desperate circumstance who were driven to violent measures just trying to survive. As he started up his car Marty tried to decide which category Richards and Everly fell into.

Marty didn't drive far. He pulled up a few blocks away in front of a diner. Inside he took a seat at the counter. When the tired looking waitress wandered over, he ordered a cup of coffee. She brought it quickly and set it in front of him. Marty nodded his thanks and threw a dollar on the counter. The woman smiled and said, "I'll get your change."

Marty replied, "Keep it." The woman was surprised as Marty asked, "You haven't seen Sam Richards or Rich Everly around have you?" He sipped the hot coffee as the woman looked at him sharply, then at the dollar and back at him again, "You a cop?"

"Naw. Private, hired by their wives."

The waitress thought about it for a moment and shrugged, "Yeah, they're regulars. They stop in most mornings, check out the want ads and go out looking. Decent enough guys, I guess."

Marty took another sip of coffee, "When was the last time they were in here?"

She took the pencil that was stuck in her hair out and scratched her head with it while she thought, "Come to think of it, it's been almost a week since they were in here; five, six days anyway."

The detective stood up and nodded, "Thanks."

Marty's next stop was a neighborhood barber shop close enough to walk to. There was a customer in the chair and another waiting with his face hidden behind a newspaper. As Marty entered the barber paused in his work and turned, scissors in hand, "Take a seat mister. I'll be with you when I get a chance." Marty smiled and said, "Not looking for a haircut. I'm looking for Sam Richards or Rich Everly. They been around lately?" The man reading the newspaper lowered it slightly to peer at Marty. The barber gave the detective a critical scrutiny, "You a cop?"

Irritated, Marty replied, "No, I'm just asking around. You know 'em?"

The waiting man spoke up, "You a private dick?"

Marty flicked him a glance and nodded, "Yeah. You know 'em?"

Before he could reply the barber spoke up, "Yeah, Everly comes in here regular like." He snipped some hair and continued, "Haven't seen him in a couple of weeks though."

Marty muttered, "Thanks," and turned toward the door. On the sidewalk he shook his head. Why did everyone think he looked like a cop? He dressed way better than any flatfoot. He looked down at his clothes and flicked a bit of fluff off one sleeve. Maybe it was his shoes. Naw, they were nearly new, could use a shine though. To his left was a shoe shine stand. Marty stepped up to it and took a seat. The aging man smiled, "Spit shine, Boss?"

Marty flipped him a half dollar and said, "Sure." The man went to work with polish and cloth. Marty watched him for a moment then reached another half dollar out of his pocket. He toyed with it while he watched. After a minute he looked up at the building across the street and spoke casually, "I'll bet you see a lot of who comes and goes in this neighborhood." The old colored man said nothing just kept at his work. Marty continued, "I'm looking for a couple of locals who might be in trouble." The old man ignored Marty and kept stropping his shoe.

"In fact, you might know 'em… Sam Richards and Rich Everly? They used to work at the shoe factory before it closed down."

The old man shifted to Marty's other shoe without a break. Finally he spoke casually, "Times is tough and a man needs to feed his family." Marty smiled and flipped him the other fifty cent piece. The shine man caught it out of the air without looking, barely slowing his work, "Didn't mean that 'zactly. I meant a man can change, take up with new people, he gets desperate."

Marty nodded, "So you seen 'em around?"

A shrug, "Seen Sam Richards." A pause, "With a new guy."

Interested Marty leaned forward, "Who? You know him?"

Another shrug, "Like I say, new guy. Ain't seen him around."

"What did this new guy look like?"

"About the same age, thin, dark hair. Kinda had that lean, hungry look, like a guy on the make, ya know." Marty nodded thoughtfully. The old man stood back and said, "There ya go, Boss."

Marty glanced down at his immaculate shoes gleaming in the pale sunshine and smiled. He stood up and held his hand out, "Thanks." The old man shook it and found a five dollar bill pressed into his palm. He nodded his thanks as Marty strolled down the street, "Thanks, Boss."

Marty continued asking around the neighborhood. His luck was poor though. The two men were well known but no one other than their wives had seen them in several days. Marty was suspicious. Where had they been lately? It didn't sound like they had been looking for work. And who was the new man who had been seen with Richards?

Running out of places to check Marty was thinking about lunch when he got a sudden inspiration. Back in his car, he made a quick left at the next light and drove two miles across Brooklyn to the closed shoe factory where Richards and Everly had been employed. The factory was closed and boarded up as he had expected. He wasn't interested in the factory itself. Instead he cruised the neighborhood looking for a certain type of business. Many nearby small businesses had closed when the factory had and the neighborhood had an empty feel to it. Few people were on the streets. Two blocks east of the factory Marty came cross what he was looking for; a neighborhood bar that was still open. He parked and went in. As his eyes adjusted to the darkness Marty decided that this place wasn't going to last long either. The only patrons were two older men nursing beers at a corner table. They weren't talking just staring into their drinks, alone with their thoughts. A bored bar tender polished a glass and looked up hopefully at

Marty as he entered. He crossed to the bar and put a foot up on the rail. He tilted his hat back and said, "Gimme a beer."

The bar tender smiled, "Sure mister," as he reached for a glass. When the foamy glass was placed in front of him Marty nodded and took a sip, "That's good, thanks buddy." He tossed a dollar bill on the bar and as the bar tender reached for it to make change Marty said, "I'm looking for a couple of guys that you might know."

The barman rang up the beer and gave Marty back his change, "Yeah? Who would that be?"

"A couple of guys that used to work at the factory before it closed." He described the two men and gave their names. The bar man went back to wiping a glass and nodded, "Yeah, I know 'em. They used to be regulars but since the factory closed I've only seen 'em in here a couple times."

Marty sipped his beer, "When were they in here last?"

The barman shrugged, "A couple of days ago. They've been here a couple of times this week."

Marty sipped again and tried not to look too interested, "Yeah? They do anything unusual?"

The barman gave Marty a look and set his towel on the bar, "Who wants to know? You a cop or something?"

As Marty reached for his wallet, he thought to himself that he would slug the next guy that asked him if he was a cop. He brought out a five dollar bill and put it on the bar but left his hand on it, "Or something. I'm looking for the two of them. You know where they might be?" The barman eyed the five and then shrugged, "Not really but that friend of theirs might."

Marty raised an eyebrow, "So they were in here with someone else? Recently?"

"Yep, I hadn't seen either of them since not long after the plant closed, and then they showed up here a week ago with another guy. Marty thought a moment, "Thin fella with dark hair?" The bar tender looked sharply at Marty and nodded, "Yeah."

Marty slid the bill a little farther across the bar, "What was his name?" The bar tender picked up his towel and glass, "Buddy, something or other."

"He have another name?" The bartender shrugged as he started polishing the glass again, "If he did, I didn't hear it. Seen him around though, I think he used to work at the shoe factory too. He use to come in here sometimes but I haven't seen him in a while… until last week." Marty slid the five all the way across and lifted his hand, "Know where I can find this Buddy?"

"What was his name?"

The barman pocketed the bill, "Don't know where he lives but I've heard him talking about shooting pool over at *The 8 Ball*."

"Where's that?" The barman gave Marty an address and went back to his glass polishing. Marty drank up and left.

Once back in his car it took Marty fifteen minutes of cruising to find the pool hall a few miles away. He finally saw a second story sign advertising *The 8 Ball* and found a place to park down the street from it. On the street he found that the pool hall was upstairs but reached through a ground level stairway below the sign. The hall was on the left at the top of the stairs. Marty pushed through the door and looked around. It was one long room: to his left windows looked out over the street, to his right was a long bar. Ahead stretched six pool tables; three were in use with a half dozen or so people shooting pool. It was quiet, just the buzz of low voiced conversation and the click of balls bumping against each other.

Marty sauntered over to the long bar. Behind it were racks of pool cues and sets of balls. There was also a couple of taps so you could get a beer here as well as shooting pool. He hadn't stopped for lunch and his stomach was complaining but it would have to be patient. As he reached the bar a man on the other side sauntered over, "Lookin' for a game?"

Marty shook his head and reached for his wallet, "I'm looking for a beer, right now."

The man nodded and filled a schooner and set in front of the detective. Marty reminded his empty stomach to pipe down as he sipped. The man behind the bar turned away but Marty stopped him with, "I'm also looking for somebody, somebody who plays pool."

The barman turned back with a skeptical look, "Yeah? A lot of people play pool."

"That's why I'm here. The guy's name is Buddy. Ring a bell?"

The man shrugged, "Can't say as it does. What's his last name?"

Marty sipped again, "Not sure. He used to work at the shoe factory across town before it closed. He's probably been in here lately with a couple of friends."

The barman frowned. Marty became aware that most of the background sounds in the hall had ceased. Suddenly it was very quiet. Marty remained calm as the barman looked suspiciously at him, "Who's askin'? You the law?"

Marty bit back a retort. Why did everybody think he was a cop? Maybe anybody asking questions just looked suspicious, "Naw, just looking for Buddy."

A man carrying a pool cue had moved up close behind Marty, his two friends had also drifted closer. The detective remained calm as the man spoke to his back, "Maybe we don't know no Buddy. Specially if you're a flatfoot."

Marty turned his beer in one hand and leaned back against the bar, "I told you I'm not with the cops. I just need to talk to Buddy."

One of the other two men leered at him, "He owe you money or something? He can't be no friend if you don't know his last name."

The first man suddenly looked hard at Marty, "You're some kind of private dick, aren't you? Well we don't like strangers nosin' around in here." Marty felt his temperature start to rise, "Yeah, I'm a private detective. Name's Marty Quade."

One man snickered, "Never heard of ya."

The man with the pool cue sneered, "I don't care if you're J. Edgar hisself. Nobody knows nothin. So why don't you blow outta here before we throw you down the stairs."

That was it. Marty's feet hurt, he had missed lunch and he was getting awfully tired of asking the same questions all day. He was also really tired of being mistaken for a cop; that was bad for his reputation! He stood up straight. The man with the cue must have taken this move for aggression because he suddenly swung the pool cue at Marty's head.

Marty threw his beer, glass and all at the man on his left's face. He then ducked under the cue and came up swinging. A left, then a right connected to cue stick's face. He dropped the cue and staggered backwards over a chair and sprawled onto the floor. Spinning around Marty met the third man rushing in with left jab followed up by a right cross. Ha! He'd show these punks some respect for Marty Quade, Ace Detective! This third would-be opponent dropped like a sack of cement.

The man on his left had caught the beer glass with his nose. Cursing he wiped the beer and blood from his face and rushed in with a raised cue. Marty took the blow on his left forearm. He grunted in pain as the cue broke in half, the front half flying over his shoulder to crash into something with the sound of breaking glass. He could hear the barman cursing as he stepped inside his attacker's reach and slammed a right upper cut into the man's solar plexus. He gasped and bent over trying to get air into his paralyzed diaphragm.

Marty spun around. His first attacker was on his knees attempting to get to his feet. Taking two long strides Marty brought his foot up into the man's stomach. He collapsed back onto the floor with a groan. Turning to the man on the right who was wiping blood off his face and looking doubtful Marty held up his fists and smiled. The man stepped back. Marty bent over the man on the floor, grabbed him by the shirt front and cocked back a fist. Through bloody lips the man blubbered, "I've had enough!"

Marty shook him like dog shakes a rat and queried, "What do you know? You seen Buddy?"

Before he could answer the man behind the bar called out, "Look, mister. I can tell you what I know. Just don't break up the place anymore."

Marty dropped the groaning man back to the floor and stepped up to the long bar. He pulled a handkerchief from his pocket and wiped his face, "So, you know this Buddy guy?"

The barman reluctantly nodded, "Yeah, he's a regular. His name's Buddy Navalle."

"Has he been in here lately with a couple new faces? Average Joes?"

"Yeah, last week or so. They keep to themselves and do a lot of talking."

Marty nodded, "You know where this Navalle lives?"

"Not exactly." The barman licked his lips nervously, "Look you didn't hear this from me, right?"

Marty smiled, "Naw, I just hear it around."

"Okay. I heard Navalle lives over on Wilson Street. Not far from the *Capital Theatre*. He said somethin' about living near there." Marty smiled again and threw a dollar on the bar, "Thanks for the beer," He swaggered out of the hall and down the stairs.

Wilson Street wasn't far away and the *Capital* was easy to find. Once parked near it Marty got out of his car and sighed. Now it would just be a matter of shoe leather.

It took nearly an hour of knocking on doors and peering at mailboxes before he located what he was looking for. It was a mailbox in an old brownstone lobby a block from the theatre that read: *Navalle 3C*. Marty rang the bell but there was no answer. He considered picking the lock and letting himself in but it was nearly five o'clock and there were a lot of people on the street probably coming home from work. His growling stomach made the decision for him; he would go find some dinner and come back when things were quieter.

●●●

The lock clicked back. Marty opened the door quietly and slipped inside. He stood in the dark listening for several moments but was convinced the apartment was empty. He had gone back to the *Baltic,* had a solid dinner, changed into a darker suit, grabbed a couple of items and was back at Navalle's apartment building by nine o'clock. It had been child's play to slip the front door lock. The apartment door hadn't been much harder.

Marty pulled out a pocket flashlight and shined the beam around. It looked like a typical cheap flop; an untidy one at that. Newspapers were scattered around. Ashtrays overflowed. Moving quietly into the kitchen Marty found dirty dishes piled in the sink and on the counters. It looked like Navalle hadn't been home in a while. Mart frowned. What was with these guys? Three unemployed factory workers spend some time together and then just vanish like smoke? Something was up.

Marty flashed his light across the kitchen table; three empty coffee cups, an ashtray and some papers were scattered around. There was also a waste basket under the table. Flashing his light over the papers he saw one of them was a drawing. Picking it up he examined it in the light. It looked like a hand drawn house plan; a simple two bedroom house from the look of it. There were also a lot of newspaper clippings on the table. Sorting through them Marty quickly realized they were all on one subject; the recent rash of bank robberies. He whistled softly.

Bending over the waste basket he rummaged through some used paper towels. He detected an unusual smell. Lifting his hand he sniffed his fingers. A very distinct and familiar smell came to his nose: gun cleaning solvent. He rummaged further in the waste basket and came up with a small card board box labeled: *50 Cartridges, .38 caliber.* It was empty and obviously new. Marty stiffened, dropped the box and reached for the hand drawn plan again. Those idiots! They couldn't have! Damn! They must have!

Dropping the plan he searched quickly through the clippings. Finally he found what he was looking for; an address scribbled in the margins of an article. He shoved the plan and clipping into his jacket pocket and made for the front door. He didn't bother locking it. For once he knew where to go and he needed to get there before anything else happened.

•••

An hour and a half later Marty pulled over to the side of the road and turned off his headlights. He was on the outskirts of a small town on Long Island east of Queens in Nassau County. It had taken some looking but the scribbled address had brought him to this lonely farmhouse on a dark road.

The house was dark and looked abandoned. With his lights off, Marty drove his car quietly a hundred yards past the house. He parked it off the road behind some bushes where it couldn't easily be seen. He got out and with his flash in one hand and his automatic in the other he crept back toward the house.

Once his eyes had adjusted to the darkness Marty could make out more details of the farmhouse as he stood in the deep shadow of a tree. It was definitely abandoned. The yard was overgrown. The front door was slightly open and a few of the front windows that he could see were broken. He moved around to one side of the house. A rickety, detached, single car garage huddled in the darkness behind the house, its doors hanging open.

The back of the house was in deep shadow but Marty could make out the back door standing half open. He stepped up onto the narrow back porch and reached for the door. As he did the old wood beneath his feet creaked slightly. He froze for a minute but nothing happened. He pushed the door open with his pistol barrel. Darkness yawned out at him. He moved forward but before he could turn on his light he knew he was in the right place. The unmistakable smell of cordite tickled his nose.

He turned on his light and flashed it around. He was in a kitchen. The first thing he saw was the body of a man, face down on the floor. He was dressed in a suit but his jacket was off. Marty knelt and felt his neck. No use looking for a pulse; this one was cold and stiff. The empty shoulder holster under his left arm told Marty everything he needed to know about the man. His white shirt was covered in blood and he had left a trail of dried blood where he had crawled through the kitchen from the room beyond. The rest of the kitchen was a mess. Empty beer bottles and crumpled sacks littered the counters. An unlit kerosene lamp stood amidst the clutter.

Steeling himself Marty stepped through the doorway and flashed the light around. It had been a living room. Worn out furniture was scattered around. A table had been placed in the center of the room. It was tipped on its side. Beer bottles and playing cards were scattered all over the floor. Chairs had been knocked over, and there were bullet holes everywhere. The two front windows were broken alright; from multiple gunshots. There were holes in walls, table and definitely in the man's chest who was propped against the wall leading to the narrow hallway.

Marty didn't need to examine this one. The pool of dried blood surrounding him told him that this one had taken a while to die. A revolver lay near the dead man's limp hand. He flashed the light around on the floor. There was another pistol on the floor near the kitchen doorway where the blood trail started. Also in the light Marty could see a lot of money scattered around. Way too much for a friendly game of poker. From where he stood he could see there were thousands of dollars scattered around the floor. Some of it blood covered.

Turning he bent over the second gunman. He slipped his automatic back beneath his arm and picked up the man's revolver. Sniffing the barrel confirmed that it had been fired recently. He flipped out the cylinder; it was loaded, with three spent cartridges. He wiped the gun off and dropped it. He then reached into the man's pants and pulled out his wallet. It contained an out of state license in the name of Bill Peters, also a lot of new cash. Marty wiped the wallet down and replaced it. He then moved back to check the man in the kitchen. His gun had been loaded but all six cartridges had been fired. This man's wallet said his name was Fred Morelli. Marty wiped the gun and wallet and replaced them where he had found them. He frowned as he stood up and looked around. What the heck had gone on here? Were these the bank robbers? Had Richards, Everly and Navalle done this? But where were they now?

He crossed to the front door. There were bullet holes in and around it. There was also blood spattered about. There was more blood on the front porch and a serious trail of it that led across the grass. A blood stained fifty dollar bill lay in the grass. Marty re-entered the house and flashed the light around again. He closed his eyes and tried to imagine what had happened. Somehow the three friends had found out where the bank robbers were hiding out. Desperate for money they had decided to go into business for themselves. They had snuck out here and caught the gunmen by surprise. Marty opened his eyes and looked at the front door. They must have crashed in the front; firing through the windows as well. The gunmen came back firing; gunfire and blood everywhere. This must have been where Richards caught the slug. What happened then? Marty thought about the fifty in the yard. He walked through the kitchen to the back door. There were half a dozen holes in the door and frame around it.

Marty rubbed his chin. The three friends must have been forced to retreat out the front. They could have grabbed some of the money as they went. But how much did they get? It looked like someone had been forced out the back door. Where had he gone?

Flashlight leading the way Marty made his way down the hall to the bedrooms. The first bedroom had two beds that had obviously been slept in. Clothes were scattered about. The second bedroom also had a used bed. There was also a table covered with guns, spare magazines and boxes of

He...tried to imagine what had happened.

bullets. There were also several hand drawn maps and some newspapers. A Tommy gun and a shotgun leaned against the wall in a corner. Peering at one of the hand drawn maps he decided it was a rough sketch of a bank lobby.

Marty shook his head. It must have been a hell of a fight. He thought for a moment. But where was the money? Richards was dead. Did Everly and Navalle have it? What about the bank robbers? If everyone had been wounded and fled under fire there wouldn't have been time to grab much money. Richards had been found with some blood stained money in his pockets but only a couple of hundred bucks.

It made sense that Everly and Navalle would dump off their buddy at the hospital if he was dying. But would they have then blown town without a trace? Especially if they didn't get the money? Navalle didn't seem to have many ties but would Everly leave his wife and kid behind? Marty doubted it. But if the money was still here why hadn't anybody come back for it? Maybe somebody would. They could be outside right now.

Marty almost reached for his gun but then relaxed and started searching. It took some work but he found what he was looking for in the first bedroom. Under one of the beds were some loose floorboards. Prying them up and flashing the light under the house revealed a pile of large leather bags. He dragged one out marked *First Bank of Manhattan* and opened it up. It was filled with cash. Pushing his hat back on his head Marty whistled softly between his teeth. He knelt there for a moment thinking about how much money there was in front of him. A lot of possibilities flashed through his mind. Finally he shook his head. Most of the possibilities involved him on the run from everybody, including the cops. Reluctantly he decided it was better to play it straight, or at least mostly straight.

He shoved the money bag back under the house and replaced the floor boards. Back in the front room he closed and locked the front door. He left all the guns, equipment and bodies just where he had found them. He exited quietly through the back door closing it behind him. He turned and was startled to find a man standing in the back yard 30 feet away. It was dark. The man wore a suit and a wide brimmed hat that left his face in shadow. Apparently as surprised as Marty, the man froze for a moment. Then they both went for their guns. Marty threw himself sideways off the porch as he drew his automatic. The unknown gunman was faster. He cleared leather and fired as Marty fell. The bullet zinged past inches from Marty's head and came to rest in the wall behind him.

Marty's first shot went wild as he landed hard in an overgrown rose bush next to the porch. The gunman fired again, his bullet slamming into the building next to Marty as he struggled to aim; the rose thorns grabbing at his clothes. He fired twice but it was dark and the shadowy figure had turned and was running into the darkness.

Cursing, Marty managed to get to his feet. He cat footed his way around to the front of the house, his gun up and leading the way. The front yard was empty. He cocked his head as he heard a car start up from somewhere down the road toward town. The sound quickly faded. He holstered his gun and turned back toward the house dusting himself off. He cursed loudly as he found several rips in what had been one of his favorite suits.

Inside Marty quickly pulled the bags of money from under the house. There were nine in bags in all. He thought for a moment. He couldn't take them back to the *Baltic*. If they were found there he would have a heck of a time explaining their presence to the police. But if he left them here they probably wouldn't be here for long. He considered calling the police but what would he tell them? He still didn't know who had done what or even where anybody was. He needed more information if he was going to wrap this one up with a bow ribbon.

Deciding, he hauled all the bags to the back door and looked out. Everything seemed quiet. Leaving the bags he cat footed his way quietly to the rickety garage. He flashed his light in and looked around. It was mostly empty except for piles of trash here and there. A few old tools lay on the ground and a pile of old newspapers occupied a back corner. Marty nodded and returned to the house. Quickly he ferried all nine bank bags into the garage. He found a broken shovel and dug a shallow hole in a back corner of the garage where he piled in the bags and smoothed dirt over them. He then stacked the newspapers over the disturbed dirt and scattered some additional trash around. When he was done he judged that the money would be safe there for the time being. He returned to the house for a final check then hiked back to his car.

On the ride back to the city Marty mulled over who he had exchanged gunfire with. It certainly wasn't the cops. Had it have been one of the bank robbers returning for the loot? Or had it been either Everly or Navalle? If it was where was the other one? He shook his head as he parked and entered the *Baltic*. Maybe things would seem clearer with a good night's sleep.

•••

After a good breakfast in the dining room of the hotel the next morning, Marty called Sgt. Donovan, "Don, I need a favor."

"When don't you need a favor Marty?"

"Hey, don't be like that, Don. If this turns out big I'll give you the inside track on it… could look good on your record."

There was a pause, "Just what are you working on Marty?"

"Something big."

Another pause, "Yeah, that's what worries me. Okay, what do you need?"

"I need to know what you can tell me about these two men." He repeated the names of the two gunmen he had searched the night before. "I think these two probably have records. I need there last known whereabouts and who else they may be working with."

Donovan came back with, "Okay. I'll do what I can but this better be important."

"Trust me. It's big."

Marty spent the rest of the morning making calls to various low-life contacts he had around town. No one knew anything about the two men he was asking about but he had put out the word and Marty was confident that somebody knew something. It might take a while for word to get back to him but eventually he'd hear something.

After a good lunch Marty's phone rang in his room. He put down the newspaper to answer it. It was Sgt. Donovan, "Marty I've got news."

"Yeah, what's the word?"

"You were right, both those mugs you asked about having long records. Mostly for strong arm stuff; assault, robbery, attempted murder. Both have done time in prison."

"Any word on what they're up to?"

"Both are thought to be in the New York area. No active warrants on them at this time."

Marty grunted and thought for a moment, "They got any friends around here? Maybe some place they might go to for work or help?"

"They're not part of any local gangs if that's what you mean. There was a name that appeared in both of their files though."

"Yeah?"

"Yeah." There was a rustling of paper, "A guy by the name of George Russell. Formerly George Russelli. Another hood with a long record. He was indicted with both the other two at various times."

Marty nodded, "Got an address on Russell?"

"Afraid not, sorry."

"Thanks, Don. I won't forget this."

"See that you don't. Oh, I almost forgot. You were asking about that Richards guy, right? We found his friend. What was his name? Uh, Everly, yeah that's it."

Marty was surprised, "You found Everly? Where?"

"Behind some trash cans, in an alley in the Bronx."

Marty was silent at this news. While he is thinking Donovan continued, "The coroner says he probably died sometime yesterday. He was shot up pretty badly. Someone bandaged him up but it wasn't good enough. If he'd got to a hospital maybe, but…"

"Have you broke the news to his widow yet?"

"So I'm told. Is it important?"

"Kind of. I'll give her a call as well. So you guys think he was involved with his friend Richards?"

"That's the way it looks. We know there were at least two more in the gang. They're still out there somewhere along with the money. It looks like somebody got greedy and Richards and Everly got the worst of it."

You wouldn't think that if you could see that farmhouse on Long Island, Marty thought to himself. He confined himself to saying, "Thanks for the info Don. I'll get back to you when I know more." He hung up and then immediately started dialing again. He spent twenty minutes calling underworld contacts and putting out the word that he was looking for George Russell. He then grabbed his hat and jacket and took to the streets.

He spent the rest of the afternoon trying to get a line on Russell. He talked to bartenders, stoolies, pimps and bookies. A couple of people had seen Russell around town but no one had seen him with anyone else or knew where to find him. His best lead came from a bookie on the lower east side. When questioned he had told Marty, "Yeah, I seen Russell around."

"Yeah? When?" Marty questioned.

The bookie shrugged, "He showed up a couple weeks ago. He was flush. He's been betting the ponies pretty heavily ever since."

This interested Marty. He slipped the man a saw buck and said, "If Russell shows up again how about letting me know. There'll be another one of those in it for you if you do."

The bookie knew Marty was a square guy and nodded, "Sure. I got your number."

Marty stood up and decided to call it a day as he left the bar the bookie was working from. He then headed back to the *Baltic* for a shower and a change of clothes. He was trying to decide where he wanted to go for dinner when his phone rang. He answered it, "This is Quade."

There was a pause and then a rough voice said, "You've got my money and I want it."

Marty was taken aback for a moment then demanded, "Who is this?"

"The guy you took a shot at last night. That's another thing I owe you for. We'll settle that later. Right now I want my money. I know just where you're holed up Quade. If you give me back the money, I won't kill you."

This was an interesting turn of events. Marty thought fast before replying, "I'll bet you're George Russell." He let that one sink in before continuing, "What makes you think I've got your money."

"Listen smart guy, you've got the money alright. It was you out there last night. I went back this morning and the money was gone and I heard you been askin' around about me. Since you haven't gone to the cops I figured you're crooked and got the cash stashed somewhere. I want my money back now!"

"Maybe I don't have it. Maybe someone else took it."

"Who? You were probably with those clowns that shot us up. Mr. High and Mighty Quade, it turns out you're just as dirty as anybody else. You were the third gun weren't you?"

"And if I told you I turned the money over to the cops?"

"I'd say you were a liar. If the cops had the money they'd be crowing over it. But they're still looking. No, you've got it alright. But I'll tell you what, you give it back and I'll let you live... for a while."

Marty's mind raced. This might be his chance. If he agreed to meet this man who he was convinced was Russell, he could give him the money and have the cops there to pick him up. He gets the reward and everybody lives happily ever after. He couldn't seem too anxious though, "Say I've got the money... why should I give it back to you? Maybe I just make a call and spill your name to the cops. You'll have to take it on the lam, and I laugh all the way to the bank."

The unknown man on the other line swore for a moment, "If they get me, I rat you out. It would look real bad if they found all that loot stuffed under your mattress. There goes your lily white reputation, Mr. Big Shot. And if they don't get me, I'll be back; maybe next week, maybe next month. But one of these days you'll look over your shoulder and I'll be there."

Marty pretended to think this over for a count of five then reluctantly replied, "Maybe it's more trouble than it's worth. But... I figure I deserve something for my trouble."

A suspicious, "Yeah? Like what?" came over the phone.

"Like ten percent."

This brought a rough bark of laughter from the phone. "Boy, do you have a set of brass balls. What makes you think you deserve anything?"

"Call it a finder's fee. I also keep my mouth shut. I forget everything I found at the farm house and your name and then we're quits."

There was another pause, "You may just be a little too smart for your own good, ya know that?" Then came a reluctant, "Alright you got a deal; ten percent. But we meet tonight."

Marty frowned, "What's the hurry? I'm kind of busy tonight."

"Then get un-busy. I don't want nothin' to go wrong. We do it tonight and get it over with."

Marty thought this over. It would mean cutting things very tightly. He was unsure if he could get everything set up in time. Unfortunately he couldn't think of a good reason to stall for time so he reluctantly agreed, "Okay tonight. Eleven o'clock."

"Why so late? What's wrong with now?"

Because I have the money stashed and it'll take time to get it."

A reluctant growl came to Marty's ear, "Okay, okay. Where do we meet?"

"The farmhouse."

Here was a pause followed by a laugh, "Yeah, why not? Eleven at the farmhouse; don't be late." The click sounded loud in Marty's ear. He hung up and looked at the phone. He hadn't planned on things going this way but it might just work out. He glanced at his watch; there wasn't much time to set things up. He left the room thinking of all the things that could go wrong with his plan.

Heading across the lobby Marty decided to catch a quick meal at a little Italian place he knew down the street. He could make some calls from there as well. He turned right as he exited the hotel and strolled down the sidewalk savoring the cool evening air. As he came abreast of a thin man leaning against the wall of the hotel, the man straightened up and stepped into Marty's path.

He was roughly dressed in work clothes that were soiled and worn. He wore a leather jacket and was hatless. His dark hair was tousled and he looked wild eyed and exhausted. Marty thought he was looking for a handout and was reaching for his pocket as the man spoke, "Are you Marty Quade?"

Marty's hand stopped and instead drifted toward his jacket and the automatic hanging under his left arm. He looked sharply at the man, "Maybe. Who wants to know?"

The man held up an open palm. "I've been waiting for you Mr. Quade. I need to talk to you."

He looked skeptically at the stranger, "I don't know you. What do you want?"

The stranger shook his head wearily, "My name's Buddy Navalle and I need your help."

Marty was speechless for a moment. This was the last person he had expected to meet on the street. He quickly found his tongue and said, "You're a hard man to find. I've been looking for you."

"I know. That's why I came here. You've got to help me," he pleaded.

"Help you how?"

"I don't know. Everybody's looking for me. I've got nowhere to go. I haven't slept in two days and I just want it to stop."

Mart frowned, "Let me get this straight. You started a war with a bunch of thugs and now you want me to help you out of it?"

Navalle wilted a little bit under Marty's hard gaze, "It's not my fault. I… uh, we didn't rob those banks. But now the cops are looking for me. They don't have my name yet but they will soon. And there's uh, other guys looking for me too. Everywhere I go people are looking for me. That's how I got your name. Somebody told me you were asking around about me. At first I thought you were somebody else but I asked around and everybody says you're honest. You've got to help me."

Marty sized the man up. He certainly looked scared and exhausted. The question was what did he want? "Maybe I can at that. But you're going to have to be straight with me."

Navalle's face brightened, "Sure, anything you say."

"Okay. I know you tried to shoot it out with the bank robbers. How did you get onto them?"

Navalle was startled by this. He hesitated for a moment before nodding, "Yeah, that's right we did. I was driving by a bank a week ago when those guys robbed it. They came out shooting, carrying bags of money. I knew who they were right away. I decided to follow them because I'd heard about the reward. I haven't had steady work since the shoe factory closed and I needed a break. Anyway I followed their getaway car. I thought I'd lost it a couple of times but I stuck with them all the way out to their hideout on Long Island. I rolled back into town figuring how much I could get from the reward."

Marty thought to himself, "Sure you did." He gave the man a hard look, "So how did Richards and Everly get involved?"

Navalle hesitated but recovered quickly, "I checked around to find out how much the reward was and I the called Sam and Richie. I bought 'em a round to celebrate my luck finally changing. They were uh, kind of jealous. I was surprised at first but I guess they were both hard up for a break as well. We kind of argued for a while and then Sam got the idea to hold up the robbers and take their money. I wasn't sure at first but the more we talked about it the better it sounded. We've all been out work since the factory closed. We really needed the money. We thought we could get the drop on those guys and..." He trailed off and shook his head.

Marty gave Navalle a long hard look. He had no doubt the man was lying or at least shading the truth to make himself look better. Everything he had learned told him that Navalle was probably the brains behind this fiasco. He spoke sarcastically, "So you guys decided to knock them off? What were you thinking, you could just walk in and hold up a bunch of professional crooks?"

"Well, things kinda got outta hand."

"Yeah, I guess so. What happened that night?"

"We had watched the place and thought we had a good plan. We waited until it was late. They had been drinking and were playing cards and then..."

"Then you crashed in and everybody started shooting."

Navalle looked guilty, "Yeah, Everybody was shooting. Richie got hit. Sam grabbed a handful of money as he was hit. We got two of them. But they were still shooting. Two more were in the kitchen. It was bad. I grabbed Sam and we all backed out the front still shooting. Sam was bleeding bad. We practically had to drag him to the car. The other robbers tore out of there in a car stashed behind the house." He paused, "Sam died before we went five miles. We dropped him outside the hospital. We didn't know where else to take him."

Marty shook his head. It had been a long time since he had heard a story that stupid, "You call that a plan? You go in shooting against a bunch of professional killers?" He pointed angrily at Navalle, "This was your idea, wasn't it?"

Navalle turned pale and held up his hands in defense, "No! Like I told you it was Sam's idea. We all uh, all kind of planned it out but..." He trailed off and looked down at his dirty shoes. Marty held his growing anger in check. He knew exactly what had happened. Navalle had followed the bank robbers and saw a chance at a lot of money. He then went to his friends and talked them into helping him. He probably made it sound easy, and his desperate friends had gone along with him. Now he was blaming them; an easy target since the dead couldn't defend themselves. He asked quietly, "So what happened to Everly?"

Navalle refused to meet Marty's eyes. He kicked at a pebble on the sidewalk, "I bandaged him up but he died yesterday. He musta been bleeding inside." He sighed.

Marty asked in disgust, "Why should I help you? You got your friends killed."

"You're the only one who can help me," pleaded Navalle. "The gunmen are looking for me. They'll kill me if they find me. You were looking for me. The cops'll be looking for me soon. There's no place I can go!"

Marty smiled thinly, "The gunmen are certainly looking for you, although I don't think they know who you are... yet. The cops are looking for you and they'll have your name soon. But me? I was hired by a couple of widows to find out what happened to their husbands." He shrugged, "Now I know, I don't care about you now."

Navalle looked surprised, "That's it? You're not going to help me?"

"I've seen what happens to friends that help you. If you want my advice: turn yourself in. The cops will protect you and you never know, you might get off lightly. But I doubt it."

"I can't go to jail!"

Marty shrugged, "That's my advice. If you don't like it, tough!"

Navalle looked shocked. Marty continued, "If you don't want to take your chances with the cops then I'd run if I were you. Get on a bus or train and run far and fast. Maybe you can stay ahead of everybody." He turned away.

Navalle reached a hand out toward him, "That's it? You're going to just walk away?"

The detective just shrugged, "I told you, I just work for a couple of widows."

"What are you going to tell the cops about me?" There was a frightened edge to his voice.

Marty looked thoughtfully back at him, "I'm not going to turn you in yet. First I'm going to speak to the widows. Then..." He shrugged, "I got plans. Maybe this whole thing will be over in a day or two if things go right. You better run or at least lie low for a while." He walked away leaving Navalle chewing his lip and looking uncertain.

●●●

"So what happened to Everly?"

At nine that night Marty was driving his car out a dark Long Island road. He had been busy that evening. He had eaten a quick dinner while he made his plans. He then had gathered up what he needed and made a couple of calls that he wished he hadn't had to. Neither Mrs. Richards nor Mrs. Everly had totally understood. They couldn't understand why their husbands had had to die. Eventually Marty hoped they would see that their husbands had done what they did for their families. That's the way it often was. People got caught in situations they couldn't handle and made bad decisions. At least the two widows knew their husbands hadn't robbed all those banks and killed those innocent people.

Lastly he made some other calls. It took a while to get a hold of the right people and longer to get a commitment but he finally got the important people on board.

Soon he reached the little town near the farm house. There was one diner still open. The rest of the town had gone to bed with the sun Marty surmised. He parked his car outside the diner and went in. He was the only patron. He slid into a booth and looked around noting the pay phone in the back on the wall. He ordered a cup of coffee and waited.

As Marty sipped his coffee he went over the plan. He would be at the farmhouse early to be ahead of Russell. He would put the money back in the house and slip out before the gunmen arrived. Before he left the diner he would call the cops. Hopefully they would arrive shortly after the gunmen did. Marty would be hiding nearby. There were several good spots near the house. He was prepared to keep the gunmen pinned down in the farmhouse if he had to. Hopefully the cops would be on time.

Time passed. At ten o'clock he went to the pay phone and put in some change. It took a couple of minutes but he finally got Donovan at home. The sergeant was plenty hot at being disturbed but listened as Marty spoke, "Listen Don, this is the real thing. What I've been working on is these bank robberies. Those two locals Everly and Richards didn't pull those robberies. They didn't have the moxie but I know who did."

"Yeah? Who?"

"Those two mugs I had you check on and their friend; George Russell. They're holed up out on Long Island. If you can get here soon you can get them all and recover the bank money."

"What? Where are you?"

"I'll tell you in a minute. Listen there are two of the hold-up gang left. They'll be armed so you better bring plenty of help. I've made arrangements with the insurance companies. You guys will get the credit for the arrest but I get the reward for the recovered money. Got it?"

"Wait! Two? Where are the others? What's going on Marty?"

"The other two are there but they won't be bothering anyone. You've got to trust me on this Don."

Donovan grumbled a bit but agreed, "So where are you?" Marty gave him directions. Then said, "The last two hoods will be there at eleven tonight. I'll be hiding near-by. Remember eleven o'clock." Donovan agreed and hung up. Marty looked at his watch; It was just after ten. He wanted to be early. He dropped some change on the table and made for his car.

It didn't take long to reach the farm house. It was dark and lonely just as the night before. He parked up the road as before and made his way back to the farmhouse. Everything appeared just as it had been. In the garage Marty found the money was undisturbed. He breathed a sigh of relief as he uncovered the bags. He had been worried that Russell might have returned here and found it this evening. He picked up several of the bags and hauled them to the house. He dumped the bags in the first bedroom and returned for the rest.

He glanced at his watch; he had only been here ten minutes. Good. He entered the second bedroom and flashed his light around. It steadied on the corner where the weapons had been leaning last night. He froze as he saw that the Tommy gun was missing. Marty slipped his hand under his jacket and came up with his automatic. He flicked off the light and stood in the darkness listening. He listened but all he heard were the sounds of crickets out in the yard.

His mind raced in the darkness. Russell had come back sometime today. He hadn't found the money and probably had taken the Tommy gun then. He had already heard that Marty was looking for him around town and assumed that Marty had taken the money after their encounter the night before. He had asked around, found out where Marty lived and called tonight to make a deal. Chances were this meeting was a trap. But for whom? Marty was setting them up but they might just be setting him up as well. In the dark he stepped into the hall and made his way quietly toward the front room.

As he reached the doorway leading to the kitchen a dark figure stepped into the house from the back porch. Behind him loomed the figure of another man. It was very dark in the house and Marty could only see their silhouettes against the open back door. He could see the gleam of moonlight on their weapons. He stiffened as he saw the long gun in the second man's arms.

There was no time for talk. Marty raised his gun and fired. The lead man saw Marty simultaneously and also fired. Their bullets crossed in the darkened kitchen. Marty fired twice more as he felt the sting of his opponent's bullet along his ribs. He staggered but kept firing. The first man was collapsing back, his gun firing into the floor at Marty's feet. The second man was bringing up his weapon as he stepped through the door.

Marty shifted his aim but the second man was already squeezing his trigger. The flash of the Tommy gun lit up the kitchen. Marty continued firing as he threw himself back out of the door way into the front room. A stream of bullets tore through walls spraying splinters and dust everywhere. One bullet clipped through Marty's right arm as the slide on his pistol locked back on empty. He dropped his gun as he hit the floor and rolled toward cover. He came up next to the sagging sofa into a ringing silence. He was deafened from all the fire but couldn't hear or see anything moving.

He waited there for a full minute but nothing moved. Grasping his wounded arm in his left hand he climbed wearily to his feet. He trudged toward the kitchen doorway and looked carefully into the dark kitchen. There was just enough light to see two additional men sprawled grotesquely on the floor. Marty walked forward. His hearing was returning a little because he heard a rasping cough from one of them. He knelt down next to the man. Marty couldn't be sure in the dark but he might have tried to raise his head a little. It was too dark to see his lips move so if he tried to say anything Marty couldn't tell. The man shuddered and was dead.

It took a minute but Marty finally located his dropped flashlight. He got it going and looked over the scene. Two hard cases that he didn't recognize lay in the kitchen. He picked up one man's thirty eight and shook his head. They had showed up early to ambush him. It was just luck that he had gotten there earlier. Carrying the revolver, he staggered into the front room and collapsed on the sofa. He wiggled out of his coat, cursing as he pulled on his wounded arm. He got a grip on his right shirt sleeve at the shoulder and tore the sleeve off his arm, thinking "Great another suit shot!"

In the light from his flash he could see he had been hit in the bicep. It had gone in and out cleanly and although bleeding Marty didn't think it had hit bone. Not that it didn't hurt like the devil, he thought, as he wrapped the torn white shirt sleeve around the wound and pulled it tight. He had to use his teeth to help knot it tightly but it slowed the bleeding. Once this was done he flashed the light at his left side. His shirt was red but a gentle probing convinced him that this wound was less serious. It looked like the bullet had just grazed along the ribs leaving a bloody groove carved along the skin.

He stuffed his handkerchief inside his shirt against the wound. As he was re-buttoning his shirt he heard the creak of a floor board. Before he could reach for the gun he had picked up off the floor he was blinded by a flashlight from the kitchen. For a fleeting moment he thought it was the cops but then a familiar voice spoke, "Well, it looks like you did me a favor."

Marty held up his wounded arm trying to shield his eyes from the blinding light, "If you mean that now you don't have to worry about the stick up men, I guess you're right."

"Two of them and only me left. Yeah, I was worried. But I had to gamble that I'd find the money before they found out who I was. I thought you might have it stashed somewhere but I didn't expect it to be here. Didn't figure they'd be here either. Did they follow you too?" He laughed shortly, "Some detective you are."

As Navalle spoke Marty was furious with himself for buying his line about being scared. Navalle had just been getting close to him looking for the money. He had been so worried about Russell and his partner that he hadn't been watching closely for a tail. He had to stall for time. The cops should be here any time.

"So I ended up doing your dirty work just like your friends. You talked them into going along with you. I'll bet you told them it would be easy. They believed you. Instead you three got in over your heads. But it was your friends that paid the price while you walked away clean. Unfortunately you didn't get the money." He paused and smiled thinly, "Well you still don't have it."

He couldn't see the expression on Navalle's face but Marty could see him stiffen. "It's not my fault that those two got killed. The bullets were flying; anyone could have caught one," he stuttered defensively. A pause, "And the money's here. It's got to be." He sounded less than sure. Marty had to feed that. He ignored the pain in his arm and shrugged casually, "Go ahead, look around. You won't find it."

Navalle and the flashlight took a step into the room. Then he stopped, "You can't pull that on me. I'm not giving you a chance to try something." Marty held up his wounded arm, "With what? I'm not even sure what happened to my gun." As he said this his left hand found Russell's gun lying on the sofa in the shadows. He kept a pained look on his face while he watched Navalle.

In a more certain voice Navalle spoke, "If the money's not here why did you bring them out here? To shoot it out? In fact why did you come out here at all?"

Marty smiled up at the man behind the flashlight, "For the reward. I called the cops and told them I'd be meeting the bank robbers. Unfortunately, they showed up early. The cops should be pulling up any minute.

At this Navalle's flashlight wavered, "You're lying!"

Marty shook his head, "No. They should be here soon. I gave you a chance to run but I guess it's too late." He paused and cocked his head to one side listening, "Is that them?"

Navalle stiffened and turned his head. Marty grabbed for the revolver. Navalle spun back and raised his gun. Marty didn't waste time lifting his. He fired upward from the sofa. The first bullet tore through the upholstered arm and went who knew where. The next bullet went straight into Navalle's chest. Then the gun clicked on an empty chamber.

The would-be thief staggered back, his gun firing once over Marty's head. He then collapsed slowly to the floor. Marty pushed himself painfully to his feet and bent over the still breathing Navalle. His face was garishly illuminated by the flashlight lying next to him. As Marty bent forward, the wounded man gasped out, "You never gave me a chance."

Marty shook his head slightly, "You were out-matched from the beginning kid. I gave you your chance earlier tonight. You should have taken it." He walked tiredly to the bedroom. He found a towel there and returned to the front room where he pressed it to the wounded man's chest. It didn't do any good; Navalle died a few minutes later.

Marty sat back and sighed. He looked at his watch in the light from his flash: nearly eleven o'clock. He found the empty revolver that he had used, wiped it down and placed it back in the stick up man's outstretched hand. He then went out the back door and searched around the dead rose bush until he found the three empty cartridge cases he had fired the night before. He walked into the field and tossed them as far as he could into the woods. Returning to the house he lit the lantern in the kitchen and another in the front room. There was no need for secrecy now. He righted a chair in the front room, sat down and waited.

He was sitting there minutes later when several squad cars pulled into the yard. Uniformed officers spread out all around the house. Detective Donovan led several through the back door. He took a look around the kitchen and whistled, "Jesus!" Marty called, "In here, Donovan."

Donovan stepped over bodies in to the front room and looked around, "What a shambles, Marty! What the hell went on here?"

Marty shook his head wearily and pointed at Navalle, "That's Buddy Navalle." He waved his hand, "The rest are Russell and the gang that have been robbing all the banks lately. Navalle, Richards and Everly tried to take on these guys."

Donovan rubbed his chin, looked around and stared hard at Marty, "And I suppose you were just standing here? What happened to us arresting them?"

Marty sighed, "It wasn't supposed to happen this way. I was tracking Richard and Everly for their wives. Navalle must have heard I was asking around and braced me. He told me he had talked his friends into helping him catch the crooks for the reward. They came out here and shot it out with them and I guess everybody lost. That's when he told me about this place. I found the money and a couple of stiffs this evening. I called you figuring they would come back and we could pinch 'em all. While I was waiting Navalle showed up with a gun."

Donovan thought about this for a moment, "They were after the reward? Sure they were. What happened then?"

"The other two gunmen showed up about then. They started shooting. I managed to get both of them but they got a piece of me too." He held up his bandaged arm. Donovan shook his head doubtfully, "Come on outside. We got ambulances on the way. They can patch you up." As Marty stood up Donovan pointed at Navalle, "And him?"

Marty pointed down at the revolver in the dead gunman's hand, "Check that gun. You should find it matches the bullets in Navalle's body." He stepped through the kitchen and out into the yard. Donovan came up beside him making some notes in a notebook. He flipped it closed, "A hell of a mess, Marty." Marty just smiled weakly. Donovan pulled out a cigarette and lit up, "Ya know Marty, one of these days your 'Honest Judge, I was just standing there' story isn't going to hold up. I hope I'm not around when it happens."

"Yeah." He shook his head, "None of it should have happened like this. Those three should have just called the cops. Instead they got in way over their heads."

They watched as an ambulance, red light flashing, pulled into the yard. "One last thing Marty, what about those two hard cases you asked me about earlier?"

"I would imagine that they're inside there." He jerked his thumb over his shoulder, "I turned up their names while I was asking around the last two days." Donovan nodded and led him toward the ambulance.

Later Marty was helped into the back of a squad car as the bodies were being loaded into ambulances. Cradling his bandaged arm, Marty leaned back against the cushions as the cruiser pulled onto the road. Donovan leaned over the front seat and spoke, "You good enough to give a statement for the record when we get back to town?"

Marty thought about how there was no one left to tell any stories but him. He nodded, "Sure Don but maybe after I get some rest. I'm kind of tired now." He closed his eyes as the cruiser headed back to the city.

●●●

The next morning bright and early Marty was at the station to going over his statement from the night before. He had told it fairly straight; leaving out only a few minor details such as shooting at Russell the first night and hiding the money. But other than that it was mostly the truth. More than a few of the cops were a little suspicious of Marty but they couldn't kick too much. The newspapers were playing up the death of the gang and praising the police for their diligence. The cops were also suspicious of the three friends. Nobody really believed that they were trying for the reward but Marty stuck to that story. He did it mostly for the widows. They needed something good to believe about their husbands.

The next couple of days passed quickly as Marty wrapped up the last loose ends. Most of the money had been recovered and the banks and insurance companies seemed pleased as well. The cops got the credit and Marty's name never came up in the newspapers at all. The really important meeting took place three days later in an insurance company office. A well-dressed and happy vice president had handed him a check. Marty glanced at it and nodded. The man looked puzzled as he held up two other checks, "Are you sure this is how you want it Mr. Quade?"

Marty nodded, "Absolutely. Half is plenty for me. The rest gets split between Mrs. Richards and Mrs. Everly."

The man waved the additional checks, "Fine we'll mail them out today."

Marty held out his hand, "Not necessary. I'll see that they get them. I'm going out to have a talk with them today, anyway." He took the proffered checks from the insurance executive and slipped them into his jacket pocket. He nodded to the man and left his office. As he waited for the elevator in the hall he wondered what he was going to tell the widows.

The doors opened and he stepped in. The truth was ugly but that might be best. On the other hand, he thought wryly, maybe it wouldn't hurt to help the truth along a little bit. The doors closed.

THE END

Twice as Good?

It's not often that I write a story twice. Now I'm not talking about revisions. There are writers out there who are good enough to write something once and be done with it: check the spelling and send it out. I'm afraid I'm not that good…yet. So I am used to revising a story once it's written, sometimes I have to rewrite whole paragraphs, but rewriting a whole story from scratch? No, I've never done that…until now.

It happened this way; Ron Fortier put out a call for stories for a new mystery anthology about a little known gum shoe detective named Marty Quade. I was between stories at the time so I looked over the character bible; a tough, wise-cracking New York detective? Yeah, I could work with that. So I put in a bid.

I grew up on Raymond Chandler's Philip Marlowe and John D. MacDonald's Travis McGee so I've always wanted to write a hard-boiled detective story. What writer hasn't? A twisting plot, numerous clues, mysterious blondes, despicable bad guys all set to the background of the mean streets of the city. Who could resist writing a story like that? I had even gone so far as to write up a rough outline for a hard bitten detective story set in L.A. (long time home of hard boiled detectives), although set in a more modern time. I dug it out and decided that a simplified and cut down version of the story would work. It wouldn't have all the complexity and atmosphere of the original novel I had planned but the plot was good; one that Marty Quade could sink his teeth into.

So away I went. The outline took a while. The story had been intended for a full novel so a lot of plot had to be revised, characters streamlined and so forth. Eventually though I had a pretty good outline to work from. I then took the time to hunt up some of the original *Marty Quade* stories to read and absorb. I also took some strong hints from Ron about the elements he wanted to see in the anthology.

The writing itself wasn't bad. I took it slow and came up with a story that I was pretty happy with. When finished, I shoved it in a drawer for a couple of weeks (standard practice, if I have the time) to distance myself from it before I started my revisions (see, I told you). There were surprisingly few. The usual assortment of clumsy sentences (Who wrote this stuff?) to clean up and a few minor plot changes were all it needed. Less than some stories I've written.

So I finished my final run through and found it good. I wrote up my writer's notes and began to think of my next project. Then disaster struck. I woke up the next morning, called up the files to send them off to Captain Ron and they weren't there.

In fact none of the files on that drive were there. Everything was gone. Story outlines, incomplete stories, everything. I don't have the words to tell you my thoughts at that moment...actually I do, I'm a writer; words are my thing. Unfortunately, all the words to describe my reactions at that moment are unprintable. When I had exhausted all my meager computer skills attempting to recover the files I hauled the drive down to my local big box store where their experts looked it over, shook their heads and sent it off to some real experts.

The long and short of it was that the drive had failed completely and all the data was unrecoverable. So I lost my original, complete *Marty Quade* story. Not to mention a whole bunch of story ideas, several complete ready to go outlines for stories and 14,000 words from my soon to be (not any more) *Purple Scar* novel. Altogether I lost nearly 50,000 words of writing.

Certainly this was a disaster of the first magnitude. It has been six months and I have yet to regenerate all the work I lost. One of the top priorities was *Over their Head*, the story in this volume. It was also one of the most difficult to re-write. You'd think that something I had just written would be easy to write again. Not so. For whatever reason, the writing went slowly. Perhaps the shadow of the original story was hanging over me. I'm not sure. Anyway it was tough but I finally got through it. I believe the new story is good; however it is different than the first one I wrote. And that's the big lesson I took away from this little disaster. I had to forget about the first story and start from scratch mentally. Trying to recreate something identically just didn't work out, for me at least.

I imagine most writers have had something like this happen to them somewhere in their career. For all you prospective writers out there; losing data is another of the occupational hazards of writing. So the moral of this story is: back up all your writing...in multiple places! I now back up all my writing in three separate places. Lesson learned.

Anyway that's how I came to write *Over their Head* twice. I'd like to say it was a lot of fun but it turned out to be a lot more work than originally planned. I'd also like to think it's twice as good because twice the work has been put into it but that would be wishful thinking. Still, I think it's a pretty good story and I hope you like it and Airship 27's first *Marty Quade* anthology. See you next time.

●●●

GENE MOYERS - studied European and Medieval history at the University of Oregon. He is a former U.S. Army armor crewman. He worked in the High Tech industry for some time and ran a store front and internet hobby shop for several years.

An avid military gamer and role player, his favorite game was *Daredevils* set in the 1930s. His love affair with the 1930s and pulps in particular stem from his first time reading a *Shadow* novel as a boy. Although interested in writing since a teen he did not turn to serious writing until 2000. He is the co-author of *GURPS Crusades* published by Steve Jackson Games. He has written a story published in *Ravenwood volume II* by Airship 27. He has also written stories that will appear in the future volumes of *Moon Man, The Purple Scar, Domino Lady and The Phantom Detective* all for Airship 27.

When not working on Airship 27 projects he is busy writing horror adventures for his swashbuckling character set in Colonial America. Gene currently lives in Beaverton Oregon with his wife and three lazy dogs.

Dead Man's Hand

By
Michael A. Black

A smoky haze hung over the table in the hotel room, but Marty Quade's face showed no emotion as he picked up the two new cards he'd been dealt. Consolidating them in his hand, he slowly spread the five of them: eight of hearts, ace of clubs, ace of diamonds, eight of clubs, ace of spades. Aces and eights... Dead man's hand. Quade resisted the urge to grin as he picked up two twenties and a ten and tossed them onto the middle of the table.

"I'm in," he said.

Karl Conroy, who was hosting the game, glanced at his cards, betraying nothing, and tossed in the same number of bills. "Me, too." His thin face twitched as he dropped the money onto the pot. Conroy was one of the few businessmen who had managed to remain afloat during the crash and Great Depression. With the dawning of the new decade almost upon them, his business leanings, a collection of commercial bakeries, seemed to be holding their own in the fragile economy.

"Gentlemen," Harold Dixon said, placing his cards face-down on the table top, grinned and picked up a stack of currency. "I'm so confident I've got you all beat," he said, making a show of peeling off ten twenties, "that I'll raise you two hundred." Dixon was a big, heavyset man in his mid-fifties. His hair was mostly gone on top, and gray on the sides, but he'd compensated by growing a thick set of mutton-chop sideburns and goatee. Quade knew he was a banker and pretty well off, but then again, in these days of house foreclosures, Quade figured Dixon was used to playing fast and loose with cash; mostly other people's money. He sat back with a cocky grin on his face and flicked his diamond studded dollar-sign stickpin on his lapel.

Wallace Myers, a prominent lawyer, scrutinized his cards before folding them and shaking his head. "Too rich for my blood." Myers had a classically handsome face with high, chiseled cheekbones and a thick crop of dark hair. Despite his complexion, he was rumored to be the mayor's fair-haired boy, and on the slate to run for public office in the next, rigged election. He was the only one of the group whom Quade knew, but they had little more than a casual acquaintance. Myers had recently dropped by Quade's home base at the Hotel Baltic and invited him to the poker game tonight. Quade had been riding a lucky streak and wanted to see how far he could extend it. He accepted Myers's invitation.

Thomas Dunn, the last member of the party, had a craggy face, the left side of which was frozen and scarred with the dark, thick pigments of numerous skin grafts. His left eye was glass and a bit over-sized, although no one mentioned it. This disfigurement was the result of Dixon having been on the receiving end of some German shrapnel during the Great War. Despite being from a very wealthy family, Dunn had enlisted in the infantry due to a time-honored family tradition. He now lived most of the time on a massive, Long Island estate that he had named Argonne, after the battle in which he'd been injured. Dunn assessed his cards briefly, then picked up some bills and tossed them onto the ever-increasing pot. He looked at Quade.

"Well, are you still in, or what?"

Quade took a deep breath and did a quick assessment. He was pretty sure nobody else at the table could beat his hand, but then again, old Bill Hickok had thought the same thing. He looked down at his reserves. Putting another two hundred on the center stack would just about drain him, but something in his gut told him that the others were bluffing. Dixon was a braggart and full of bluster most of the time. The twitch in Conroy's face had been a "tell" that Quade had picked up earlier. He was in for the penny, but Quade doubted Conroy had the cards to make it a pound. And Dunn was born into money, so he really had nothing to lose, even if his cards were mediocre. This was just pocket change for him.

Quade picked up the bills from his stack and tossed them in.

All eyes fell on Conroy, whose nose twitched again. He took a deep breath.

Linda Conroy, Karl's knockout wife stepping over to the table and put her left hand on her husband's shoulder. Her right held a bottle of Scotch. "Anybody want a refill?"

"Honey," Conroy said, "not now."

"Oh, hell, Karl," Dixon's voice boomed. "This next hand is about to clean some of us out. Why not celebrate with a drink?"

"Sounds good to me." Quade grinned and held up his glass. As Linda Conroy moved around the table, Quade placed his cards face-down.

"Well, Karl," Dixon said. "You in or not?"

Conroy compressed his lips, saying nothing.

His wife gently clicked the top of the bottle against Quade's glass as she poured the amber liquid into it. He stopped her after two fingers.

"That's good. Thanks."

She smiled down at him. It was an alluring smile. She was a good looking woman with blond hair and a full figure. She reminded Quade of a mature version of that young actress, Lana Turner, he'd seen recently. "The Sweater Girl," they called her. Both of them were lookers. As she withdrew the bottle the back of her hand brushed against his. His eyes shot upward in time to see her smile widen, accompanied by a quick wink.

Quade was used to reading signals from the opposite sex, and he was no stranger to the ladies either. What he was not accustomed to, however, was a woman flirting with him while her husband sat only a few feet away. Taking a deep breath, Quade lowered his gray eyes and stared at Karl Conroy, who had yet to indicate if he was in or out. Conroy glared at his wife, who turned and left the room.

Quade brought the glass to his mouth and took a sip. He had the feeling Dixon was right. This was most likely the last hand for him, especially if he walked away with the substantial pot.

With a sudden burst of energy, Conroy set his cards aside and counted out several twenties from his now meager cash reserves. His hand shook as he dropped the bills onto the stack and said, "Call."

Dixon's head lolled back in laughter.

"Just what I like," he said, his voice sounding like he was talking through a megaphone. "A man who hosts a good game and has the backbone to see it through. Right, Tom?"

Dunn's stoic face betrayed nothing as he said, "Oh, hell, show us your damn, fabulous hand, Harold."

Dixon grinned and licked his lips. "Read 'em and weep, gents." He spread his cards out displaying the seven of clubs, the eight of diamonds, nine of clubs, ten of clubs, and the jack of diamonds. Dunn dropped his cards to the table in disgust, as did Conroy.

Dixon laughed and began reaching for the pot.

"Hold on," Quade said, putting his hand over Dixon's and halting the other man's progress.

Dixon's smile faded and he was just about to mutter something when they all heard Linda Conroy's scream. Quade turned, starting to reach for the .32 caliber Beretta in his shoulder holster, when three men in dark jackets, hats, and with bandanas over their faces came bustling into the room. Each was holding a big .45 semi-auto. The thin man in the center also held Linda Conroy by the hair.

"Everybody just keep your hands flat on the table, palms up," the guy in the center said. His body was long and lanky, and he was a lot shorter than the other two, who were very good-sized. But the man in the center moved with a cat-like grace, and something told Quade that he was not only the leader of this trio, but the most dangerous as well. He stepped forward with the woman, and shoved his pistol an inch from Quade's face. "Especially you, tough guy."

Quade looked at the gaping darkness of the barrel a few inches in front of him. He could see the hammers on the other two men's weapons were cocked back, and assumed the third man's was, too. Quade gave a curt nod and sat motionless.

One of the other men produced a burlap sack from his pocket and tossed it onto the table top.

"Okay, gorgeous," the center man said. "Start filling it up."

Linda Conroy grimaced in pain as the man pushed her face into the pile of greenbacks.

"Hey, don't hurt her," Conroy said.

The center man released Mrs. Conroy and stepped around in back of her husband. His left hand shot out, the palm smacking Conroy in the nose. Blood bubbled from the seated man's nostrils.

"Pretty bold move for a guy holding a gat," Quade said, letting the sarcasm edge into his tone. "Pushing around a woman and punching a defenseless man."

The thin man stared directly at Quade now, and the detective made a mental note of the man's eyes, which were the only thing visible between the low-slung fedora and the upper edge of the folded bandana. The eyes were dark brown, almost black, and Quade noticed the lashes were very full, almost like a dame's. He was sure he'd recognize them again, with or without the bandana, and he intended to remember them.

"What you looking at?" The thin man came around and clipped Quade across the right temple and cheek with the .45. The detective felt the sting of the blow, and seconds later the wet flow of warm blood down his face.

Before Quade could say or do anything else, he felt the barrel of the pistol being pressed against his right temple.

"Lean forward, buster," the man said. "All the way with your arms over your head."

Quade complied and felt the man's probing left hand doing a pat-down. Seconds later, Quade felt his .32 semi-auto being pulled from his shoulder holster.

"The rest of you do the same," the man said. "Strip off your watches, rings and wallets, too, and toss 'em on the table."

Myers slipped off his college ring, Harvard, Class of Twenty-Seven, and set it on the table.

One of the big thugs grabbed it, and then leaned forward and pulled the gold chain of a pocket watch from Dunn's vest. He muttered a protest: "That watch has been in my family for generations. One of my ancestors carried it throughout the Civil War." The closest gunmen slapped him. Quade noticed the both of the big lugs had light blue eyes and cauliflower ears.

"Shaddup and do what I say," the thin man said, "or I'll give the good side of your face the strawberry treatment."

Dunn's mouth pulled into a tight line, but he said nothing.

"Just take what you want," Harold Dixon said. "But don't hurt any of us."

"Hey, that's the spirit," the thin man said. He nodded to one of the big guys. "I like that stickpin of his."

The big guy plucked the diamond dollar pin from Dixon's lapel.

"Wait, please," Dixon said, flashing a nervous smile. "That pin has great sentimental value to me, but it's not real."

"Oh yeah?" the thin man said. "We'll check it and get back to you."

Dixon pursed his lips and lowered his gaze to the table and they stripped off the rest of their valuables and wallets, which Linda Conroy then placed on top of the money in the burlap sack. She stood straight in defiance and handed it to one of the gunmen.

"Your rings, too, doll," the thin man said.

Linda Conroy's neck tightened. "My rings?"

The thin man came around the table, slipped Quade's .32 into his coat pocket, and grabbed her left hand pulling the rings from her finger.

"They'll look good on you," Quade said.

"Please," Karl Conroy said, his voice pleading. "Don't take her rings. They belonged to my mother."

"Just be glad that's all I'm taking," the thin man said, and brought his hand up to Linda Conroy's full breasts and squeezed.

"Hey," Conroy shouted. "That's my wife."

"She'll be your widow I hear one more peep outta any of you." The gunman's voice was a vicious snarl. "Now, we're leaving, and if any of you pops his head out the door, we'll shoot it off." He motioned to one of his big compatriots, who grabbed the telephone and ripped the connection from the wall. Quade caught a quick glimpse of a thick scar along the man's right wrist. All three gunmen backed out of the room, keeping Linda Conroy with them until they reached the door. The thin man groped her again, and shoved her to the floor.

"Next time, doll," he said, and they slipped out the door.

Quade immediately rose to his feet and rushed to the fallen woman.

"You all right?" he asked as he helped her to her feet.

Her face looked pale and drawn, but she nodded.

"Oh, my God," she said. "You're bleeding."

Quade wiped at his cheek and his hand came away red. He moved the door and opened it a crack.

"Marty, no," Conroy yelled. "They'll shoot you."

Quade ignored him and pulled the door open a crack.

The hallway was empty. He slipped out and moved cautiously toward the three elevators, their gold-colored doors were all closed. This was the twelfth floor and Quade didn't figure the masked trio would be taking the stairs. He pressed the elevator button and waited, wondering why none of the elevator operators had thought it strange that three darkly clad men had ridden up to the twelfth floor, and were now riding down again. But they probably hadn't been wearing their bandanas on the way up or the way down. It was possible that an alert elevator operator might recall their faces. But how had they just departed from this floor so quickly? Quade had reached the door in a few seconds, and the hallway had been empty.

Then it dawned on him: the freight elevator. It was located in the rear of the building, and rarely occupied. The trio most likely ascended in that one, left the doors open, assuring it would remain on this floor, and descended in it afterward.

The elevator doors finally opened and Quade stepped inside. The operator's jaw dropped when he saw Quade's face.

"What happened, mister?" the kid asked. "You're bleeding."

"One of those new safety razors," Quade said. "Now take me to the lobby and don't stop at any other floor."

The operator closed the doors and rotated the handle to descend as fast as he could. When they got to the bottom he slowed it to a stop and reached up for the lever to open the doors.

"Does it hurt?" the kid asked as he opened the doors.

"Only when I laugh," Quade said.

He ran to the front doors. The hotel lobby was pretty much deserted. Outside, the doorman was helping a lady out of a limo. Quade moved close and tapped the guy on his shoulder.

"Hey, Mac," Quade said. "You see three tough looking mugs come in or outta here in the last ten minutes?"

The doorman ignored him and walked to the doors with the lady. Quade stepped behind him and grabbed his arm.

"I asked you a question, bud," Quade said, tightening his grip. "Two big guys and a shorter, thinner one. All dressed in black and carrying a burlap sack."

The doorman recoiled, then turned to Quade with a pained expression. "Carrying what?"

"Never mind," Quade said, and ran back inside. He went to the front desk and slammed his palm down on the service bell. The clerk came hustling up.

"Yes, sir, what can I do for you?" The man's eyebrows rose when he saw Quade's bloody face.

"You got a hotel dick working tonight?" Quade asked.

"Yes, sir."

"Well, call him for me. I need to talk to him."

The clerk's gaze lowered to the counter and Quade looked down. Several drops of blood were dotting the counter top. Quade took out his handkerchief and held it to the wound.

"Want me to call the cops, too?" the clerk asked.

"Just the hotel dick for now," Quade said. "I'll let you know on the other."

●●●

Quade watched as Linda Conroy sat crying in one of the chairs by the poker table. Her husband stood by her side, his hand on her shoulder.

"The freight elevator?" Dixon said, frowning. "Are you sure that's how they got away?"

Quade nodded. The hotel dick had taken him through the back rooms of the hotel, through the kitchen and storage areas to the area adjacent to the loading dock. When they arrived the freight elevator sat unoccupied, its big horizontal doors standing open. The rear exit door to the loading dock was ajar. Quade went over and pushed through it, taking note of the locking mechanism and the door jamb. Both were intact and in working order. The rear alleyway was as empty as the elevator. The robbers had been very familiar with the layout. This operation had taken some shrewd planning, not to mention the timing.

Having jettisoned the hotel detective on the way back up to the 12th floor, Quade reviewed the robbery and the events leading up to it in his mind. Karl Conroy had hosted the game, but Quade had actually been invited by Wallace Myers. Quade knew the lawyer slightly, having done a bit of investigative work for him on a case about six months ago. They'd run into each other at the Hotel Baltic, and Myers remembered that Quade had a reputation as a good poker player. The rest, as they say, was history. Except Quade didn't particularly like the way this game had turned out.

"Why the hell didn't you shoot them, Quade?" Harold Dixon asked. "You had a gun, didn't you?"

"Didn't seem like a good idea at the time," Quade said.

"Oh, leave him alone," Karl Conroy said. "They had the drop on all of us."

"Well," Dunn said, "are we calling the police, or what?"

"Don't be a fool," Wallace Myers said. "Call them and say we were involved in illegal gambling." He put a cigarette between his lips and flicked the wheel on his lighter. "I can see the headlines now. *Mayor's Nominee for City Treasurer Robbed at Illegal Gambling Den.*"

"That's a pretty long headline," Quade said.

"But a valid one," Harold Dixon said. "I'm in the same boat, being vice president of the bank. I can't afford to have this getting out."

"But what about our money?" Conroy said. "We're all out a substantial amount. That may not bother the rest of you, but I'm a businessman. I can't afford to ignore a loss like that."

"Maybe you should have thought about that beforehand," Dunn said.

Quade looked at each of them. He remembered the old saying about poker games: if you look around the table and can't figure out who the sucker is, it's you.

"I think we're overlooking an obvious solution here," Myers said. He blew out a cloud of smoke and pointed to Quade. "We've got one of the best private dicks in New York standing here. Let's all pitch in and hire Marty to get our money back."

Quade shifted his gaze over the four faces, gauging their reactions.

"Excellent idea," Dunn said. "How about it, Quade?"

Quade said nothing. Instead his gray eyes kept scanning the faces of the others.

"Find them, Quade," Dixon said. "Find them and get us our money back."

"You think you can do it?" Conroy asked. "Maybe we would be better off contacting the authorities."

"Hogwash." Dixon popped one of his big cigars into his mouth and picked up Myers's lighter. "Like Wallace said..." He held the flame to the tip of the cigar and rotated it as he puffed. "We've got an ace detective here... We'd be foolish not to avail ourselves of his services and expertise."

The four men looked at Quade. He shrugged.

"I accept, but I was intending to look into this anyway," Quade said. "Not only did those rats take my hard-earned pot, but they took my gun, too. It's personal."

"Your pot?" Dixon said. "As I recall, I had the winning hand. A straight."

Quade shook his head and walked over to the table where his five cards still lay face-down. He flipped them over.

"Aces and eights," Myers said with a grin. "Dead man's hand."

"Only if someone shoots you in the back," Quade said.

●●●

Since it was close to midnight when the agreement to hire Quade had been reached, and Quade's pronouncement that nothing further could be done that night, the group agreed to leave and confer again the next day. The Conroys, who had rented the room for the game, decided not to stay in it either. Quade felt a bit naked without his trusty .32 in his now empty shoulder rig, and that became his number one priority early the next morning when he walked into Police Headquarters and asked for Lieutenant James J. Brannigan.

"First things first," he said to himself.

The desk sergeant lifted an eyebrow and asked, "You got an appointment?"

Quade shook his head and said, "Tell him it's his old buddy, Marty Quade."

The sergeant smirked and picked up the phone. After a brief conversation he set the phone back in its cradle and pointed to the stairs on the left. Quade strode up the flight to the familiar room. He'd helped Brannigan out a year or so ago by locating one of Brannigan's indiscretions who was in possession of a very special broach that Brannigan's wife thought was in her jewelry box. It took Quade a week of hitting the bars and wining and dining the lady in question until he conveniently made his way up to her place. Quade delivered the broach back to Brannigan the next morning in exchange for a marker to be cashed in at a later date.

Quade figured that the date had arrived.

The big Irishman had a thick mat of bright red hair and an unkempt mustache. He sat behind his desk, his uniform blouse draped nearby on a coat rack. Brannigan's shirt sleeves were rolled up exposing massive forearms covered with reddish hair. He leaned forward over a desk awash in paperwork and extended a big hand toward Quade.

"Well, laddie what brings you here this fine morning?" Brannigan asked. His eyes narrowed and he pointed to Quade's temple with his left index finger. "I hope the other fella looks worse."

Quade shook his head. "Not yet."

Brannigan motioned for Quade to sit in the chair opposite the desk. He did so and took out his silver cigarette case, offering one to the lieutenant.

Brannigan popped two smokes from the case and nodded a thanks. Quade offered his lighter, but Brannigan shook his head. He opened his desk drawer, dropped one of the cigarettes into it, removed a wooden kitchen match, and flicked it with his thumbnail. The match ignited and Brannigan held it to the end of the cigarette.

Quade lighted his and then sat back as Brannigan shook out the burning match and dropped it into an ashtray. He drew in a prodigious amount of smoke and expelled it with a sly grin.

"It looks like I'm gonna be able to finally get rid of that marker that's been hanging over me head like the sword of Damocles, eh?"

Quade blew out a plume of smoke. "I'm looking for a couple of guys. One of them's got dark brown eyes with a set of lashes Carole Lombard would envy. The other two are about the size of Max Baer and his brother, Buddy. One of them's got a mean looking scar on his right wrist, and they both got cauliflower ears."

Brannigan smirked, put the cigarette to his mouth again. "Sounds like a likely combination. What'd they do?"

"They took my gun."

Brannigan's brow creased. "That little Italian thirty-two automatic of yours? Where did this happen?"

Quade shook his head. "Not important. I'm getting ready to deal with them. But I need a favor."

Brannigan blew twin plumes of smoke out his nostrils. "Listen, if you think I'm gonna be looking the other way while you conduct some kind of vendetta ...."

Quade laughed. "A vendetta? Do I look Italian to you?"

Brannigan leaned back in his chair and took another long drag. "No, you look like a mick who's holding a grudge. You got any Scot in you, by any chance?"

"How about if I promise you not to do anything untoward?"

"Untoward?" Brannigan laughed. "To paraphrase Race Williams, you ain't gonna shoot nobody what don't deserve it?"

"You been reading too many pulps," Quade said. "What I need is another roscoe."

"And do I look like the local gun store?"

Quade winked as he drew on his smoke. "No, but I do remember that cameo broach that your wife is so fond of..."

Brannigan snorted and stuck the cigarette, which was down to about an inch now, between his lips again. He leaned forward, pulled open the bottom drawer of his desk, and reached down. His big hand came up with a blue steel .38 revolver with a four-inch barrel. He flipped open the cylinder, checked it, and then handed it over the desk to Quade.

"It's high time you had yourself a dependable gun for a change."

Quade accepted the weapon, which he noticed was fully loaded, and snapped the cylinder back into place. "Thanks. I'll get this back to you when I get mine back."

"And I'll be sure to let the rightful owner know that, if and when I ever run into him again." Brannigan took one more puff on the cigarette, then pinched the butt between his fingers and stubbed it out in an ashtray.

Quade smirked, leaned forward. "I don't suppose you'd have any more ammo and a holster to go with this?"

"Big time PI, you can afford to buy your own damn ammunition," Brannigan said. "And as far as a holster, trade in your suspenders for a good, solid belt and keep it in your pants."

"Good advice," Quade said, taking one more drag on his cigarette before stubbing it out in Brannigan's ashtray. "You should try that yourself sometime."

Brannigan laughed. "Get outta here you damn mick, before I throw you out meself."

Quade stood, dropping the big .38 into his coat pocket. It felt good not to be naked anymore.

•••

Quade took a taxi to see Maxie Levin, who owned a pawn shop on 42nd Street. When Quade opened the door the little man looked up from behind the counter, lifting a pair of magnifiers off the frame of his regular glasses.

He was a small man of late middle age, with a thinning crop of gray hair and a hook nose. Quade thought the pawnbroker resembled a human-sized rodent, but he had a reputation as the preeminent pawnbroker in the city.

"Well, well, well," Maxie said. His voice had a squeaky sound to it. "What brings the king of the private eyes to my humble abode?"

"I'm looking for something," Quade said, taking out his silver cigarette case and walked through the aisles, which were full of glass cabinets housing layers of shelves littered with items ranging from costume jewelry to old military medals. One space held a set of full dentures and several partials, which were labeled *Real Gold*. The place had a fusty smell, and dust motes floated in the air as Quade made his way toward the back counter, which was surrounded on three sides by a heavy, wire cage. The door of the cage was on a hinge so that it could be slammed shut at a moment's notice.

"Well, you've come to the right place," Maxie said with a laugh.

Quade put a cigarette between his lips and held out the case, offering it to Maxie.

Maxie's eyes swept over it, then back to Quade's face. "If it's solid sterling, I can give you twenty."

Quade frowned.

"Okay, okay, twenty-five," Maxie said, raising his hands in a conceding gesture. "But that's as high as I can go. Take it or leave it."

"I'll leave it," Quade said. "Besides, I was just offering you a smoke."

Maxine's face twisted into a smile. "Oh, in that case, I don't mind if I do." He plucked one of the cigarettes from the case and reached down behind the counter and took out a gold-plated lighter. It ignited on the first turn of the wheel and Maxie extended the flame. Quade leaned forward, his smoke between his lips, and held the tip in the fire.

"How's tricks?" he asked exhaling a smoky breath.

The little man lit his own cigarette and shrugged. "Could always be better. Times are still hard. With Hitler taking over Europe, it don't look like it's gonna get much better."

Quade nodded. "I need you to put the word out. I'm looking for some merchandise."

Maxie laughed and waved his hand over the glass counter top. "Take your pick."

Quade shook his head, then said, "Specifically, a set of yellow gold wedding and engagement rings, size five, with the initials *LRC* on the

"I'm looking for something."

inside of the band, a Harvard, Class of Twenty-Seven ring with *WDM* inscribed inside, a diamond studded stick pin shaped like a dollar-sign, that may or may not be real, and a vintage gold pocket watch on a chain. Purportedly a genuine Civil War artifact."

Maxie nodded. "Okay. The watch got any specific identifiers?"

"I'll have to check on that and get back to you," Quade said. Actually, the watch had Dunn's family crest engraved on it, but Quade wanted to hold something back for verification purposes. Plus, Dunn had not been keen on news of him being involved in an illegal gambling game to become public knowledge. "It belongs to a very important person, and I'm sure he's more than willing to pay a good finder's fee, but keep that on the QT."

"Got it," Maxie said. The tip of the cigarette glowed red.

"The guys peddling these things might also be in possession of a thirty-two caliber Beretta semi-automatic."

Maxie's eyebrows raised. "Say, ain't that the same kind of roscoe that you carry?"

Quade said nothing.

Maxie shrugged. "What else you need, shamus?"

"I need a line on the three guys trying to peddle the stuff."

Maxie drew on the cigarette again, and blew a stream of smoke out of the side of his mouth.

"These guys sound like real bad news," he said. "But anybody that could give a shiner like that to a tough guy like you would have to be somebody to step aside from."

Quade flashed a sardonic grin and felt the sudden sting in his still-tender cheek. He smirked anyway.

"Hell, Maxie, how do you know I didn't just run into a door?"

●●●

Quade watched as the two big men, one white and one black, circled each other in the ring and made tentative, jabbing moves. Behind them, the staccato beat of a row of speedbags was accompanied by the grunts and expelled breaths of a couple more boxers working the heavy bags. The smell of sweat was pervasive. Danny O'Toole stood on the ring apron watching and shouting instructions. His neck was cradled by a towel and an unlit cigar dangled from his pendulous lips. Quade was standing a few feet behind him, and from his position, had a pretty good view of the combatants through the ring ropes.

"Come on, come on," he yelled. "Jab, jab, right cross, left hook. Show me something."

The white fighter responded with a lackluster combination.

"Now it's your turn, Leroy," O'Toole shouted. "You got something?"

The black fighter nodded.

"Then show me what yah got, dammit!" O'Toole shouted.

The black man shot out a quick jab, then smacked home a solid right. The white fighter staggered back, his nose leaking blood.

"You guys look like a couple of ladies in there," O'Toole yelled. "You show me something, or you're out."

The two men stood in the center of the ring exchanging punches at a furious rate.

A smile twitched O'Toole's mouth.

"That Negro might have some promise," Quade said. "Got a good right."

O'Toole nodded, not taking his eyes off the two fighters.

"He could probably be a contender some day," O'Toole said. "But he ain't no Joe Louis."

The bell rang and both men dropped their gloves and stood in the center of the ring. O'Toole stepped through the ropes and slipped a towel from around his neck. He wiped off their faces, shifting the towel to mop up the blood still cascading from the one man's nose.

"Clancy," O'Toole said. "You got a nose that's made for punching."

The fighter grunted.

"Don't blow it, dammit," O'Toole said. "Your eyes will swell up."

O'Toole told them to do some shadow boxing, and stepped down the stairs. He flipped the towel back over his shoulder, shifted the cigar to the other side of his mouth, and looked up at Quade. "So what brings you over to Brooklyn? Looking to go a couple?"

"Not my style," Quade said.

O'Toole snorted and pointed to Quade's swollen cheek. "Looks like you already went a few rounds with somebody."

"Something like that. I'm looking for a couple guys. Big lugs. Both of them have cauliflower ears, and the bigger of the two has a nasty scar on his right wrist. They hang out with a thinner guy, who's got the moves, and a mean disposition. Sound familiar?"

O'Toole laughed and waved his hand around the gym at the plethora of good-sized men working out. "Take your pick."

"The two big guys are about the size of the Baer brothers."

"Max and Buddy?" O'Toole whistled.

Quade nodded.

O'Toole took the cigar out of his mouth and rolled his tongue over his teeth. After gazing over toward the ring, he looked back at Quade and shook his head.

"Can't think of nobody like that I seen recently," he said.

"These guys might be a bit past it."

O'Toole pondered a few seconds more, then shook his head again. "Nah, I ain't seen nobody like that for a while." He scrunched up his nose and squinted. "You know Roger Fellers?"

"Can't say I do. Why?"

"He's got a gym over in the Bronx. Was tied up with that theater place that closed down."

O'Toole started to put the cigar back in his mouth, and then stopped and looked at it. The end was a masticated, wet misshapen mass. He frowned and tossed it on the floor.

Quade took out his cigarette case and opened it, offering to the other man.

O'Toole shook his head and plucked a fresh cigar out of his pocket. "I don't smoke 'em as much as chew 'em. Don't want the smoke to bother the guys." He unwrapped the cigar as he talked. "Like I was saying Fellers was running a *rasslin'* card outta that old, theater place. I think it was called the Aragon Ballroom, or something."

"Wrestling?" Quade said.

O'Toole grinned. "Yeah, I know it's a joke, but it's got a lot of big guys. Mostly washed up bums what can't cut it in the ring any more. Primo Carnera was doing it for a while, after he got demolished by Baer."

"And the Brown Bomber," Quade said.

O'Toole nodded. "That dumb *dego* didn't belong in the same ring with neither of 'em." He snorted and popped the fresh cigar into his mouth. "But for what it's worth, that might be a place to start. Tell Roger I sent yah. Come to think of it, he did have a couple of big polack brothers that might fit your bill."

"I'll do that," Quade said. As he turned to go, O'Toole called after him. Quade stopped and looked at the other man.

"Some of them *rasslers* can be pretty mean." O'Toole tapped his right cheek, and then pointed to Quade's. "Remember to keep your guard up next time."

"You can count on it," Quade said.

●●●

Quade stopped in a diner and bought himself a ham on rye and a cup of coffee. He left a quarter for the waitress and took the rest of his change to the phone booth at the back of the place. After dropping in a nickel, he dialed Maxie Levin first.

"Any news for me?" Quade asked after the other man answered.

"Nothing so far, but I got my feelers out. Told my network of associates what I was looking for."

"Okay," Quade said. "Keep me posted."

He hung up and picked up the phone book. The Aragon Ballroom was listed, but when he tried the number it came back as disconnected. He looked up the listing for Roger Feller, dropped another nickel into the slot and dialed. The phone rang half a dozen times before a man answered with a muffled, "Yeah?"

"Rog?"

"Who's this?" The voice sounded suspicious.

"I'm looking for Roger Feller."

"Yeah? Who is this?"

"Marty Quade."

The line was silent for a bit, then the man said, "He ain't here. I'll let him know you called."

The dial-tone buzzed in Quade's ear.

Quade hung up and wrote both numbers and addresses down in his notebook. He stuck the phonebook back in its slot and glanced at his watch: five-fifteen. Taking the subway or a taxi to the Bronx to try and tag up with Roger Feller didn't seem too appealing. It had been a long day, he felt tired, and his face hurt. Quade wanted nothing more than to go back to his room at the Baltic Hotel, relax in a hot bath, and put an icepack on his face. After all, he'd laid most of the necessary groundwork today. Now, it was a matter of waiting until something clicked. He pulled open the folding doors and started to step out of the booth, then stopped. He sat back down on the stool and fished out another nickel.

Maxie Levin answered on the second ring.

"What time you closing up shop?" Quade asked.

"Huh? Quade, that you?"

"Yeah. I need a favor."

"Another one? Whaddya want now?"

"Write this number down," Quade said. He read off Roger Feller's phone number.

"Okay, got it. Now what?"

"Call it when I tell you."

"What do I do if somebody answers?"

"Ask for Ira."

●●●

Quade ducked into the drug store across the street from the three flat and found the row of payphones in the back. He dropped in another nickel and dialed Maxie again.

"I need you to make that call in exactly five minutes," Quade said.

Maxie sighed. "*Oy vey.* My wife's gonna be waiting for me with a frying pan for being this late, and it ain't gonna be for making *latkes.*"

"Tell her you've got my undying gratitude."

"Like I can take that to the bank." He sighed. "Okay, five minutes and I call."

Quade hung up, checked his watch, and set off for the building across the street. Inside the vestibule he looked at the names on the mailboxes. Roger Feller lived on the third floor. The entry door to the stairway was locked, so Quade took out his lock picks. He managed to get it open after about a minute of raking the tumblers, and glanced at his watch again. Four minutes and thirty-five seconds had elapsed. Hopefully, Maxie would be exact in his timing.

Quade ran up the three flights and came to a stop outside apartment 302. Struggling to get his breathing under control, he placed an ear against the door. Inside he could hear a phone ringing: once, twice, three times…

"Hello," a voice said.

Even though it was muffled by the door, it sounded like the same man who'd answered when Quade had called before.

"Who?" the voice said. "Nah, you got the wrong number."

Quade heard what sounded like the phone being slammed down into its cradle. He took in a few deep breaths, and was starting to feel fully recovered from his run up the stairs. Lifting his hand, he knocked sharply on the door, then placed his thumb over the peephole. This garnered no response, but Quade thought he heard movement inside. He knocked again, this time harder, and yelled, "Open up."

"Whaddya want," came a voice from the interior.

"Health Department," Quade said in a gruff voice. "The super let us in. We gotta check all the apartment for rats."

"I'm fine. Get outta here."

"Either you open the damn door or I'll get the super up here to do it," Quade said. "In which case you'll be getting a citation."

Several seconds went by. Quade kept his thumb over the peephole. He heard a scratching sound, then the door opened slightly. A thin, angry face appeared in the crack between the door and the jamb. Quade lurched forward, hitting the door hard with his left shoulder. It bounced back and the momentum carried Quade inside. The apartment was a wreck, with stacks of old papers and magazines scattered everywhere. Dirty clothes were draped on furniture, and rows of empty beer bottles lined the floor. The place smelled like the interior of a tavern.

A slim man Quade assumed to be Roger Feller jumped forward throwing an awkward, looping right at Quade's head. The detective blocked it with his left and stepped in, putting his weight into good belly punch. Feller folded in half and sunk to the floor, emitting a hissing groan. His mouth curled into a snarl as he looked up at Quade from a fetal position on the dirty rug.

"You ain't from the Health Department," Feller said through clenched teeth.

"No," Quade said, glancing around. "But from the looks of things, I should be."

"Whaddya want?"

"I told you, I'm checking for rats." Quade bent down and grabbed Feller by his shirt. The detective lifted the wispy man to his feet and walked him over to a chair. Quade brushed a bunch of girlie magazines onto the floor and shoved Feller into the seat. "Must be the maid's day off, huh?"

Feller responded with a bit of profanity.

"I'm looking for a couple of guys," Quade said. "Wrestlers. They're both good sized, and one of them has a nasty scar on his right wrist. Both have cauliflower ears."

"Hell, show me a rassler what aint' got 'em."

"They hang out with a smaller guy that's got eyelashes that Loretta Young would kill for."

Quade thought he saw a flicker of recognition in the other man's eyes.

"Give me their names and I'm outta here," Quade said.

Feller repeated the profanity.

Quade grabbed him by the shirt again and lifted him out of the chair. "Listen, palie, I'm more than able to go a couple more rounds, if you want."

Feller expelled a couple quick pants. His breath was a foul as a country outhouse. Finally, he looked away, and said, "Go ahead, beat me if you want, but I ain't saying nothing."

Quade saw the resignation in the other man's face. He shoved him back into the chair.

"All I want is their names."

Feller shook his head.

Quade looked around. Searching this place would be like trying to find an Indianhead penny in Fibber McGee's closet. He decided to try a bit more intimidation. He reached into his pocket and took out the .38, holding it down by his side.

"Give me the names," he said, transforming his voice into a low growl.

Feller's eyes widened as he looked at the gun. He swallowed, expelled a few more rancid breaths, then shook his head again.

"They'll kill me if I start talking," he said, looked up at Quade. "You got no idea who you're messing with."

Behind them, Quade heard a woman's angry voice filtering in through the still open door.

"Mr. Feller," the woman said. "What's going on up here. It sounds like…" There was a pause, then a high-pitched scream. "Oh, my God. I'm calling the police." She ran off.

Quade frowned and pocketed the revolver. He pointed at Feller and said, "I'll be in touch. And next time, I'll expect those names."

He turned and left, taking the stairs at a rapid, but not excessive pace. When he exited the building he went back across the street and went into the drug store to the pay phones. He dropped a nickel into the slot and dialed Feller's number. After hearing the buzzing of a busy signal, he hung up and left the store, stripping off his overcoat before he went out and slung it over his arm. Feller hadn't wasted any time calling someone, and Quade doubted it was the cops. As he walked down the street he heard the distant sounds of sirens, but Quade made it all the way to the subway stairs by the time the sounds grew louder.

•••

The ringing of Quade's phone jarred him from a fitful slumber. He rolled over and turned on the light next to his bed, then realized he didn't need it. A bright line of sunlight was pouring into the room through the slit in the heavy hotel drapes. The light hurt his eyes, and then he realized the pain was going to continue whether the room was dark or light. His head felt like it had been run over by a garbage truck. The clock next to the bed told him it was a quarter after ten. A bare, feminine arm extended from under the covers next to him, and he felt her hand caress his shoulder. Shaking his head, he grabbed the phone and was greeted by Maxie Levin's squeaky voice.

"*Oy vez*, did I wake you up? Didn't your mother ever tell you that the early bird catches the worm?"

"Yeah, but I didn't listen," Quade said. "You got something for me?"

"Why else would I be calling? You think I have nothing else to do? I've got a business to run."

"Yeah, yeah," Quade said, reaching for his cigarettes and lighter. He lit one up and inhaled, feeling better immediately. "Spare me the lecture, okay?"

"Whoizzit, honey?" the doll said, then dozed back off.

"Who was that?" Maxie asked. "I take it you are not alone?"

Quade's mind spun over the events of the previous night… The incipient exhaustion he'd felt as he rode the subway home had given way to the urge to stop for just one drink at the hotel bar to mull over the case. The dame had been sitting alone on a bar stool, and mentioned she'd just arrived in the Big Apple from Philly. Being a gentleman, Quade had bought her a "Welcome to New York drink." After all, no one wanted to drink alone? One drink had led to two, and so on, and so forth. He barely remembered their trek up to his room.

Quade removed her hand from his side and she flopped on her back. A few seconds later she was snoring. Quade tossed back the blanket and swung his legs out of the bed. He took another drag on the smoke.

"So what you got for me?" He exhaled a stream of smoke toward the ceiling.

"Maybe some good news, maybe some not so good news. You be the judge."

"Quit talking in riddles, dammit. I had a rough night."

"Egads, it sounds like it," Maxie said. "Snoring like that would wake the devil."

Quade reached over, grabbed a rather substantial hip, and rolled her onto her side. It required a bit of effort and he noticed that she was a kissing cousin to a nude in a Rubens painting… not his usual taste in a woman.

"The more you drink, the prettier the girls look," he said. "Now will you please tell me why you called?"

Maxie sighed heavily. "Have you forgotten that you asked me to put the word out about my desire to acquire certain items of interest?"

This perked Quade up. "You got something?"

"Possibly. I got a call this morning from an associate in our neighboring borough. It seems a gentleman, a very large gentleman, entered his establishment last night trying to sell a family heirloom with which he had tremendous sentimental value."

"What kind of heirloom?"

"A gold pocket watch that his great grandfather had faithfully carried throughout the Civil War." Maxie paused. "Ironically, my associate says that the sentimental giant sounded like he just got off the boat."

Quade took another quick drag on his cigarette. "Tell me more."

"As I had instructed, my associate offered the huge fellow a less-than-modest price, but did say that he knew of a certain merchant who might offer him more, due to an acute interest in such things."

"And the guy went for it?"

"Apparently so," Maxie said. "I received a call this morning from someone that sounded like he'd grown up in Warsaw. I told him to bring the described item by one o'clock."

The recumbent female rolled onto her back again, and the snoring started once more. Quade rolled his eyes, took one more drag on the smoke, and stubbed it out in the ashtray.

"Okay, Maxie, you did good. Give me a little bit to tidy things up here, and I'll be right over."

"I hope you're at least going to buy that poor girl breakfast first."

Quade listened to the reverberating snore and winced. Becoming a teetotaler might have some advantages.

●●●

An hour later Quade was in the process of hailing a cab when he heard someone call his name. He turned and saw Lieutenant James J. Brannigan strolling down the sidewalk wearing a overcoat, a derby hat, and a rather sour expression. An unmarked police car followed along by the curb, a young, uniformed copper at the wheel. Quade grinned.

"If you came to take me to lunch," he said, "I'll have to take a raincheck."

Brannigan did not look amused. He jerked his thumb at the squad car and opened the rear door.

"Oh, good," Quade said as he got into the back seat. "This'll save me finding a cab."

"You'd be doing well to dispense with the jokes, laddie," Brannigan said, getting in after Quade.

Quade pulled out his cigarette case and popped it open, offering one to Brannigan.

The big cop squinted, frowned, and then grabbed four smokes. He dumped three in this shirt pocket and stuck the other one between his lips. Quade took out his lighter, but Brannigan was already holding a wooden kitchen match in his hand. He raked his thumbnail over the primer and the match ignited. "Bright and early this morning I was reading the crime reports from last night."

"Commendable. Shows your dedication to public service."

"There was a murder over in the Bronx last night," Brannigan said, holding the flame to the end of the cigarette. After drawing on it, he shook out the match and tossed it out the window.

"Just one?" Quade asked, placing a smoke in his mouth and flicking his lighter.

"Just one that piqued me interest. Name of the decedent was Roger Feller. Somebody broke in his place and shot him dead."

Quade said nothing.

"Seems this guy, Feller, was a small-time operator," Brannigan went on. "Used to run con games mostly. Also did a couple of fight cards at the old Aragon Ballroom. Ever hear of him?"

Quade drew deeply on his cigarette, as if trying to check his memory. He exhaled the smoke through his nose and shook his head. "No, can't say that I have. But I had a dog named Feller once."

Brannigan frowned.

"You say the guy was a small-time thief?" Quade asked.

Brannigan nodded. "He had an arrest sheet as long as your grandmother's nightie. Should've been cooling his heels in the big house, except some high-priced mouthpiece talked the D.A. into probation instead."

"Shakespeare had it right," Quade said. "First, kill all the lawyers."

Brannigan kept the cigarette in the corner of his mouth, inhaling on it, and then letting the smoke leak out of his nostrils. He leaned back and crossed his big arms. "He was shot to death, and they found a shell casing next to the body. Want to offer a guess as to the caliber?"

Quade blew out a plume of smoke and shook his head again. "I left my crystal ball up in my room."

"It was a rather obscure caliber," Brannigan said. "A thirty-two. Not too many tough guys carry a roscoe like that."

"That's true." Quade clucked sympathetically. "Sure wish I could find mine."

"You say the guy was a small-time thief?"

"That'll make two of us," Brannigan said. "Another little tidbit from the overnight reports… a suspect was observed at the scene about an hour or so before the homicide. Roughed Feller up a bit when the landlady saw him." His cigarette was barely a glowing nub now and Brannigan pinched it out between his forefinger and thumb. "Funny, the description fits you to a T. And this guy also was holding a gun, too."

"Really?" Quade asked. "What kind of gun?"

"She didn't know. Said it looked pretty big, though, and I somehow got a sneaking suspicion that it might look a lot like a certain thirty-eight caliber revolver that I loaned to somebody."

Quade smiled. "Maybe you can have her look at a gun line-up."

Brannigan snorted. "Can you account for your whereabouts last night?"

Quade smiled again. "Sure. I can give you her name if you want. In fact, you can talk to her. She's sleeping it off in my room right now."

Brannigan's frown was evident, even under his bushy mustache. "Give me another one of them smokes, Quade. And then get out at the next corner."

Quade took out his cigarette case and handed one cigarette to the big cop. "So I take it that a ride to the business district is out of the question?"

Brannigan grabbed the cigarette and stuck it between his lips. "Just remember what I told you about staying out of trouble." He reached into his pocket and took out another kitchen match. "As far as our previous bit of business, we're square, and it never did give you a license to run around causing trouble."

"Heaven forbid," Quade said. He turned to the driver. "You can let me out along here and it'll be fine."

The car slowed to a stop and Quade gripped the door-handle. "Lieu, it's always a delight to see old friends."

"Get the hell outta here." Brannigan flicked the match. "And remember what I said. Stay out of trouble."

"You know what Philip Marlowe always says," Quade said as he got out of the car. "Trouble is my business."

●●●

"*Oy Vez*, how did I let myself get talked into this?" Maxie Levine said, holding his head in his hands. "You're not going to accost him inside my store, are you?" He was standing behind the main counter by the cash register, the wire mesh surrounding him on both sides.

"We'll see," Quade said. He'd been waiting forty minutes for the guy to show up. "If he shows, that is. You sure he said one?"

Maxie blew out a long breath. "Well, it's not like these guys punch a time-clock."

"Yeah, but he supposedly wants to sell you a watch." Quade grinned. "You'd think a guy peddling a time-piece would be a bit more sagacious."

They were the only two in the store and Quade glanced at his watch. He had little choice but to play the waiting game some more, but he did begin to wonder whether the caller had suddenly gotten cold feet. This question was answered a few seconds later when a huge shadow eclipsed the light shining in through the wire mesh fastened behind the glass window of the front door of Maxie's shop. The big guy's hat almost bumped the top of the door jamb as he came in.

Quade saw that the guy was the right size. Buddy Baer's twin brother, probably just a hair under six-foot-eight, with a chest like an icebox. Shuffling off to an adjacent aisle, Quade pulled his hat down a bit and pretended to be looking in one of the cases. The wooden floor creaked under the giant's weight.

"Good afternoon, sir," Maxie said. His voice quivered a bit. "How can I help you?"

Quade cast a quick peek. The big guy's head was rotating like a ball on a pivot. Light blue eyes, cauliflower ears. Quade tried to look for an accompanying scar on the giant's right wrist, but the positioning was wrong. Still, Quade was sure the big guy was one of the three who'd robbed the poker game. Quade shifted his body slightly and looked away, trying to masquerade as just another customer.

The big guy just stood there, saying nothing.

"What are you interested in?" Maxie asked in his most obsequious tone. "I'd be glad to help you select something."

The big guy shook his head and leaned over the counter. "I no want buy. I want sell."

"All right," Maxie said. "Whacha got?"

"I call you before about watch. Very fine watch." He reached into his pocket and took out a gold pocket watch attached to a chain. Even from a few feet away, Quade was sure it was the same one that had been stolen at the robbery. He put his hand in the pocket of his overcoat and gripped the handle of the .38.

"Ah, yes," Maxie said, letting a bit of avarice seep into his voice. "It appears to be a very high quality. May I examine it a little closer?

The big guy seemed reluctant, then handed the timepiece over. It looked about the size of a silver dollar in a hand the size of a catcher's mitt. Maxie stepped back to his desk and flipped on a lamp, holding the item under the light. "What's this engraving here? Looks like some kind of family crest."

"No matter," the big guys said. "Watch is gold, no? You tell me how much you pay."

Maxie walked back over to the counter and set the watch down on top of the glass cage. "I could go with twenty-five dollars."

The big guy's face twisted into a scowl. "No, I want hundred."

"A hundred?" Maxie said. "Forty, and that's as high as I'll go. The inscription devalues it. Is it a family heirloom?"

The big guy held out his hand. "Give me watch."

As Maxie started to hand it back, Quade stepped out of the shadows of the adjacent aisle.

"Hey, that is a nice watch," Quade said, moving over next to the giant. "Much too nice for a big ape like you to have acquired legitimately."

Maxie's face turned ashen and he stepped back into the recesses of his wire mesh cage and slid the door across, separating him from the other two men.

The big man's head turned on a neck the size of a grand piano leg. "You talk me?"

Quade saw a flicker of recognition flash in the light blue eyes. "I know you. You detective, but no gun."

"Wrong, buster," Quade said, holding up the .38. "Now you and I are going to have a little talk in the alley, and you're going to tell me where your partners are at."

The big man look down at Quade, his eyes lowering to the revolver, and then back up again. His huge face twisted into a menacing smile. "I think no. I think you no shoot. You maybe strong, but you no strong like Otto strong."

The man-mountain turned with a quickness that belied his size and pushed Quade into a towering stack of old radios. As the shelves crashed to the floor, Quade tried to bring the gun around, but the big man was already reaching out. He grabbed Quade by the shoulder and pushed him into another set of shelves, which also went crashing down. Maxie screamed that he was calling the police.

"No cops!" the giant yelled, turning his head toward the caged pawn merchant. "You no call, or I kill you."

The brief respite was all Quade needed to get to his feet and level the revolver at the huge torso.

"Get your hands up, King Kong," Quade said. "Or you're dead."

The giant's face curled into something between a grimace and a snarl. The big body lurched forward, huge arms outstretched, the immense hands grabbing for Quade.

Quade pulled the trigger. The .38 roared, and the smell of burnt gunpowder was accompanied by a haze of smoke. It seemed to have no effect on the giant. The big hands grabbed Quade's head and shoulder, pulling him close to the refrigerator chest.

Quade shoved the .38 against the big torso and pulled the trigger again. The sound was a bit muffled this time, and still seemed to have no effect. One of the big hands closed over the top of Quade's head, the other around his neck, and they moved in opposite directions. Quade felt like his head was about to be torn from his body.

He pulled the trigger two more times.

The numbing pressure continued. Black dots swarmed in front of Quade's eyes. He shot into the expansive chest again, but felt his air being cut off. The black dots grew thicker, and Quade struggled to try to recall how many rounds he'd fired. Five? Six?

Hoping that it was only five, Quade used his last bit of strength to lift the gun upward and jammed the end of the barrel against the underside of the giant's jaw. Just before he blacked out, Quade heard the last report.

Suddenly the blackness evaporated and he found himself lying on the floor under what felt like a streetcar in a detritus of shattered clocks, radios, broken glass and costume jewelry. Warm blood ran down the side of Quade's face, and he saw a pair of light blue, dead eyes, staring directly into his own. After several seconds that seemed like an eternity, Quade managed to extricate himself from underneath the huge carcass.

"*Oy vai iz mir*," Maxie was saying. "Look what you did to my shop."

"Yeah," Quade said, staggering to his feet. "But we got the watch back."

•••

Hours later, Quade leaned against the seat as the taxi turned off the main road and went between the two, large stone pillars that marked the entrance to Argonne, Thomas Dunn's palatial estate. The paved driveway was as smooth as a road, and Quade watched as the headlights illuminated the finely manicured shrubbery and well-trimmed trees on either side of the drive. It had taken Quade the rest of the afternoon to square the shooting with the police, not admitting to anything other than being in

Maxie's store when the big guy had come in, apparently to rob the place. Neither he nor Maxie mentioned the watch. The cops kept grilling Quade until Lieutenant Brannigan arrived and took charge. His face twisted into an ugly frown as he told the uniformed officers to "bag the gun for evidence." Brannigan then leaned close to Quade and whispered into his ear, "Now you really owe me one, laddie."

After giving his statement at the precinct house, Brannigan told Quade he was free to go, but not to leave town.

"I wouldn't dream of it," Quade had said, and left feeling mentally relieved, but physically drained. His neck and shoulder, where Otto Levinsky had damn near dismembered him, felt tender and sore. Again, Quade wanted nothing more than to go back to the Hotel Baltic and relax in a hot bath, but he knew he had to keep moving. He was still a couple of laps behind, and had to maintain his momentum if he wanted to run his quarries to ground.

The cabbie pulled up in front of the pillared mansion's front doors. The house was two massive stories, and about half-a-block long, like something out of *Gone With the Wind*. Quade paid the cabbie and got out. He walked up the white, wooden steps to a front door with an ornate knocker and a doorbell that looked like it could pass for one of the crown jewels. He pressed it and heard some distant chimes ring inside. Presently, a shadowy figure appeared behind the frosty glass pane next to the door. A man in a butler's uniform opened it and stood looking at Quade with hooded eyes.

"Mr. Quade, I presume?" the butler asked.

Quade nodded.

"Master Thomas will receive you in the library," the butler said, and turned on his heel.

Quade followed him through an expansive foyer large enough to host a stickball tournament. The butler stopped outside a pair of oak doors and told Quade to wait there. Quade nodded and sized the place up. Oil paintings of men in uniform with battle scenes from conflicts ranging from the Civil War to the Great War lined the walls. The last one sported a flattering portrait of Thomas Dunn in Army uniform against the background of a verdant forest. Quade noticed that the rich man's face and eye weren't depicted in their present, deformed state.

"I was once a very handsome man, wasn't I?" a voice said.

Quade turned to see Thomas Dunn standing there in a purple dressing gown, a fancy glass tumbler in his right hand. He shifted it to his left, and extended his right. Quade shook the man's hand and they stepped into the adjacent room.

It had a long mahogany table with a dozen finely crafted chairs. Book cases lined the walls, sporting seemingly endless volumes of finely bound leather volumes. Quade didn't ask if they were ever read. Dunn walked over to a smaller end-table and pointed to an ornate glass decanter.

"Would you care for a drink?" he asked.

"Don't mind if I do."

Dunn removed the glass stopper, poured two fingers of amber liquid into a glass, and handed it to Quade. "So, you said on the phone that you'd recovered my watch?"

Quade sipped the drink and felt the burn all the way down to his stomach. He reached into his coat pocket and removed the pocket watch, handing it to Dunn.

The other man's eye widened and he cocked his head slightly. When he looked up, the unfrozen side of his face curled into a grin.

"This is it. It's been in my family for generations. Thank you."

"There's a little matter of a finder's fee," Quade said, taking another sip of his drink.

"Of course," Dunn said. "Name your price."

"Two thousand dollars."

Dunn's good eye narrowed and he looked askance. "A bit steep, isn't it?"

Quade smirked and sipped his drink again. "Actually, you're getting off cheap. I almost got my neck broken in the process of getting your watch back, and an associate of mine lost a substantial amount of goods as well. I also had to kill a man."

Dunn stood silent for several seconds, then asked, "And were you able to keep my name out of it?"

"I was," Quade said.

Dunn nodded. He went to a bell cord that hung next the fireplace and pulled it. Quade heard nothing in the way of bells ringing in the other parts of the house, but the butler knocked and entered the room after about thirty seconds. Dunn told him to fetch the checkbook. The butler left as unobtrusively as he had entered.

"You say you had to kill a man?" Dunn said.

"One of the big lugs that robbed us at the game. Otto Levinsky was his name."

Dunn poured himself more liquor. "How did it happen?"

Quade recounted the event.

Dunn picked up a wooden box on the table, opened it, and offered it to Quade. He took a cigarette and waited while Dunn lighted it, and then his own. The rich man leaned artfully against the wall next to the fireplace.

"It's an interesting experience, watching a man die," he said. "Isn't it?"

"I don't know if I'd put it exactly that way."

The good side of Dunn's face flashed a smile. "I saw quite a bit of that during the Great War. We were all being moved to the front lines for what was to be the principal allied engagement. The Meuse-Argonne Offensive. The Argonne Forest… One point two million men… All intent on ending the stalemate… Kicking the Germans back to the Rhine." He paused and shook his head. "A hundred days of pure hell. At its finish. We sustained over twenty-six thousand fatalities, over ninety-five thousand wounded, including …" He pointed to the side of his face. "I re-named our estate Argonne, after that battle."

"Must have been pretty rough," Quade said. "I'd say you were one of the lucky ones to have survived."

Dunn turned his head and looked at him. "Survival, like all other things, has its price." He tossed down the rest of his drink just as the butler came in with a silver tray upon which was a leather-bound checkbook and a fountain pen. Dunn pulled out one of the chairs, sat down, and wrote out the check. "Does this close things out?"

"Huh-un," Quade said. "I still have to run some more people to ground."

"You know who they are?"

"Not all of them. I have to figure out which one of the five of us set up the robbery."

Dunn looked at him. "You think one of us was involved?"

Quade folded the check and stuck it in his shirt pocket. "Mind if I have another drink? It's been a long day, and I still got a ways to go tonight."

Dunn nodded and Quade poured himself a double. "Somebody had to tip off the three jokers as to the time of the game and which room we were in."

"Who do you think it was?"

Quade took a slug from his glass and shrugged. "The only two I'm sure are innocent at this point are me and you."

Dunn smiled. "I'm glad you don't suspect me."

"I never did, actually." He patted his shirt pocket. "And this proved it to me. You've got too much money to go to all that trouble to steal a few grand. Plus, your watch was one of first items to turn up on the pawn shop circuit. If you'd been involved, it wouldn't have."

"Good point."

Quade drank some more, then asked, "Who invited you to the game?"

"Harold Dixon. I've played with him and Conroy before."

"Poker?"

Dunn didn't answer immediately, and then said, "Among other things."

"What's that mean?"

Dunn pursed his lips. "Both of them are compulsive gamblers, although Harold's a bit more circumspect than Karl. Conroy's got a lot of outstanding debts, and he goes to extreme measures sometimes to pay people off."

"Extreme measures?"

Dunn sat silent for several seconds. "He was into me for quite a bit. Over a thousand dollars. I had his IOU, but soon realized that it wasn't worth the paper it was printed on. So we made another arrangement."

He stopped talking. Quade waited about ten seconds, and then asked, "What was that?"

"Mrs. Conroy," Dunn said. "She's a very attractive woman, as I'm sure you noticed."

"She is."

"Conroy rented her out to me," Dunn said. "Two sessions to wipe out his debt. It's not something I'm proud of, but when you've got a face like mine, the attention of a beautiful woman for a night can mean a lot."

Quade considered this. "How did you two come to that arrangement?"

"Harold approached me with it. He and Conroy are quite close. Apparently, I wasn't the only one that Conroy paid off by pimping out his wife." Dunn turned toward him. "I assume that all of this will remain confidential, as per our agreement?"

Quade nodded. "What else can you tell me about Conroy and Dixon?"

●●●

The dark sea water slapped with regularity against the hull of the boat as it cut through the waves toward the bright, welcoming lights of the *Siren's Song*. Quade stood near the back, watching the handful of other people anxious to lose their money on the floating casino that lingered just outside the three-mile limit of the harbor. The ship's lights grew sharper as they approached, seeming to change from pure white to the softer edged red, green and blue hues that decorated the vessel. The boat's engine whined and rasped as it slowed and the pilot steered it up next to the floating platform that was affixed to the side of the ship. Quade waited as the giggling couples stepped onto the platform first.

He wondered how much giggling they'd be doing on the return trip.

Two servicemen stepped off the dinghy next, and then Quade. They all crowded into a special elevator lift, and a burly looking attendant pulled a metallic safety curtain across the front entrance. The elevator chugged upward at a leisurely pace.

At the top, the attendant unfastened the corresponding metal curtain that allowed them access to the main deck.

"Enjoy your stay aboard the *Siren's Song*, ladies and gents," the attendant said. "There's a boat leaving every forty-five minutes for the return-trip."

Quade hung back and let the people filter ahead of him. He'd been on the gambling ship before, but it had been a while and he wanted to get his sea-legs. The ship was an old luxury liner that had been transformed into a floating casino. Because it stayed, more or less, just outside the legal limits of New York Harbor, the authorities tolerated its presence. Word was that on weekends it had been known to cruise to Jersey upon occasion. Quade followed the merry group down the brightly lit main staircase. At the bottom of the stairway the main room opened up into a maze of slot machines and roulette wheels, as well as sections of craps and poker tables. A restaurant and bar were to the left, complete with a dance floor, a full orchestra, and a girl singer in a low-cut dress. She was singing an Ira Gershwin tune that Quade recognized. He kept walking through the casino area, the singer's mellifluous voice floating after him. When he got to the casino's rear wall, which sported a row of mirrored windows above an open section with a stairway, he was accosted by two tough looking mugs in tuxedos. From the bulges under their jackets, Quade could tell that they were both packing heat.

"This is off limits to the customers," one of them said.

"I'm not a customer," Quade said, affecting an official tone. "I'm here to see Big Jim Dandy." He held up the black wallet with his generic and totally fake badge and identification. "New York Gaming Commission."

At the sight of the ersatz credentials and the mention of his boss's name, the mug's head jerked slightly. Now obviously unsure of himself, he licked his lips. "You got an appointment?"

"I don't need no appointment, greaseball," Quade said. "Now lemme through, or you're gonna find yourself in real trouble."

The tough guy rubbed his nose, suddenly not looking so tough anymore. After a moment, he blinked and told his partner to escort Quade to the boss. After trudging up a set of metal stairs they turned right onto a second deck and the escort knocked on a solid door.

A voice from within said, "Come," and the hood opened the door.

"Hey, boss, this guy wants to see ya. Says he's from the gaming commission."

Jim Dandy sat behind a big, teakwood desk smoking a pipe. He grinned, showing a line of exceptionally straight, white teeth. "Bring him in."

The hood stepped aside and Quade went into the sumptuous office. Jim Dandy was already standing, extending his right hand across the desk.

"Well, well, Marty Quade, as I live and breathe."

Quade shook Dandy's hand and cocked his head over his shoulder in the direction of the door. "You really ought to hire better help. I got past those two with a song and a dance. What if I was really somebody intent on causing you some harm?"

Dandy snorted a laugh as he plopped down in his chair again. "I seen you coming a mile away." He jerked a thumb over his shoulder and added, "One-way glass."

Quade nodded appreciably.

The other man leaned forward on the desk, taking the pipe out of his mouth. "So whaddaya want, shamus?"

"Information. Do the names Harold Dixon and Karl Conroy sound familiar?"

Dandy raised an eyebrow. "Why you want to know?"

"Just wondering if we have some mutual friends."

Dandy's pipe had gone out and tapped the ashes into an ashtray on his desk. "So what if I do know 'em? I know lots of people. No crime in that."

"I'm trying to collect an overdue debt for somebody. I was wondering how successful I'm gonna be. Like how deep Dixon and Conroy are in to you?"

Dandy took out a tobacco pouch and began packing his pipe. He sat in silence until he was finished, then stuck the pipe into his mouth, flicked a lighter, and held it over the packed bowl. "Quade, you and me go back a long way," he said, between puffs. "A long, long way. So I'll be straight with you. Both those two are regulars here, but as far as them owing me," He paused and blew out a prodigious cloud of smoke. "They don't owe me squat."

It was Quade's turn to lift an eyebrow. "Their luck that good?"

Dandy laughed. "Conroy's a loser. Always has been, always will be."

"How about Harold Dixon?"

"Dixon?" Dandy laughed again. "Well, let's just say I overlook a lot of stuff. It never hurts to have a banker by the short hairs."

"So I take it he's into you for a bundle, too?"

"Was," Dandy said. "I don't even let him play here no more. The guys a blowhard. As phony as that *diamond* stick pin he wears."

"And Conroy?"

Dandy's face scrunched up as he blew out another plume of smoke. "That's more complicated."

"How so?"

Dandy puffed on the pipe, expelling smoke through his nose. "Ever seen his wife?"

"I have. She's gorgeous."

Dandy nodded. "She's also my sister's girl. Step-daughter."

"Your niece?"

Dandy shrugged. "I gave her a job singing here. Talking to the customers... Just that kind of light stuff. Nothing dirty."

"And?" Quade asked.

Dandy seemed to ponder his reply, then stood and motioned for Quade to follow him over to an array of framed pictures on the wall of various women in a low cut evening gowns, showing a lot of cleavage. One of the pictures showed Linda Conroy, Harold Dixon, Karl Conroy, as well as another familiar face: Wallace Myers.

"She met Conroy here?" Quade asked.

"Yeah, it was a real storybook romance, all right." Dandy smiled. "She thought he had dough, and she swept him off his feet."

"So she quit working here when they got married?"

Dandy nodded.

"And you wrote off his debt as a wedding present?"

Dandy smirked. "Conroy has some... business dealings with me and some of my associates."

"In other words," Quade said, "He does some laundry for you?"

Dandy lifted an eyebrow. "No comment."

"What about his wife?"

"Linda's a sweet kid, and I wished her well. She still comes by, from time to time." He grinned. "You know, to work off some of her husband's debts. Being nice to Uncle Jim."

Quade recoiled. "Your own niece?"

The other man laughed. "Everybody needs a write-off, from time to time, right? Besides, we ain't blood. She's only related to me by marriage."

"Speaking of debts," Quade asked. "Who you got doing your collecting nowadays?"

"I gave her a job singing here."

"Pete Tantros. But he don't do no freelancing."

"He work with a pair of big ex-pugs named Levinsky?"

Dandy shook his head. "Nah, he always works alone."

"Know where I can find him?"

Dandy's face acquired some ugly creases. "No. What's your angle, Quade? I got a feeling you ain't being above board with me."

"Above board." Quade laughed. "Nice nautical metaphor, especially from a guy who spends all of his time on a kissing cousin to the Titanic."

"So that's the way it's gonna be, huh?" Dandy said. "At least you could go out on the floor and lose some money."

Quade smiled as he walked to the door. "Keep your life preservers handy."

●●●

Quade was beat when he got back to the Hotel Baltic and decided to just get a sandwich from the restaurant to take up to his room. As he walked across the expansive lobby the desk clerk waved to him. Quade moved over to the front desk.

"Mr. Quade," the clerk said, "I've got some messages for you."

Quade heaved a sigh. "Let's have 'em."

The clerk handed him three pink message slips. All of them were from Brannigan.

"He say what he wanted?" Quade asked.

"Only that it was important."

Quade nodded and went into the bar. After taking a quick glance around to make sure his Rubens' girlfriend wasn't anywhere in sight, he ordered a bourbon and branch water and told the bartended to rustle him up a ham on rye and the telephone. The bartender nodded, poured the drink, and set the phone on top of the bar. Quade dialed the number for the precinct and asked for Brannigan.

"He ain't here," the desk sergeant said.

"This is Marty Quade. He was trying to get ahold of me."

"Quade? Yeah, he did say something about that. Gimme your number and I'll see if I can catch him at home."

Quade repeated the hotel bar phone number and hung up. The bartender came back and said the sandwich was in the works. He reached for the phone, but Quade put his hand on top of it and shook his head. "I'm expecting a call soon."

The phone rang about three minutes later. Quade answered it and heard Brannigan's Irish brogue. "Well, well, well, laddie. I got some good news for you. We found your gun."

"Yeah? Where?"

"In the hand of one Karl Conroy. It was used to shoot him in the head."

"Suicide?"

"Could be, but we're investigating. He was clutching some phony diamond stickpin shaped like a dollar sign. Sound familiar?"

"Huh-un," Quade said. "He leave a note?"

"No. His missus found him. Pretty little thing was all broken up." He chuckled. "I thought about trying to comfort her a bit, but me Irish manners prevented it."

"Yeah, I'm sure."

Quade was trying to process this information. If Conroy had Quade's gun, and Dixon's ersatz stickpin, that meant he'd been in on the robbery.

"It still don't explain how he ended up with you gun, laddie. I'm gonna need you to explain that little development before I can tie this one up with a pretty little bow."

"Beats me," Quade said. "I barely knew the guy. Plus, I told you my gun was missing."

"So that's how it is, eh?"

"What are the chances of getting my gun back?"

Brannigan laughed. "Well, let me see… I'd say the chances are slim and none, and your buddy slim left town." He roared with laughter.

"It's a good thing you're such a hot-shot copper," Quade said. "Because you'd never make it as an Irish Jack Benny."

He hung up.

●●●

Quade tried to call Mrs. Conroy the next morning, but got no answer. He spent the remainder of the morning at the Hotel Baltic restaurant, nursing a cup of black coffee, pondering the case, and ducking Brannigan's calls. The big Irishman called four times, and each time the hotel staff covered for him. During the last one Quade could hear Brannigan's booming voice a foot away from the phone: "Tell him to get his *arse* down to headquarters now, before I send somebody to pick him up."

Quade decided a stroll around Central Park might be in order. He was in his room putting on his overcoat when he got another call. This one was from Mrs. Conroy.

"My condolences," Quade offered. "How you holding up?"

"I'm all right," she said.

"If there's anything I can do..." Quade started to say.

"Actually, there is." She paused. "I'm in my husband's office in the factory. I closed everything down and was going through his desk." She paused again, then said, "I think I've found the money from the robbery. It looks like mine and Mr. Myers's rings, too."

It was Quade's turn to be silent, then he asked, "You called the cops?"

"No, not yet. I... I'm not sure what to do. I thought perhaps you could come here and help me sort things out."

"I'll be right there."

●●●

Quade took a taxi to the Conroy's factory in Brooklyn. The place was more like a small warehouse where teams of bakers labored through the night to assure that the fleet of trucks could make their early morning deliveries of biscuits, bread, and sweet rolls. When the cab let him out, the place looked deserted and was dark inside. It was only early afternoon, but this seemed logical. Mrs. Conroy had told him she'd closed everything down. Quade guessed that a lot of restaurants would be without pies that evening. He went to the front door and saw a hand-printed sign next to a doorbell that read: *RING FOR SERVICE*. Quade rang it. He could see a shadowy shape moving inside through the filthy window pane of wired glass. Thinking about the rolls he'd had for breakfast that morning, Quade grimaced, hoping the interior would be a bit more pristine.

"Who is it?" a feminine voice asked over an intercom.

"Marty Quade."

The heavy door buzzed open, and Linda Conroy was standing just inside. Her blonde hair had been pulled back into a pony tail, but she wore full makeup and mascara. Her full breasts strained at the cotton prison of her blouse.

"Thanks for coming," she said.

Quade followed her through the deserted foyer to a pair of double doors that led to an enormous room housing an array of huge ovens, tables, and large cans overflowing with sweet-smelling baked dough. Large, fifty-pound bags of sugar and flour were stacked along the back wall. They went through another pair of swinging doors that separated the baking area from a warehouse section. To his right, against the far wall, Quade saw a distant loading dock. The rest of the room was filled with rows and rows of metal shelving upon which more big paper sacks had been neatly stacked. The stacks extended about fifteen feet upward, toward the high ceiling, which was criss-crossed with an extensive network of open piping. Quade guessed it was a sprinkler system. Several posted signs admonished: *ABSOLUTELY NO SMOKING. FLAMMABLE SUBSTANCES PRESENT.*

They came to a small, lighted office and Linda Conroy opened the door and went in. Quade followed. She pointed over the large desk toward some filing cabinets.

"In there," she said. "The middle drawer."

Quade walked over and pulled it open. He saw a several neatly stacked bundles of currency, each secured with a thick rubberband.

"The rings are in the desk," she said.

Quade moved to the desk and pulled open the top drawer. The two wedding rings, and the thick Harvard, Class of Twenty-Nine ring, lay amongst an assortment of pens, pencils, and paperclips. He picked up a pencil and hooked the class ring, bringing it up so that he could see the inscription: *WDM.*

She moved closer to him. So close he could smell her delicate perfume.

"There's something inscribed on the inside," she said.

Quade let the ring slip off the pencil and fall back into the drawer. "You're trying too hard to get me to pick it up, sweetheart."

She stepped back. "I don't know what to do. I thought about calling the authorities, but I'm not sure that's such a good idea. That would mean all of you would lose your money, right?"

"Yeah, especially since you were in on the whole shebang."

Her head jerked back. She looked at him with widening eyes. "What? How can you say that?"

"Easy. It was always obvious that somebody in the game had orchestrated the robbery. How else would the three thugs have known where and when?"

She took a half a step back. "But that was Karl, not me."

"That's a pretty good delivery. You should've been an actress. You're good looking enough."

"You've got to believe me. I had nothing to do with it."

Quade laughed. "Who pulled the trigger on your husband? Tantros?"

"I don't know who that is." Quade had an uneasy feeling in the pit of his stomach. He'd been operating "naked" ever since Brannigan had taken back the .38 revolver. Quade scanned the dark warehouse through the row of windows that ran the length of the walls on either side of the door.

Obviously, Karl Conroy had been a boss who'd liked to look out on his busy employees.

"Save it, sweetheart. There was no forced entry to the door to the room. You said there was a knock, and you just opened it. Three hoods wearing masks… You didn't take the normal precaution of looking out through the peephole."

"It was dark. I couldn't see."

"Plus, you knew the thin man, Tantros. From your days as a lounge singer for Jim Dandy."

"Who?"

"Your friendly step-uncle." Quade grinned and picked up the telephone. "Tell it to Lieutenant Brannigan." He started to dial.

"What are you talking about. I'm about to bury my husband."

"Yeah, I'll bet the poor jerk was comforted going to his last reward knowing one of his poker-mates was going to be squeezing you. Where's your boyfriend at?"

She jumped forward and jammed her fingers onto the cradle of the phone, disconnecting the call. "Get in here now!" she screamed.

Three men who'd evidently been standing in the shadows in the warehouse bustled through the doorway. The first one was Tantros, holding a .45, the second was Wallace Myers, and the third was the hulking Levinsky brother.

"Good to see you again, tough guy," Tantros said. His face twisted into a cruel looking smile.

Linda Conroy immediately went to Myers, who embraced her.

"He was calling the police," she said, her voice a whisper.

"Bad boy," Tantros said, waggling the barrel of the semi-auto back and forth.

"It's all right, darling," Myers said to her.

"Don't forget to take your class ring," Quade said.

Myers pursed his lips.

Quade figured a rush to the door was fruitless with the giant Levinsky brother blocking it, Quade knew he had to keep talking. "It wasn't hard to figure out. When they robbed us, how did slick here know I was armed?" He pointed to Tantros. "No one knew I was a private dick except one person… the guy that invited me."

Myers considered this, then nodded.

Quade laughed. "Wallace, you woulda made a good politician. Too bad you'll never get the chance."

"Shut up," Myers said.

Quade continued, stalling for time. "The question I had was, why was I invited in the first place? The only explanation I can think of is that I was a safety check to see how well you'd covered your tracks. If I investigated, and turned up any loose ends that needed to be tidied up, like good old Roger Feller, they could then be taken care of." He stared at Linda Conroy. "Plus, my gun provided the convenient connection between me and your husband's staged suicide. After I conveniently disappear, it'll look like I killed him and took off with the dough, especially after you plant the ring with my fingerprints on it."

"Interesting theory," Myers said. "Have you shared any of this with the police?"

Quade didn't answer.

"We'll get him to talk," Tantros said, leveling the gun at Quade's chest. "Let's go, tough guy."

"Peter," Linda Conroy said, "He knows too much."

"Yeah, yeah." Tantros reached forward and patted Quade down. "No roscoe, huh?"

Quade said nothing.

Tantros shoved Quade toward the big man, who raised his massive fist and brought it down of Quade's head.

The blow knocked Quade to the floor.

"You kill my brudder," Levinsky said. "Now I kill you."

"Wait," Tantros said. "Not until we find out what he told the cops."

Levinsky grunted and bent down grabbing Quade. The detective felt himself being lifted like a sack of potatoes and being slung over the big man's shoulder.

"We'll be back in a bit," Tantros said. "We need to use one of those wooden tables for our interview session."

"Make sure you clean everything up" Linda Conroy called after them as they went through the door. "I'm going to open the bakery back up tomorrow."

Quade had been feigning unconsciousness. Tantros exited the office first, followed by Levinsky. As they strode toward the doors leading to the baking area, and the big tables, they were walking alongside the adjacent shelves with the sacks of flour and sugar.

Quade knew he had to make his move. He reached out grabbing the edge of one of the metal shelving units, at the same time churning his legs. His knee caught Levinsky in the face and Quade managed to slide off the big man's shoulder. Quade continued kicking as he hit the floor, catching the giant a couple times in the shins and knees. The big man danced out of range, which gave Quade the few seconds he needed to get to his feet. The huge man-mountain lumbered toward him, arms outstretched, his open hands the size of twin frying pans. Quade turned and ran. Behind him, he heard Tantros yelling for Levinsky to get out of the way.

The crack of a shot tore the air as a bullet whizzed past Quade's head. The detective reached a small space between the shelving and squeezed into it. The giant attempted to come after him, but the space was too narrow to accommodate the big man's girth. Swearing, Levinsky extricated himself and ran down toward the wider expanse. Quade continued to edge through the break in the shelving units. He emerged in time to see Levinsky rounding the corner and heading down the aisle toward him. Knowing the giant would be on top of him in seconds, Quade grabbed the edges of the closest shelf and climbed upward, feeling Levinsky's huge hands narrowly missing a grasp. As he crested the edge Quade scrambled over the heavy, paper sacks. The top area formed a platform of stacked bags about twelve feet square

Another bullet tore through the sacks near Quade, and an eruption of fine, white mist filled the air.

Flour… He was sitting on top of sacks of flour.

"Get the ladder," Tantros shouted. Quade glanced to his left and saw the top of a ladder being moved down the aisle. The wooden frame plopped against the top edge of the stack and Quade heard Tantros say, "Go up there and get him. He ain't got no gun."

Quade saw the frame dig into the paper sacks, indicating an enormous weight was now ascending the ladder. In desperation, he glanced at the torn sack and the white powder that had spilled forth. Quade rolled onto his back and lifted his feet above the torn sack. He brought his heels down with repeated kicks, further rupturing the opening. The powdery haze filled the air.

One huge hand was now gripping the top of the ladder. Quade grabbed the ruptured sack. Another big hand emerged. Quade lifted the ripped sack and thrust it toward Levinsky's massive head as he crested the stack. The white dust was everywhere and Quade hoped the particle concentration was sufficient. Reaching into his pocket, he withdrew his lighter, pausing a few seconds to position himself to take cover as best he could in between the unopened sacks. He then flicked the lighter and threw it toward the giant, recalling the posted warnings: *FLAMMABLE SUBSTANCES PRESENT.*

The particles of flour ignited with a crackling, concussive wave, sending a searing blast of heat washing over everything. Quade felt a burning sensation sweep over his legs and back. His pants were on fire. He quickly rolled over and smothered out the flames. More fire curled over the tops of the stacks. A bellow came from below and Quade caught a glimpse of Levinsky, whose clothes were on fire. The giant lifted himself off the floor, screaming as he ran toward Tantros.

"Get away from me," Tantros yelled. "You stupid idiot."

The blast from the .45 echoed five times.

Quade heard a gurgling roar, punctuated by a final shot. He mentally calculated that it had been eight rounds and peeked over the edge. About fifteen feet below Tantros was dropping the empty magazine from the pistol. The slide was locked back.

Something clicked above Quade and suddenly the sprinkler heads above the burning sacks of flour began sending out a cascade of water.

Brushing the drops out of his eyes, Quade grabbed the nearest sack of flour, noticing that the weight, *55 LBS*, was printed beneath the block letters *F-L-O-U-R*. He moved closer to the edge and threw the bag over the side. Tantros looked up through the rain of droplets as the bag struck him in the face. He crumpled to the floor and Quade picked up a second bag and hurled that one down as well. It landed with a thud, accompanied by a muffled grunt.

"One more for good measure," Quade said and pushed another bag down on top of the fallen thug. Swinging his legs over the side, Quade jumped, landing on top of the haphazard stack. Tantros screamed in pain. Quade pulled the bags away from the thug and grabbed the .45. After regaining his footing, Quade delivered a solid blow to the thug's temple with the gun barrel. Tantros's eyes rolled back into his head, and Quade repeated the blow.

Finally, satisfied that Tantros was no longer a threat, Quade straightened up and muttered, "I owed you that last one, palie."

As he emerged from the stacks he hit the release button, sending the slide forward. He doubted that Myers and Linda Conroy were armed, but they didn't need to know that the .45 was now empty.

The pair was just inside the office, watching his approach in wide-eyed terror.

"Marty," Myers said and Quade strode through the door. "Thank God you're okay. They made us go along with them. You have to…"

Quade grinned and looped a left uppercut into the lawyer's gut. The man sank to his knees. Quade waited a second more, then added a second blow with the butt of the pistol. Myers crumbled to the floor.

"They made me do it," Linda Conroy said.

Quade smirked.

Her face took on a look of desperation and she ripped open her blouse exposing her breasts. "I'll do anything you want. Anything."

Quade walked past her to the desk. "Put your Princess Alberts back in the can, sweetheart. Maybe you can play Lady Macbeth in the prison theater."

He picked up the phone and dialed Brannigan.

●●●

A week later Brannigan and Quade sat opposite each other at a table in the Hotel Baltic Restaurant. "How many blackbirds you bake in this pie, Quade? Three dead and three in the can?"

The waiter came by with the bottle of wine, opened it, and handed Quade the cork.

"I hope that smells better than those cock-and-bull stories that you slung on me last week, laddie," Brannigan said.

Quade set the cork down on the table and nodded to the waiter, who filled their glasses.

"I told you," Quade said, shrugging. "It was… complicated."

Brannigan sampled the wine. Frowning, he shook his head and said, "That's more fitting for a woman than a man."

Quade laughed. "You're welcome to take the bottle home to your missus if you want."

Brannigan's frown slowly dissipated and he leaned forward, placing his big forearms on the table. "Well, now that this one's pretty much all wrapped up, I'll admit you did help me out a tad. So, to show me appreciation, I'll see what I can do about getting your gun back to you." He paused and grinned. "As soon as the trial is over, that is. And as long as you promise to quit leaving dead bodies all over the place."

"I never make promises I can't keep," Quade said. "Besides…" He pulled open his coat displaying the butt of a .32 semi-auto in a shoulder holster. "I figured that's what you'd say, so I got myself a new one."

Brannigan lifted an eyebrow. "Another one of those little Italian numbers, I see."

"I always stick with a winning hand," Quade said, flashing a grin. "After all, I got an image to uphold."

THE END

The New Pulps

Alittle over a century ago, back when writers were really writers, a market for genre fiction existed like no other, before or since: the pulps. These magazines were printed on the cheapest of paper (called "pulp paper"), but they had magnificently painted, full-color covers. The magazines spanned a variety of genres from western to romance, from sci-fi to mystery, offering a wide variety to readers, as well as a host of opportunities to writers. The publications paid a penny a word, and allowed a writer to make a meager living turning out the pages, if he could write quickly. While some writers sought to increase their paychecks by increasing modifiers and fluffing out their prose, others only sought to turn out a decent story. Not only was it a viable marketplace for a wordsmith, but it offered a place to learn. As the great Elmore Leonard said, "The pulps gave you a place to be bad." They gave fledgling writers a chance to hone their craft, to learn how to tell a story, to learn how to write. These mags were the proving ground for some of the greatest writers of the Twentieth Century. Isaac Asimov, Ray Bradbury, Raymond Chandler, Dashiell Hammett, John D. McDonald, Ed McBain to name a few... They all cut their writing teeth with the pulps.

When the new editor of *Black Mask Magazine*, Captain Joseph T. Shaw, took over the helm of the magazine in 1926 he put the word out that he was trying to elevate the quality of the material. One of his writers, Samuel Dashiell Hammett, subsequently came to him with a new manuscript that he thought might fill the bill. The title of the work was *The Maltese Falcon*. Shaw immediately recognized its potential, and it was published in three parts in *Black Mask*. Later it was picked up by Alfred Knopf and published in book form. It went on to become known as one of the 100 greatest novels of the Twentieth Century. On the opposite coast, Raymond Chandler, a failed oil executive in California, began submitting stories featuring tough guy PIs. His stories were so well written, with muscular prose and crackling similes and metaphors, that Chandler never received a rejection slip. Chandler later transformed his pulp detectives into Philip Marlowe, one of the most enduring private eyes of all time.

But not all the writers were in Hammett's or Chandler's class. Many struggled in obscurity, churning out decently written stories with less than memorable characters. While they were not the first string of emerging talent, these writers churned out entertaining yarns that readers enjoyed.

One of them was a man named Emile Tepperman. His private investigator character, Marty Quade, falls into that "second string" category. Unlike many of his contemporaries, Tepperman wrote the Quade stories in the third person. While Chandlers "Mallory" and Carrol John Daly's "Race Williams" and "Two-Gun Terry" wisecracked their way through their cases with engaging, first person narrators, the Quade stories were more laconic and reminiscent of Hammett's Sam Spade.

A few years ago I had the pleasure of meeting Ron Fortier, the main editor and driving force behind Airship 27, which has almost singlehandedly reinvigorated an interest in the pulps, both old and new. The more Ron and I talked, the more I realized that he and I shared a deep appreciation of the pulp characters, and Airship 27 was introducing a new generation to the thrills of those incomparable old mags. I knew I wanted to be a part of it. I was honored when he invited me to submit a story for this anthology.

Writing "Dead Man's Hand" proved to be quite a challenge. Ron sent me the Marty Quade "character bible," which laid down the specific rules for writing the about the character: "a no-nonsense, tough guy, loud mouthed private eye with a quick trigger finger." The style had to be in the traditional pulp style, and written in the third person. Intrinsically, the use of the third person establishes distance between the reader and the characters. The first person narration provides an immediate identification between the reader and the narrator, which is why that POV has been used so often in tough guy private eye mysteries. Writing a PI story in the third person was a bit of a challenge. The main character has to be illuminated by means other than the on-going, internal monologue, so there is a seeming built-in disadvantage using this POV. However, there are numerous variations of this point of view, as well. While the "omniscient narrator" was predominant in the previous centuries, it has fallen out of style for current writing. In today's writing, the more character illuminating "third person limited" (one character's POV per scene) is the most popular point of view. That said, there is another third person POV alternative that Hammett and some of his pulp contemporaries (like Tepperman), used effectively. I call it the "third person objective." In this POV, the story is told without getting into any of the character's heads. It's reminiscent of watching one of those old, black-and-white, noir movies unfold before you. That's primarily how I saw "Dead Man's Hand" evolving as I wrote it.

It's my hope that the readers will experience this nostalgia as well as they read all of the stories in this fabulous anthology... That they can sit down with this book and be transported back to that bygone era, when tough men prowled those mean streets... Men who were neither themselves mean, nor were they tarnished or afraid... Men who were not white knights on horseback, or heroic supermen. Men who had strengths and weaknesses, but operated by a personal code of honor that didn't always coincide with society's dictums... Men who didn't always get it right the first time... Men who would answer with a wisecrack, a punch in the gut, or a bullet... Men like private investigator Marty Quade.

Enjoy the read.

• • •

MICHAEL BLACK - is a life-long aficionado of the pulps. He is the author of 26 books, including the Ron Shade mysteries and the Leal and Hart police procedural series. Black also co-wrote two novels with television actor, Richard Belzer (TV's *Law & Order SVU*), the Doc Atlas neo-pulp series with his friend Ray Lovato, and the novel, *Dead Ringer*, with bestselling writer, Julie Hyzy. Black is currently writing the Mack Bolan Executioner series under the name Don Pendleton (*Dragon Key*, *Desert Falcons*, *Uncut Terror*, and *Missile Intercept* are his most recent titles). His last novel under his own name was the hit thriller, *Chimes at Midnight*. He was able to fulfill a life-long ambition to write a Sherlock Holmes story when Airship 27 published "A Most Unusual Dichotomy" and "The Dark Visage in the Mirror" in *Sherlock Holmes, Consulting Detective, Volume 6.*

In the middle 1930s, Chicago was one of the fastest growing metropolises in the country. Situated on mighty Lake Michigan, it was the home to millions of hard working Americans looking to better themselves. The Windy City was also shackled by its bootleg history, a time of violent gang wars that had permanently established a brutal underworld empire second to none. Corruption was the order of the day and both the police and government were in the pay of the mob bosses.

Frank "Mac" McCullough was a foot-soldier in one of the city's toughest families until he was ordered to rough up his uncle; a decent man with a gambling problem. The innate decency in Mac rebelled and suddenly he found himself up against the very men he had once admired and followed. Determined to put an end to their lawlessness, he put a bag over his head as a crude disguise only to become labeled the Bagman by the press.

Now writer BC Bell tells the amazing stories of old Chicago's most unique hero. Aided solely by a tough, black WW I veteran named Crankshaft, Mac wages war against the mobs in fast-paced, non-stop action tales pulp fans will cheer. Airship 27 Productions is thrilled to present pulpdom's newest avenger, THE BAGMAN.

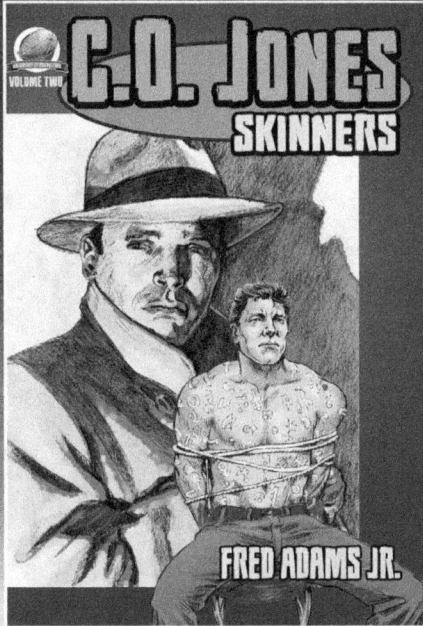

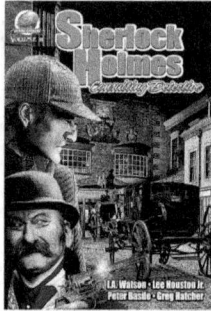

www.ingramcontent.com/pod-product-compliance
Lightning Source LLC
Chambersburg PA
CBHW051119260626
47170CB00005B/1581